Francis of the Filth

George Miller

This book is about a character.
It has no relation to the author.

Francis of the Filth

Chapter 1

A long time ago in a dimension far, far away there was a collective of midgets fighting over a hummus snack, who have nothing at all to do with our story, which really begins in a small and very unhygienic bedroom in what humans call 'New York'. It was at first appearance a common habitat: last Tuesday's ramen floating on a carpet of used tissues, unwashed socks, chewing gum-clogged USB sticks and bottles of urine stacked up in a pyramid; poorly written Japanese calligraphy scrolls hanging on the walls between cracked mirrors and old proudly displayed high school detention slips; and semen stains on the ceiling.

Yet on closer inspection, there was, at the same time, something unique about this habitat as well. Grotesque to the point of disfigurement, and disconcerting to the point of alarm, there lay in the middle of it all — rather happily — blending in as though one with it, Francis of the Filth. He was covered in nothing but phlegm and a pair of Sponge Bob underpants which could stand on their own and would most certainly shatter like glass if thrown at a hard surface. Though dead to the world, he would occasionally whimper utterances which were a window into the mind of filth that beheld his name and title:

No, Juelz Santana please don't touch me there.
Female comedians are very funny.
Must eat more hummus.
The other kids won't let me play in the park.
It's my turn to ride the chocolate man.
The school bus is responsible for their deaths, not me.
Yes, it was I who left the steamy surprise.
My step-dad was a veiny individual.
Need more rats.

Curiously, and without warning, a second voice could be heard whispering through the dorian-scented air of the room.

Ochin chin ga dai suki dayo.

For a moment the words just floated in the air like they were struggling to cut through the stench. They were repeated.

Ochin chin ga dai suki dayo.

This time they reached the ears of our protagonist, yet they remained muffled till he instinctively picked at his ear and pulled out a log of wax the size of a date.

A third calling brought the desired effect and Frank sat bolt upright, with that terrified look that only comes from hearing Christian rap played in the morning and seeing the dark lord himself.

Ochin chin ga dai suki dayo.

Part of the ceiling then opened up like a wet pouch, pulsing and pushing out what looked like, for lack of a better description, a black fetus. Still screaming, it slid onto the ground and began to unfold. Dressed completely in black, it was as though he was the very source of darkness itself. His presence seemed to bring a distortion of the space-time continuum and when he spoke it brought both shadows and chills. He prowled slowly before Frank on all fours like a frog with chronic arthritis. His tongue occasionally darted in and out, almost in rhythm to the Tourettes-like flinching of his tightly wrapped black head. Everything about him incited dread: his darkness, his movements, his uncut finger and toe nails. But most of all it was his eyes. Weird and freaky to the core, they were simultaneously present and ethereal, penetrating and all-knowing, and they stared out from their sockets with spastic abandon.

"Chin chin! Dark lord! Why have you come to torment me? Have you come to send me into the abyss?" Frank asked, paralyzed with fear.

Now, Frank lived across a backstreet from a morbidly obese lady called Mrs. Montez who pretended to be a widowed pole dancer but was really a PETA agent determined to catch Frank in the act of animal abuse. She was, however, actually widowed. That part is true. She had also had a miscarriage. She observed Frank through a humongous telescope which was really quite unnecessary because the back street was only five feet wide and their windows directly faced each other. She would sit for hours watching Frank lie comatose from huffing jenkem, just as he would sit for hours keeping a protective eye on that ten year-old boy with the nice little ass living across the street in front of his apartment. She befriended Frank by telling him she was simply checking on his fibre intake and occasionally throwing fruit through his window, whether it was open at the time or not.
When she saw the horrors of Chin Chin unfolding in Frank's room she threw open her window and cried out for mercy. "Leave him alone! He's just a boy!" Within moments, other neighbors with similarly large telescopes were throwing their windows open and hurling their emotive pleas toward the dark lord and soon the whole back alley echoed with the words, "He's just a boy!" "He's just a boy!" "He's just a boy!" much like any Italian neighborhood.

Ochin chin. The dark lord continued with his demands.

"But I have made the sacrifices you asked for," said Frank. "The blood and pubic hair and nail clippings of a thousand youths were all duly provided with video evidence. I can show you right now."

9

Dai suki dayo.

"Why do you need extra sacrifices? Weren't those I made enough?" Frank was quivering with trepidation.

Ochin chin. Ochin chin.

"I swear I have no more. I have given you everything I had. I have no more chromosomes to give."

"He's just a boy!" the cries continued to ring out through the alleyways and over the building tops.

Ochin chin ga daaaiii suki.

He placed his hand on Frank's trembling heart and absorbed the remaining chromosomes from him. With that, he quickly crawled back into his giant wet ceiling pussy, leaving Frank a quivering empty shell on the bed.

Once the shock waves had subsided and the space-time continuum had returned to normal, fear departed and life returned to normal in Frank's bedroom. That is, Frank sat on his bed and scratched his balls. He looked around to re-orientate himself. Then, very faintly at first, other activity began around the room. Initially, it started with just the lightest of movements from the cupboard door. It budged just a fraction; then a fraction more; then it peeped ajar. Finally the door swung open and out jumped a semi-naked little runt carrying some rosary beads.

"Alpha Centurion!" Frank exclaimed. "Good to see you, my friend! Thanks for all your support a minute ago when Chin Chin was here!"

He waddled over to Frank and sat on the bed beside him. "Good to see you too, Frank, fucking tool. Good thing I wasn't here a minute ago when that dark lord was here or I would have snapped his dick in two. I would have pounded those creepy black eyes of his all the way to the back of his head. I would have reached into his chest, pulled out his still-beating heart and held it up to his face so he could see how black it is."

"Alpha Centurion, what are you talking about. I saw you hiding in the cupboard. Also, you owe me money. You came up short." The clock on the wall suddenly opened up and from it a tiny, wrinkled human stuck his head out and said, "That was a great joke, Frank. Seven out of ten!". They aggressively winked at each other. The little guy returned back into the clock, never to be heard from again.

Before the runt could respond, the bedroom door swung open to the sound of disabled grunts, and in hopped a demented looking guy, pink from head to toe. "Pink Guy! It's you! You're here too! You made it! You just missed all the action by the way. You're a pussy, too, you know that? You and Alpha Centurion are both a couple of pussies — leaving me to face Chin-Chin all on my own. It was pretty scary for a while there." On hearing the dark lord's name, Pink Guy's eyes were stunned wide open. He could not understand how Frank ever had the courage to say Chin Chin's name out loud.

At that moment a rustling noise came up from under Frank's bed. "Come out Salamander man, I know it's you."
"Nyeessss!" came the reply as the huge humanoid salamander peeped out from under the bed.
"Salamander man, what are you doing under my bed? Have you any idea of the filth that lies under there? I tell you, there's some nasty stuff down there."

"Nyeessss!" He pulled himself fully out and immediately began to caress his nipples. He was now completely back to his normal self. All his lacerations had healed and his nipples were back to full erection. Whatever wretched woundings had previously disturbed him, he was back to his normal, cheerful self again. "Nyeessss!" he cried and immediately inserted a recorder into his left nostril and broke into a rousing rendition of a tune from his glory days.

Before Alpha Centurion could start dancing to the music, or Frank could compliment him on his playing or his general good looks and SICK moves, the door was kicked wide open and in strolled a strange Japanese man wearing brown spectacles, a Hawaiian shirt and a safari hat. "Wow!" he declared. "Wow, Franku!"

"Safari Man!" cried Frank, ecstatic that his whole posse was reunited once again. "I thought you were still back in…"

"No, no! Let's not go there! Suffice to say, being married to a negi was never going to work out for someone like me ha ha ha. She had no pussy. Can you imagine aggressively trying to make a dent in drywall with your dick? Not for me." He was shadowed by Drone who hovered just above his left shoulder.

Frank gestured for them all to come together. They embraced in a tight and passionate group hug, with Alpha Centurion burrowing with pleasure into Pink Guy's thighs. With the six of them now together, the circus was pretty much complete again. And there was much rejoicing until late in the night with laughing and dancing and general scat.

But Frank's dilemma remained and his interest was piqued. He was still capable of multiplying his chromosomes and he was still greatly troubled by this, not merely the capability but the reasoning behind it. Why would any god want to see the multiplication of his chromosomes and no-one else's? Why had Chin Chin, the all powerful god chosen him? Why was Frank so verbally and sexually aggressive all the time? He was no closer to finding out why. There had to be more. Beyond the peace lords, there had to be an Ultimate God. Frank was more determined now than ever before to find Him, confront Him and demand the answers to his questions. And so his quest became all-consuming. But this is by no means where it had begun.

Chapter 2

All children, except one, grow up. And all children, except one, are born of woman. In the spring of 1945, a fetus-like infant was retrieved from an open-air sewer beneath a public toilet in a slum in the Lorong Village of Jakarta. He was named Fransiskus (meaning 'freed from filth') and from the first moment of his existence, and in spite of his squalid genesis, he demonstrated an unparalleled genius. At first there was a moment of crying, then cooing, very shortly followed by clear linguistic utterances. By the time the authorities arrived some hours later he was writing quadratic equations on the wall in his own excrement (excrement on walls was nothing new to the locals) and explaining them in Aramaic to the crowd which had gathered.

For the next two weeks he was taken in by a family of twenty-eight running a local temple. They lived over a feted brown creek with the smell of a pig farm, and there he was fed and clothed and loved. Because of his brilliant mind and progressive knowledge, he was quickly treated as a god in the village and people would line up to pet his head in the hope of having knowledge imparted to them. He thrived in the grime of his environment, growing rapidly in stature and intellect, and soon had the appearance of a toddler while engineering sanitation, transport systems and birth control for the whole community. This way, he no longer needed to circumcise the women.

Word spread quickly about Fransiskus and soon the Indonesian military were on where his doorstep would be if the temple had had a door step. There was much wailing and moaning as the young prodigy was ripped from their arms and a torrent of semi-naked bodies followed along the vehicles as they departed, banging on the windows and doors and begging them to return him to them. Their hopes were never realized. They were gunned down, all of them: the temple family, their neighbors and all who had come out to protest, their bodies piled as high as horses shoulders for as far as the eye could see. "Salaaang kalamankang!!" a soldier yelled at the families. This was not Indonesian. He had a speech impediment.

Fransiskus was taken to a top secret facility deep in the mountains where, after a brief period of quarantine, so-called experts (though they had never seen anything of Fransiskus' like before) began to feed his voracious curiosity, intellect and abilities. They were in awe. They began with Little Golden Books and tic-tac-toe but were before long working on James Joyce and global thermonuclear warfare. Apart from the odd foray into hentai and erotic art, Fransiskus adhered strictly to academic and ethical pursuits.

Scientists from all over the world began to hear rumors of this prodigy and would try to arrange secretive visits to Fransiskus' cell. There, the lucky few would marvel over the possibilities he brought into the world. Was he a god? they wondered. A mutation? Should he be encouraged or stopped? Their audience with Fransiskus was inevitably inspiring and humbling, and was often coupled with an intoxicating agenda.
Despite the highly classified nature of the 'project' (to which Fransiskus was now referred), and the isolated location of its facilities, one day several months into operations, a blonde-haired man in a very dark suit turned up unannounced at the front gate. He flashed some identification and was escorted into the heart of the complex. There, he was introduced to the overseer of the program. Looking his Indonesian colleague in the eye with a curious expression that could have been mistaken for contempt, he removed his spectacles and raised a palm. "Heil Hitler."

~

In the summer of that year, the Pacific War was brought to an end with two cataclysmic explosions. They destroyed everyone and everything for miles around and left a simmering, scorching layer of radiation to last for the ages. The lucky ones were those right under the detonations who were immediately reduced to ashes and outlines etched in concrete. It was those who survived the initial blasts who learned the true meaning of suffering. They wandered about aimless, hopeless, with melting flesh, groping about in near or total blindness for help. None came and that which did, came too late and with little or no means of alleviating their agony.

(The torture was not short-lived. For years, even decades to come, those who had been exposed to the radiation suffered numbness, loss of fingernails, blood spots under the skin, tumors, leukaemia, kidney and liver dysfunction and so on. The list of after-effects was almost endless, and for those who suffered from them, so was the pain.)

Such widespread and severe affliction hastened the surrender of the Japanese forces, and with the capitulation of the other Axis powers earlier in the year, the ceasing of worldwide hostilities was now complete. For the general populace, exhausted and depleted, it couldn't have come soon enough, and with the exception of a couple of skirmishes in Guam and a few other remote areas, peacetime was welcomed by victor and loser nations alike with great relief and vigor.

But not by all.

Not everyone was pleased with either the outcome of the war or the means by which it had been achieved. There were some who believed that the Axis powers still retained the ability, the manpower and most of all the technological savvy to inflict revolutionary damage on the Allied forces and alter not merely the outcome of the war, but both history and the future together.

16

Soncorp was one such organisation. A secretive, privately-owned Japanese company based in Okinawa, it was bitterly opposed to the Japanese surrender and continued to work unabated in technological, ideological and biological warfare. Though the rest of the country labored in poverty, Soncorp remained flush with funds for its operations. A little known fact regarding the end of the war in the European theater concerns the demise of the Fuhrer. In that bunker in Berlin just before he put the pistol to his temple, Hitler uttered his final words: "Gib alles zu Soncorp" ("Give everything to Soncorp").

As such, the Okinawan company had available to them near-unlimited resources from war loot and retained communication with its sister allies in Germany and Italy to pursue its goals of supremacy. Given these objectives, one could hardly overstate the joy that reverberated along their corridors when they received word from the Fatherland that a new resource of immeasurable capacity had been secured.

And so it was that Fransiskus was removed from Indonesia at a very young age and transported to Okinawa, where he was to spend the remainder of his adolescent years. There, his name was shortened to 'Frank' because the Japanese seemed incapable of pronouncing the 'siskus' part of his name, and he was put in a lab working toward various means of Axis domination.

This enigma of a young man grew to about 180 centimeters tall and developed a well-defined body thanks to chasing monkeys and boars around the lab whenever they escaped (which was often). He would wrestle them to the ground or knock them out, sometimes with the aid of a porcelain sink, a trick he had learned from a Slav. He had a shock of thick black hair which gave him an aura of tremendous virility. He wore silver wire-rimmed glasses upon a nose that had more than once identified him as having Jewish ancestry, an association he vehemently denied. And he always wore the same blue shirt. It had never been washed.

Frank's secluded upbringing gave him a peculiar perspective on the world. He tended to see people and events in extremes. He divided folk into 'creators' and 'consumers', 'leaders' and 'followers', 'thinkers' and 'dumbasses' and 'bullies and their 'prey'. No-one really sat in between any of these paradigms. People were either one or the other and once they were one, it was virtually impossible to change to the other. Frank saw himself as the consummate creator/leader/thinker/bully in almost any environment he found himself in.

And then there was his voice. Much has been hypothesized about the raspiness of Frank's voice and why it came to be so. Some have assumed it to be a purely genetic anomaly. Others are certain it is the result of a bacterial infection caught from any number of the animals he was experimenting on. On occasions, Frank told people that it was from swallowing thumbtacks after losing a bet in a drunken stupor. But the truth of the matter is that for a short stint in Frank's formative years, he took to singing Christian heavy metal, a phase he quickly grew out of to the relief of everyone in the lab and the local area, but the constant shrieking and growling took its toll on poor Frank's virgin vocal cords and alas, they never fully recovered.

Young Frank had interests and ideals that extended way beyond the walls of the lab. He was fascinated with midgets and aliens and black people in Paris. He found unusual dialects from the Congo, Peru and the bowels of South-east Asia to be of particular interest. Rap and opera filled his musical library. And he develop a particular distaste for non-Japanese who attempted to infiltrate Japanese society, professing a knowledge of the culture whilst demonstrating a profound ignorance of it. There were many artisans and thinkers, musicians and poets who inspired him, but none more so than Schrödinger and some guy named Mozart, who down the line would become the ancestor of Fred Durst.

Biologically speaking, Frank himself was, it turned out, an even more mysterious figure than his filthy origins would suggest. Though dredged up from an Indonesian sewer, DNA testing revealed that he was primarily of Japanese and German extraction. This explained some inherent traits in Frank like his insatiable appetite for takoyaki, sudden bowing and a penchant for rajio taiso early in the morning. On the Kraut side, Frank would immerse himself in bratwurst diets for weeks on end, find secret relief in listening to recordings of the oom-pah-pah bands of Munich, and was without any sense of humor. Yet there were other genetic markers in his DNA that were unidentifiable and it was these which started the rumors and fears amongst his colleagues in the lab.

There was only one man that Frank answered to in the lab and that was Tsubasa Honda. Honda was a graduate from Tokyo University who excelled in bio-engineering. He originally joined the Imperial army because, nurturing the psychopath within, he wanted to create bio weapons to 'see what happens with them'. A quietly spoken man, he was once well built, yet now rather rotund as he approached middle age. He almost became a professional baseball player before the war, primarily because smashing things with a bat was marvelous release for someone who was otherwise extremely reserved, yet he quit baseball at the last minute because he didn't want to give in to a dirty American tradition. When the war came to its fireball end, Honda was offered a job at Soncorp, a position he received with enthusiasm and gratitude as, philosophically, it involved continuing service to the Emperor and, in practical terms, it involved destroying things.

His relationship to Frank was simple. In awe of Frank's genius and his moral failures, his job was to leave Frank alone to do the work that he had been specifically employed to do and to question neither the Germans nor the Japanese board of Soncorp about it. In this sense, Honda was the perfect supervisor for Frank: loyal yet without ethics, nationalistic yet without any sense of restraint, and brilliant without any desire to use it for the greater good.

There were fifteen other employees in the lab to clean and to perform mundane duties but to Frank they were all faceless drudges, as boring as a feminist at a dinner party and about as funny as a fart in church. Yet there was one presence in that facility who stood out to Frank and who become very nearly the sole focus of his attention. His name was Ichiro. Ichiro mattered, not in the sense that he was important or intelligent or helpful. On the contrary, Ichiro was a useless idiot. He was the very antithesis of Frank, the 'consuming dumbass follower' type who was the prey for Frank's inner bully. He was the necessary evil in Frank's small world and Frank worked him without mind or mercy.

A little contemptuous man with a basketball head and round glasses, he looked like some kind of bootleg Japanese Harry Potter doll you would win at a second rate carnival. He had 'kick me' written all over his fat, poxy face. Simply put, he looked fucking retarded. Ichiro was Frank's whipping boy, his dog, his right hand wiper. In almost every sense of the word, Ichiro was Frank's bitch. This explains why Frank never referred to him by the name his mother gave him at his sorry birth, but called him, without exception, Bitchiro. Whenever Frank needed someone to mop up spillage, he called for Bitchiro. Whenever Frank wanted someone to pick up the pieces of a rat, he would bellow for Bitchiro. If he needed a bottle to piss in, Bitchiro would hold it at the ready.
"Bitchiro hand me the generator."

"Bitchiro, pick up that spleen."

"Bitchiro, stick that knife into the toaster."

With every command Bitchiro would bow and scrape and respond with, "My nama Bitchiro." And whenever Frank defecated he would watch as his turd was flushed away and say, 'Goodbye Bitchiro'.

The laboratory itself was like no other. A perfectly square gray building, it looked like a rundown Japanese public school. There was nothing in its design to please or inspire, save for a few palm trees which grew on the boundaries of the property. Rising up behind it was a mountain range covered in jurassic vegetation and still-unclassified fauna. It teemed with monkeys, boar and habu snakes, yet most of its natural resources remained undiscovered. The building contained three floors, with the top floor at tree top height. Vines and other vegetation ran along the outside wall of the lab, weaving in and out of the windows and ventilation systems which no longer worked. The sultry air was a perfect incubator for all this foliage and a common source of fatigue amongst the employees on any given afternoon.

The top floor was all Frank's and he was given unfettered access to complete his tasks. It contained line after line of computers and various other equipment, most of which no-one, other than Frank, knew how to operate. But Frank, with an intellect that itself was fast approaching Singularity, ran them all with ease and with distinction. His preferred fields of research were diverse, including bacteriology, horology, pharmacology, biochemistry, cosmology, endocrinology, spectroscopy, haematology, mycology and of course gelotology. But if there were a pet area of research and design that meant more to Frank than any other, it was radiobiology; that is, the study of the action of ionizing radiation on living things.

As such, the lab was strewn with cages containing (or which contained) animals of all sizes and kinds. Primates, birds, reptiles, amphibians, insects were all loved equally for their willingness to serve a greater good. Presently, a small newt sat gingerly in the corner of a clear container, occasionally looking up at Frank as its god and scratching its chest. And then there were the rats. Frank hated rats with a passion and found a great pleasure in reserving his most terrifying experiments for them. Some moved about in their confinement with knowing concern while others were no longer able to; and some were no more than organs or appendages on a table.

On more than one occasion, Frank would tie a rat to three or four pigeons, then release them to the skies. The pigeons would fly off in different directions tugging the rat back and forth in mid-air, the rat would be writhing and screaming, the birds would be scared to death of the noise the rat was making and fly even harder, which made the rat's screams reach fever pitch and so the circus would go on till it came to it's grisly demise. Frank would just shrug and chuckle.

These episodes marked a beginning. Indeed, the socially repressive lab life began to take its toll on Frank. He would drink copious amounts of beer and then abuse the animals in the lab for what he claimed was a node. He would disappear for hours on end in the evenings to go to dog fights, cock fights, bull fights and midget boxing. He would drunkenly harass the hookers in the red light district, yelling 'I got Molly, I got white!" and "Gang gang, free my nigger guwop" while being dragged away by the police and/or the off-base U.S military. In short, while Frank was a genius and a biological phenomena, his environment was making him filthy.

Yet the greater change was from within. Frank had been pouring his heart and soul into radiobiology, and all the while unwittingly, he poured radiobiology into his genetic vulnerabilities. The interaction of radiation on the unknown genetic markers in Frank's DNA brought about changes which Frank could never have imagined; dark changes; menacing changes; changes that reached far further than Frank could ever have imagined. At first it was just aches and pains, but then his urine turned orange and he began to have hallucinations - sometimes happy, sometimes terrible, always weird. Aware of these changes, Frank decided to secretly test himself, certain that he now had some form - or forms - of cancer.

It was not without fear then, that he lay the syringe on the table, sterilized his arm with a swab of alcohol and slapped his skin to bring up the veins. On finding the best one, he slipped the needle in and watched the red essence fill the test tube. He filled a second just in case. Before the blood on his arm had dried, he had the sample mixed with testing solutions and placed under a microscope. There, to his horror, he watched nucleic acids behave in a way that he had never seen before. They were wriggling - writhing - and then pulling apart as though in self-rejection, before completely splitting down the middle, a process which appeared to be repeating ad infinitum. This discovery made cancer look like the common cold. With cancer, the cells multiply uncontrollably. With Frank, his chromosomes were now multiplying uncontrollably. He was, in effect, becoming an entirely new species. He continued to look into the eyepiece wondering - hoping - that this was another hallucination.

He called his little rodent friend over to confirm the findings.
"Bitchiro! Get over here!" He was in front of Frank immediately.
"Look into this microscope and tell me what you see."
"My nama Bitchiro."
"Well, what do you see? Don't hold back. Tell me everything."
The simpleton began to sweat and look decidedly nervous. "My nama Bitchiro."

"So you see it, too?" Frank asked. "You see the chromosomes multiplying?"

Bitchiro could no longer control his bladder. "My nama Bitchiro. My nama Bitchiro."

Frank turned away in distress for a moment, then looked back to his underling and held out a stern finger.

"No-one hears about this, Bitchiro. You got that? No-one is to know."

"My nama Bitchiro."

"If anyone - anyone at all - gets wind of this, I will stew you up and serve you with fries while you're still breathing!"

"My nama Bitchiro."

"Now what are you still doing here?! Piss off!"

The weasel scampered off with one last "My nama Bitchiro."

Frank diligently took samplings every morning and evening and kept daily notes on the progress of his condition. What he failed to do, however, primarily because he just didn't care, was test Bitchiro who had also been regularly exposed to the uranium.

"Bitchiro, bring me that sea cucumber," he called to him one fine morning.

"My nama Bitchiro."

Frank looked at his little dolt as he held the dripping echinoderm in his trembling hands. Bitchiro looked different this morning. He had an aura of greater patheticness, greater nervousness, as though he was expecting to be beaten far greater than he had ever been beaten before. Frank enjoyed this enormously.

"My nama B…"

"What?" said Frank. "Spit it out, boy."

"My nama B…"

"What in the name of scat is wrong with you?"

"My nama…" and before he could get any more out, his head jerked back in such a violent manner, the crack in his neck could be heard down on the second floor. With a sound like the branch

24

of a tree breaking, his jaw and mouth ripped apart with such incredible force that the crown of his head began to split open. There was momentary resistance before Bitchiro's entire body from his head down to the base of his torso ripped in two and a new naked and slimy Bitchiro emerged, slithering out of what was now a crumpled carcass lying on the floor.

"Hmmh," said Frank. "Cool." He then turned to continue on his own testing.

"My nama Bitchiro," said this new Bitchiro, identical to the previous one though still covered in a thick slime.

"Yeah, I know," said Frank. "Now piss off."

This metamorphosis was not a singular event. In fact, Bitchiro fast fell into a natural routine of excruciating death and slimy rebirth once a week or so and Frank, more amused than concerned in any way at all, would take fastidious notes each time it happened. His concern remained more for himself. He knew that he and Bitchiro were changing, the only difference was that no-one cared about Bitchiro. And as soon as Bitchiro had completed a metamorphosis, Frank would tell him to hurry and clean up the mess he had made on the floor and to incinerate the putrid carcass that he always left behind.

Chapter 3

All happy families are alike; each unhappy family is unhappy in its own way. Frank was beginning to get very tired of sitting by his assistant in the lab, and having nothing particular to do other than radiobiological experiments. Once or twice he had peeped into his journals, or those of others, but nothing much took his interest or shook his world. He kept a small, ancient wireless on one of the window sills of the third floor. He loved the juxtaposition of such a crackly old piece of equipment having a place amidst the hum of all the latest technology. The weather report sputtered to life in the fading afternoon light as Frank turned the volume up.

"Typhoon," he heard. "Massive" with wind, rain and tsunami warnings. This would explain the cool gusts which had started to blow and the metallic smell of imminent rain. Frank looked out the open window at all the foliage. It would be grateful for the downpour it was about to receive. The jungle behind the lab fell into an eerie silence - literally the calm before the storm - as all the animals burrowed their way into holes and crevices and knots and cracks, behavior not unlike Frank's. Sirens from the military bases began to wail in the distance as if to herald some ominous calamity. This was actually truer than most would realize.

Frank woke the next morning, badly hungover, after a harrowing night of tempest. The typhoon had fully passed leaving a whisper quiet and sunny dawn. Groaning, he slowly sat up to recollect the previous night's antics before the tranquility was shattered by the rumble of vehicles approaching the compound. He squinted through the slats of the blind as a beam of light shot through. He adjusted his eyes to see four large army jeeps and a tank pull up in front of the lab. Even from the third floor he could hear the thumping on the door.

"Who the fuck is in charge and do any of you Japs speak English here?"

At that moment, Honda ran through the lab door and looked at Frank alarmingly. "I do not speak English," he said with beads of sweat growing above his eyebrows. "I need you to take care of this." Gathering his thoughts, Frank nodded and made a dismissive waving gesture at Honda, implying that he would handle it.

The banging on the door got louder as he trotted down the concrete stairs. Frank opened the door to see Sergeant Benson, a large man with a beer gut and a piggish face staring at him. His nose was as red as a strawberry and his eyebrows were intense, as if he were about to eat the meanest ass of all time.

"Do you own this facility?" he bellowed.

"No sir. This facility is run by my supervisor, Mr. Masayuki Honda." Frank looked over at Honda who gave him a firm nod. "We're a private research facility."

"In the mountains of Okinawa?" Benson asked, smiling as if he had found something good.

"Yes."

"Documents, now!"

"May I ask why you are visiting?"

"I said documents, Jewnose Jap, are you fucking deaf?"

"I'll get them right away, sir."

Frank rushed back to his lab and hid whatever evidence he could.

"Bitchiro, I need to give them our documents. Hide everything."

"My nama Bitchiro," he replied.

Frank returned with his passport, some files containing the breeding habits of starfish in the Ryukyu waters, and the results of the weekend boat races in Osaka. Benson perused the documents.

"Well shit, boys. We hit the jackpot. We got ourselves a Japanese German."

The soldiers standing behind Benson smirked and widened their eyes.

"I don't see an issue here, sir," Frank said.

"Why would they have a Japanese German working in a lab like this? In Oki-fucking-nawa!"

"We are privately owned. We do peaceful scientific research"

"What exactly do you do?"

"Cancer research, sir, since, you know, you guys really fucked us with that whole radiation thing."

"Don't get smart with me." Benson rammed the clip of his rifle into the back of Frank's head and he fell to his knees. He held Frank's head up by jamming the forestock of the rifle into his neck. Frank's nose began to bleed.

"You're the two things I hate most combined into one you sorry son of a bitch, and whatever the fuck is going on here, I don't like it." He then spat in Frank's face and walked out of the room.

"I'll be back," he said as he kicked a table over. After the rumbles of the jeeps faded into the distance, Honda came back into the room.

"I'm terribly sorry you had to go through that," he said as he handed Frank a tissue to mop up his bloody nose."

"People fear and despise what they don't understand," Frank said as he stood and put an ice pack to his head wound. "He was raised that way, like an American. I cannot blame a man for his upbringing."

Honda nodded and looked down at his feet.

"Plus, next time I'll be ready to fight back. He took me by surprise."

"That won't be necessary," Honda interrupted quickly. Benson will do whatever he can to have this place shut down. If you show weakness and fight back, he can cancel all operations here for unruly conduct. We are a private company, after all. We would hate to see all our funding—not to mention your talents— go to waste."

Frank tasted blood in his mouth. He was biting his lip out of frustration.

"Fair enough. I will continue as planned."

From that day, Sergeant Benson came every week without fail. The only surprise was the time of day. Sometimes he'd kick the door in at the crack of dawn; at other times it was right in the middle of dinner. On the odd occasion he would enter through the back door at midnight. Regardless of the time, he would constantly hold a gun up to Frank's face and proceed to turn the lab inside out. Benson knew something was up, and he didn't like it. He was totally obsessive about it. Even the other soldiers viewed Benson's frequent visits as a fanatical hate crime. He kept saying "A Jap-German in Okinawa working with radiation. Does that not sound suspicious to you at all?"

Frank was rarely the sole target. He would sometimes terrorize Bitchiro, bombarding him with questions.

"Who the fuck are you?"

"My nama Bitchiro."

"Do you speak English?"

"My nama Bitchiro."

"Yes, I know."

"My nama Bitchiro."

"What the fuck?"

"My nama Bitchiro."

"What is wrong with this guy?"

"My nama Bitchiro."

"Shut the fuck up."

"My nama Bitchiro."

Two months after the first visit, Benson drove up to the compound more aggressively than normal. He stormed out of his jeep and burst through the door holding his rifle. It was quite clear that he had been drinking.

"You two, up against the wall,"

He yelled at two young employees—no older than twenty-four. They did as they were told and lined up.

"Benson, you can bully me all you want but please don't bring the employees into this," Frank calmly said. "They're just janitors."

"How come I never see your notes or clipboards lying around anywhere, Frank, you autist?" Benson replied.

"We mail them off to HQ every day."

"Where is your HQ?"

"I don't know, Sergeant Benson."

"Bullshit. And stop twitching your fingers like that."

"I really don't know, sir. It's classified."

"I don't see any point to your research, Frank. You can't cure cancer."

"I believe we can. I also believe our nations can help each other with this new research."

"Yeah, when pigs fly."

"Yeah who am I fucking kidding, you'll never fly."

Benson's eyes widened and his lips stiffened. At that very moment, for the first time in his life, Frank regretted his sharp wit.

"This is your fault; your doing," Benson said as he lifted his rifle and shot both of the employees multiple times in the chest. A canvas of blood splattered across the gray concrete wall. Frank watched their bodies drop on top of each other. Honda was looking out the window, waiting for the nightmare to end. "Next time it'll be you and your little Bitchiro friend." Benson began to head out. "I would have killed you but I like to see you suffer." He and the other soldiers strutted out, leaving the lab pin-drop quiet. They'd all seen death before, but not in a while. For Frank it brought back with a scream all the suicides he'd seen in Okinawa during the war; line after line of men, women and even children taking their own lives rather than suffer at the hands of the enemy. Frank saw this so vividly he began to tremble. Everyone immediately went back to work. It was all they could do.

"Eyyyy boy" said Bitchiro.

Frank buried both of the employees later that night. He didn't ask anyone to help because he felt responsible for their deaths. It was still typhoon season, and it had just stopped raining a few hours before. It made the soil soft and easy to dig through. Frank took a break from the shovel and looked over at the bodies. They were pale and limp. He laughed. It was a defence mechanism that worked for him. "It's all cancer, everything is fucking cancer," he said, laughing to himself. "I work with cancer, act like cancer, and by saying 'cancer' I get people killed. I AM cancer." His laughter echoed up into the mountains and all the chirping crickets and birds went dead silent. He continued to dig.

Frank wasn't afraid of Benson, but he was afraid of not being able to complete his research. But he knew that the moment it was done, he would have his revenge on Benson. "I'll fucking kill him," Frank would say to Bitchiro after another one of Benson's weekly visits. "After we complete the research and take back our land, I will literally slit his throat in front of his wife and children." Saying things like that made him feel better, and motivated him to finish his work. If he ever felt discouraged at any point during the day, he would daydream about the blissful release that would come with murdering Benson. What would his blood taste like? Would his children die too? Would his wife's pussy be tight? All kinds of dark questions swam through his head.

Frank would spend every day by the graves, watering a couple of flowers that had managed to sprout from the compost. Frank never cared for other people. In fact, he didn't even know the names of the two employees buried in front of him. "I don't care about these people. Why am I still here every day?" Frank asked as Honda emerged from the trees.

"You're a compassionate person who was driven to narcissism by your environment. You care, but only because you're responsible for their deaths. Otherwise it wouldn't be an issue."

Frank laughed. "Yes. I'm quite rotten."

"Quite filthy."

"Bitchiro should have died instead."

They both laughed.

"Eyyyyy," said Bitchiro from inside the building.

"Listen, Mr. Honda. I need to tell you something, but you can't tell the board until I've completed my research."

Honda was listening.

"I am most likely dying. At first I thought my cells were multiplying at a rapid rate but I discovered that it is actually my chromosomes which are splitting." He went on in detail that night, explaining everything to Honda about his research to date.

"I've never heard of chromosomes duplicating before," said Honda. "That should instantly kill you."

"It doesn't matter," said Frank.

"We can use your gift for other things. There is no point in attempting to create a weapon that may or may not work if there's a chance of you dying before that. We should get you out of this lab right away. Especially away from Benson."

"I'm going to die anyway. At least let me finish my research. I know I was born to finish this. I'll leave blueprints to a wiser generation."

He never got the chance. It began in the midnight hour of a Tuesday. Frank, watching phlegm react to bursts of radiation, suddenly got mind-splitting headaches. Clutching his cranium, he dropped to his knees and let out an agonising cry before staggering to the refrigerator and grabbing a bottle of milk. He quickly downed it before collapsing onto the bed to sleep. But sleep was his tormentor that night. As he tossed back and forth the nightmares came to him. These were not, however, your run-of-the-mill nightmares of falling or being chased or drowning or of clowns. If only Frank were to escape that lightly. These nightmares were so vivid it was impossible to distinguish night from day, spirit from matter, or reality from virtuality. The pain inside his fracturing head was unbearable.

And then they came. Numbers. Clusters of numbers tumbled across his field of vision. Stream after stream of them. He had no idea what they were or what they meant; he only knew that there was no escaping them or the fear that manifested when they came. For hours, Frank would lie, rigid with terror, watching the numbers scroll and hoping with all his heart that they would stop. Occasionally in the dreams, he would also see images; a silhouette effigy, a tree on a hilltop, a dark figure of unknown origin and nature but clearly powerful and mighty. This dark, fearful form was fused to the tree as though crucified on it; repressed by it yet somehow sustaining it. The image conveyed an ancient mystery, tragic and formidable, of agony and wonder, and it horrified Frank to his very core. In the end, he would wake in the morning light, feeling a sense of total depletion, and lie there until his strength returned. And when it did, and he needed to unleash his fear and frustration at the visitations, Bitchiro was there.

The nightmares lasted for months and drove Frank to the brink of insanity. Had it not been for Bitchiro's purulent presence, Frank would have slid into certain madness. Yet there was another element to the nightmares that brought a slither of intrigue amidst the dread that Frank experienced. Every night, the nightmares would conjure up their numbers, but Frank began to notice that it was the same number segments being revealed to him each time. He began to agonize over them, analysing them, reciting them, but their meaning eluded him.

33

One night, tormented by the nightmares, Frank resisted the urge to go into town and hustle, and instead spent the evening crunching the numbers once again. Yet his inability to decipher them was more than his erudite mind could handle. He began to smash beakers and test tubes around the lab, overturning equipment and hurling animals. Bitchiro was madly trying to clean up after him. In his fury, Frank was unaware of the gash that had opened down the side of his hand or of the blood that was streaming from it. He began to spin in circles, reciting the numbers over and over. The claret flowed from his wound forming a circle of crimson on the ground around him. Again and again he intoned the numbers, spinning and spilling and recalling and chanting.

All of a sudden, the floor beneath him began to rumble and pitch. The tiling cracked and the walls split. The ceiling caved in, first in small clusters, then in huge panels. Enormous steel beams fell to the ground, smashing everything beneath them. The lights on the ceiling flickered off, but an ethereal luminescence, now coming from a source beyond the lab, remained. A violent shaking and a howling wind followed from which deep chasms opened up all around him, and the equipment, the lab animals and the flooring crumbled away. The very foundations of the facility became brittle and started to break, dropping away into the darkness below. The noise which accompanied all this was thunderous, shattering ear drums and arresting hearts, as though a trumpet heralding an apocalypse.

The world as they had all known it, ceased to be, exterminated in seconds. Bitchiro clung for his life to an ultracentrifuge that stubbornly held to Frank's central work station.

"My nama Bitchiro! My nama Bitchiro!" he screamed with wild eyes. Nothing remained of the lab but the circle of flooring that Frank was standing on, still encrusted in crimson, and that was fast fragmenting under his feet. Everything then fell away completely into infernal suffering.

A thick soupy darkness surrounded him, and deformed hands, aged and tormented, reached up from it, grabbing and pulling. Voices called in falsetto screams and guttural moans, begging for release and salvation. The awful cacophony of destruction had subsided, leaving an eerie sound vacuum which amplified the cries of the tormented souls. A chilly wind blew. The contorted limbs and distorted heads with their unhinged jaws, stitched up eyes and melting flesh, were of human and beastly forms, their only fellowship being in their writhing and their agony. Again and again they desperately reached up, flinching and twitching in rage and wretchedness.

Plumes of toxic odors, acidic and pungent to the very back of the throat, wafted up in ever greater dispersions. There seemed to be a lawlessness to the senses so that what could be seen could also be felt, what could be heard could be tasted and what could be smelt could be seen. As such, the sulphuric stench contained an anaemic glow which rose up into what had, until very recently, been air, giving everything a dull, rotting appearance. It seeped into every crevice and orifice. Screaming was one's only release, yet it only served to exacerbate the suffering.

Other than Frank, Bitchiro was the last semblance of life to remain. Chest-deep in damnation, he held fast to Frank's ankle but the soulless hands were on him and around him, pulling at him, wrenching his garments and gouging their gnarled digits deep into his flesh. The young turd had fight in him. "My nama Bitchiro! My nama Bitchiro!" he continued to shriek. He swung wildly at the ogres and even tried to bite them but it had no effect other than to further excite them. In the end their appendages entered his ears, his mouth and his eyes and with one final shake of his leg, Frank flicked him off into the abyss for good. He fell into the darkness with a final blood-curdling, "My nama Bitchiro!" An overriding sense of misery extinguished any remaining flicker of hope or reprieve for Frank.

He looked up into the portal that was opening above him. A circle of ominous light, it was in no way inviting and invoked terror almost equal to that of the blackness beneath him. He feared for his life to enter the gateway, but the overriding dread of the engulfing abyss below, with its fill of destitute souls and screaming remorse, left him with no choice. He would go. He raised his palms and ceased to resist. "Habere eam viam vestram" he said. And then he was gone.

Chapter 4

The boy with greasy, unwashed hair lowered himself down the last few feet of rock and began to pick his way towards the sea. He had no idea where he was. It was perfectly still, perfectly quiet and the landscape appeared in silhouettes. The expanse above him was shadowed yet without cloud. It was impossible to make out any sort of distance in relation to it. He sat on an ice-cold rock and looked out over a sea of liquid so black it could have been crude oil. Gnarled and twisted hands continued to reach up out of it as they had before, but this time in silence. He watched them grasp in desperation, yet he felt no emotion. Only emptiness. This place was weird. Dreamlike. It had a stronger sense of reality than he had ever known but it was hallucinatory as well. In this realm, there was nothing other than a huge frozen rock and an ocean of lost souls stretching out from it. There was no atmosphere, no warmth, no color, no fear, no joy, no desire and no time. As such, there was no telling how long he had been here or how long he would be here.

Presently from within the confines of the shadows, something dark was fumbling along. He wasn't sure what to make of it at first, and watched till the intentness of his gaze was able to form an image. Then the creature stepped from mirage onto clear ice and he saw that the darkness was not all shadow but mostly flesh. The creature, an unsightly humanoid, was of singular matter, and one color from head to foot. He drew near and sat beside the boy. Though a total stranger in a foreign world, there was neither any sense of alarm nor of relief. The two observed each other for a period and then the creature spoke.

"Frank," he addressed the boy in a deep, rich tone.
"How do you know my name?"
"I was sent to you."

"By who?"

"By higher powers."

Frank sat and observed the entity before him. "Am I in hell?"

"No."

"Surely this can't be heaven."

"No."

"So what is this place?"

"We are in between worlds. Off the map. Literally nowhere."

"And what are we doing here?"

"Nothing, of course. But I have been sent to you to bring revelation."

"Revelation? Revelation of what?"

"Revelation of the beginning and of the paradigms."

"What about the end?"

"I don't have that authority."

"What happened to my world?"

"Your world no longer exists and I'm tempted to say that it never did, but that might be misleading. Suffice to say, you're no longer in that frequency and never can be again."

Frank studied his companion closely. His face was rimmed as though by a tight circle of light and his head occasionally gave a mild twitch. He seemed serene but occupied.

"Who are you?" Frank asked.

"My name is Freygarður Geirtryggur Þjóðleifur Lúthersdóttir.

"You've got to be shitting me."

"I'm also known as Pink Guy."

"I think I'll go with Pink Guy."

Frank assumed in the gray hues of that place that his flesh, in the right light, had to be a shade of pink.

"Listen carefully, Frank. Life as we know it, in all it's fullness, is to now be revealed to you."

"Speak on, dear friend." All of a sudden the gravity of the situation made Frank start to speak like an idiot.

"All life and matter is contained within three known omniverses, each of which contains any number of universes. The omniverses are divided into dozens of dimensions, and each dimension is divided into millions of realms." He looked at Frank to see if he was comprehending. The pink creature spoke with a voice that seemed not his own. Indeed, in most other realms, he would only have been capable of communicating in a series of grunts and squeals, but here he spoke with a somber tone and a beautiful timbre.

"Are there any black people in these omniverses?" asked Frank.
"What do you think?" asked Pink Guy. There was a pregnant silence before they both burst out laughing.
"This really must be the future then," laughed Frank. Despite being flung into an unknown world of darkness, Frank's garbage 1940's humor stayed intact.

"There are many lifeforms throughout the omniverses, Frank," the pink character said returning to sobriety. "Many. And these entities essentially fall - or are placed - into one of seven Tiers of Being."
"Who decided that?" Frank asked. Pink Guy ignored this question as one of utter stupidity. He continued. "The bottom tier contains the Wretched. The Wretched are those who have been confined to the abysses and the infernos. They exist but only in a form that knows suffering and pain."
"I'm guessing these hands..." he said gesturing out to the sea.
"Yes. They have been condemned."
"For what?"
"For ...," he struggled to find the right word. "For damages."

Frank looked off the edge of the rock, as one of the many wretched humanoid shadows swam towards him, reaching out with those skeletal hands, asking for another chance. Its mouth opened, but nothing came out. Frank could feel the warmth leaving its body as if its soul was being chipped away by the second. He quickly broke eye contact.

Pink Guy saw Frank's discomfort and cleared his throat. "The second tier from the bottom contains the brute beasts. Lower than humans and other humanoid creations, they exist but in a lesser form and with nominal consciousness. They can neither be elevated from their level nor condemned from it. They toil all their days as servants of those who exist above them. To those above them they are dominated and pitied. To the Wretched, the Beasts are free and secure, and the envy of their sorry souls."
As he said this, Frank continued to watch the knotted limbs stretching up from the black sea. He was still not entirely comfortable with this entity before him and so watched him with a cautious eye. "The third tier," Pink Guy continued, "hosts the mere mortals. You would be familiar with these. A somewhat sad and conflicted mob, they live a quasi existence in worlds in which they procreate and kill, create and destroy, love and hate. No-one really knows quite what to do with them. There's minimal intervention at this point. They are a sort of work in progress."
Frank looked down as he heard this. "I was trying to make the world a better place," he mumbled. "Mm," said Pink Guy. "By melting flesh." He moved on without another word.

"The fourth tier (and fourth from the top) are the rankenfiles. This includes entities like you and me, Frank."
Frank looked up, perplexed. "I'm not a mere mortal?"
"Far from it, Frank. You are a rankenfile. What's more," he looked intently at Frank as he said this, "you are the only one who has ever transcended from mere mortal to rankenfile. Suffice to say, there is a lot of interest in you."
"I'm the only one?" The corner of Frank's mouth broke into a proud grin. "That makes me kind of special then, doesn't it?"
"Whether this turn of events is fortunate for you or unfortunate, is yet to be determined. I strongly suspect the latter." Frank's

shoulders slumped at hearing this. "I warn you that this situation has developed not necessarily to your advantage." He looked at Frank with steely eyes. "That's why I was sent to you. I have come to get you before..." he grew nervous and his voice trailed off to a whisper "...before others do."

"Who sent you?"

"I don't know."

"What do you mean you don't know? Why would you come if you didn't know?"

"I felt compelled."

"How did this happen?" Frank asked. "I didn't work for this. I didn't seek it out or want it."

"It's impossible to tell. Maybe you were just in the right place at the right time (or the wrong place at the wrong time); maybe you are a pawn in a plot orchestrated by higher powers; or it's possible that you were never even human from the start."

Frank pondered these possibilities. None of them appealed to him. "So, I'm a rankenfile," he mused. "What does that even mean? How am I any different from a mere mortal?"

"Rankenfiles can appear in many different forms - including humanoid form - and are able to travel between omniverses, dimensions and realms."

"How?" Frank asked.

"It's what humans would call... chromosomes. Chromosomes are everything beyond the world you were living in. Chromosomes are the universal means of currency, time, travel and power. When your chromosomes began to multiply, you became a full rankenfile and this made you both an asset and a target. Your chromosomes are still progressively multiplying at a dangerously fast rate. Entities will fear you and hunt you for your chromosomes. And whenever they are used, sold or stolen, you will need to replenish them quickly or terrible things will happen." He paused before looking out over the iceberg they were sitting on. "I know," he said forlornly.

"The fifth tier are the chimpillas. The chimpillas are powerful. They travel the realms shadowing the rankenfiles, pursuing them for their chromosomes and pressing them into their service." Pink Guy began to sweat as he said this. "They are many and they can be savage." He was whispering now and looking about as though simply uttering a name could bring devastation. "Several of them are pursuing me ruthlessly and have sworn to pursue you as well. There is no escaping them. They will find you. All you can do is delay it for as long as possible and hope that you can escape without too much loss."
"Chimpillas?" Frank asked. In a flash Pink Guy had his finger to his lips. "Say nothing of them."
"But who are they and why would they want my chromosomes?" Frank wondered.

Pink Guy continued, dismissing the question as more mindless drivel. "The sixth and seventh tiers are shrouded in mystery. Nobody in the tiers below can say, with any certainty, who or what reigns in these two tiers (or even if there are two tiers). Rumor has it that the sixth tier belongs to the peace lords but few would even dare to state that publicly."
"The peace lords?" Frank repeated. "I'm guessing the chimpillas are the bad guys and the peace lords are the good guys?"
"Then you guess like a moron. Some chimpillas are good, others are evil and some are yet to make their allegiance known. What you have to understand, Frank, is that there are hostilities in the omniverses. And loyalty is currently a very fluid notion. The peace lords are extremely powerful yet no-one knows where their allegiances lie, certainly not us and perhaps not even amongst the peace lords themselves. Some are the very essence of evil, yet wrap themselves in light. Others are pure goodness, yet veil their loyalties with clouds of darkness and deception."

"Who is at the top tier? Who has supreme power?" Frank was agitated as he asked this.

"The top tier," said Pink Guy. He stopped there, lost for words, and Frank looked at him agog.

"Tell me about the top tier! You're here to reveal this to me, right? Who or what is at the top Tier of Being?" Frank glared at Pink Guy as he asked this. Pink Guy appeared reluctant to speak on, as if revealing any such names or identities or titles or presence could see him instantly thrown amongst the Wretched. "At the top tier," he said with a holy awe, "if the stories are true, is the Ultimate God." Pink Guy held Frank's tricep tightly and pulled him near to conclude his revelation. "We think the Ultimate God is Chin Chin," he whispered firmly in Frank's ear. Frank sat in wonder as he heard these words. "The Ultimate God," he mouthed. " Chin Chin!"

"Or so we think," whispered Pink Guy, leaning in again. They both sat there in reluctance. "The Ultimate God is the creator, the owner, the Lord of all. He is The Great One." Pink Guy paused again. "But the peace lords are becoming very powerful and they are uniting and amassing many chimpillas to serve under them. They have an untold number of chromosomes in their arsenal and they are rebelling against any force that opposes them. No-one knows anymore where the real power might lie. No-one knows who is in control."

He lowered his voice back down to a whisper again. "The tiers are shifting," he said, excited and horrified. "The natural order is changing. More and more entities are resisting their innate position and are storming other tiers. They do this by stealing chromosomes. It's the ultimate moral depravity. And it can, in effect, not only elevate them to higher tiers but potentially alter the constitution of others, destining them to lower tiers."

"But the peace lords," said Frank. "Won't they condemn those who do these things?"

"As I said, Frank. The tiers are shifting. Dimensions and realms are warping. This has never happened before. The omniverses no longer have the order that we once knew. Some are even becoming too powerful for the peace lords. Frank," he said looking about. He reserved his greatest gravity for this summation: "Some are contesting the Ultimate God."

The air in which they were sitting suddenly felt colder and damper. There was not a breath of wind but Frank felt a coolness run across his brow.

"One more thing, Frank." He looked at Pink Guy. " Chin Chin himself is coming for you. Your transition has provoked him."

"Do you mean he is coming for me to get me, or he's coming for me to help me?"

"Frank, you are completely expendable and Lord Chin Chin will spare nothing to get your chromosomes to secure his own position. Believe me, the Wretched will have nothing on you. Once Chin Chin is done with you, you will wish you were swimming in that abyss." Frank swallowed hard. "That's why I'm here. I'm here to protect you from Chin Chin; to take you to the furthest realms and deepest recesses of the omniverses to keep you from being found."

Frank sat in silence, processing all this. The iceberg they were sitting on remained static and the sea around them continued to display its silent agony. What Frank said next took Pink Guy completely by surprise. "I don't want to be a rankenfile."

"What?"

"I want to go back down to being a mere mortal. I want to return to what I once was. I don't want to be a part of this. I don't want to be hunted by Lord Chin Chin. I want to go back."

Pink Guy snapped at him. "It's too late for that, my friend. There's no turning now. You are what you are and you must live the life that you now have."

"Why? Why does it have to be too late? You said yourself you can't be sure what the upper tiers hold. The peace lords are still powerful. They might very well be forces for good. And what of the Ultimate God, whoever he is? Why wouldn't he have the power and the inclination to restore me? Between them all, there must be a way. Surely they can make me mortal again. They can stop my chromosomes from multiplying and return me to the life I had."

Pink Guy wanted to ignore this as another sentiment of monumental idiocy, but he could see how determined Frank was. "That might be true," he said. "But what is possible is not the same as what is probable. And the whim of a rankenfile is no match for the will of a Lord."

"I want to meet one of the Great Powers," Frank said, as though stating a universal right. "I want to meet a peace lord." He paused again, processing, and then he came out with it: "I want to meet the Ultimate God. I want to plead my case."

Pink Guy shook his head. "You're such a damn fool. You understand nothing. Leave that idea right now, I tell you. Leave it and have nothing more to do with it."

Frank stood and wiped his hands on his shirt as though to signal cessation in the matter. "We can't stay here forever," he said. Pink Guy rose with him. "Let's see what else this place has." They walked off without another word, side by side, yet the conversation trailed behind them like a chest being dragged by a chain. They passed along slippery narrow gullies with jagged icy daggers protruding at head height, and small stalagmite formations under foot. The landscape would change in appearance but not nature. They walked along broad open glacier-like fields, climbed walls of glass and stepped down into bulky gorges. Yet there was never a sound, nor a smell, nor a sense of fear or excitement. It was as though they were in their own bubble, separated from all other life and matter, all other sentiment and spirit.

Whilst there was no point in staying put, there was, clearly no point in continuing either. Eventually Pink Guy spoke. "I have co-ordinates for you Frank." They stopped walking and faced each other. "These coordinates will take you to a safe place. It's right off the grid. No-one will find you there."
"That's not necessarily good news," Frank returned.
"It's good news for now," he said looking at the limbs reaching up from the expanse around them. "Just recite them as I give them to you, and create the same circle of blood and you will be taken there."
"And what about you?"
"My work is done."
"You're not coming, too?"
"I don't have enough chromosomes to travel further and this place allows for no more replenishment." He looked stoic. "This is the end of the road for me. They will come. They will find me."
"You came to warn me on a suicide mission?"
"Suicide, no. But there is no more life ahead for me. My future ceases to exist here."

Though he barely knew Pink Guy, and he had never really cared for anybody before in his life, hearing this was like a stab in the chest.
"I will come back for you," said Frank with a newfound ethic.
"It will be too late. They will find me here before you return and they will condemn me without a moment's hesitation."
"Use my chromosomes," Frank insisted. "If you use mine, then we could both go through."

Pink Guy shook his head. "That wouldn't leave you with enough chromosomes to travel on if you needed to. And that would be a very dangerous state to be in."

"But the place I'm going to is safe, right? I could stay there until my chromosomes replenished and then move on."

Pink Guy considered this with caution. It made sense but it was not part of the plan.

"I have no idea where I'm going," Frank continued, "what to do there, or when and where to move again. I need you to come with me. Surely we're safer together?"

Pink Guy squatted before his new friend, deep in thought. "Let's go then," he said looking up. He stood shoulder to shoulder with Frank. "You will need to cut your hand and create a circle of blood around us, as before. I will recite the co-ordinates."

"What if you get the coordinates wrong?" Frank asked casually, almost as a joke. Pink Guy responded with a look that shook Frank to his very core. "Then heaven help us," he said breaking out into another sweat." This passing question of Frank's led to a flurry of others which suddenly took him to dark places. Who was this Pink Guy really? How did Frank know he could trust him? What if he were one of the lackeys of an evil peace lord? What if he were a peace lord? What if he were Chin Chin himself?

Frank, caught up in the moment, came right out with this last question and barked it to Pink Guy's face.

"If I were Chin Chin,"he retorted, "I would have stolen your chromosomes and finished you off in a flash. You would be bathing with our friends right there in the sea of infernal suffering."

Frank, still breathing heavily, looked Pink Guy in the eye. "Good answer," he said through clenched teeth. "Good answer." Frank walked over to a shard of ice and ran his hand along it. The life force flowed freely from the wound. He returned to Pink Guy who had already begun reciting the co-ordinates. Frank made the crimson circle around them both before standing back-to-back with his comrade. Over and over Pink Guy called the numbers and letters, louder and louder, with increasing zeal. Frank prepared for destruction. As Pink Guy continued to call, Frank continued to brace. On and on he called with a voice that rose up over the sea. It soon reached fever pitch, bursting with prolepsis.

Then suddenly, he slumped. "What happened?" asked Frank.
"I don't know. It's not working. Nothing's happening."
"Are sure you got the coordinates right?"
"Are you sure you used the right blood?" Pink Guy shot back, offended.
Frank began to move from his spot and as he did, he felt the squelch of soft ground beneath him. "It's soft," he said.
"So it is," Pink Guy returned. Indeed, the land outside the circle remained as hard as a diamond but the ground inside continued to soften and liquify. The more they trod within the circle, the more pulpy the ground became until before long they were ankle deep in water. To hasten the process they began to jump up and down, being very careful to stay within the confines of the red band.

Neither of them were aware of the rate at which they were sinking into the hole so suddenly being waist deep in water took them both by surprise. The greater shock came moments later when Frank found himself on his own, in near-total darkness, overtaken by torrents of water. He was drowning. At first his sole awareness was of his impending death. Yet this fear was easily surpassed by the torment of the Wretched as he brushed by them. Souls of children long deceased, yet still perishing grabbed at his fingers and toes, begging for help, pleading for mercy, wailing and cursing, tossing about in their torment and laying hold of him. They stared at him through empty eye sockets and wailed through stitched mouths. They would float by him, writhing and holding their bellies in agony as they inflated and then burst open.

From the wound, new infants would ooze out before their bellies swelled and ruptured, and so the nightmare would go on. Other babies, gliding with awkward flinches through the murkiness, would suddenly stop and then turn completely inside out. Muscle and bone would remain frailly bound together, but strings of intestines and sinew would be flung off into the swell. As such, the current surrounding him was a thick amniotic soup.

The infants were instinctively grabbing and gnawing on each other as they drifted about. Yet a sad semblance of compassion developed in which they would pull out their own teeth to spare the others, but their teeth would rapidly and constantly grow back. Frank felt their agony. He felt their pain in all its forms and degrees. His screams became bawls. "I'm sorry!" he roared. "I'm sorry I can't save you!" The grasping and calling, the sorrow and the sobbing continued unabated until Frank took one final gasp, filled his lungs with the fluid and floated off to his quiet end.

Chapter 5

It was like so, but wasn't. Frank came to, but didn't. He was conscious but of the sort that might accompany an out-of-body experience or an animated suspension. The first thing he perceived was that he was floating through an entirely new dimension - one of previously unknown physical qualities. He was free of gravity and completely weightless. His skin tingled as though he were being lightly caressed all over. The light around him was distorted in an other worldly way and made everything look soft and beautiful. Pretty shadows and reflected lights danced around him. Time ceased to exist and a beautiful silence encapsulated him. For Frank, it was a rare, beautiful moment, shattered only by the realisation that he was floating face down in a swamp and about to choke.

He rose from the waters, coughing and spluttering and retching and crying. He needed a few moments to regain full awareness and when he did, misery was there with a comprehension that traveling between realms was like death and rebirth each time. He sat in the shallow water amidst a vast forest of mangroves. Strips of seaweed fluttered in slow motion under the water, tickling his calves and wrapping around his toes. Small fish darted under and out of the roots of the trees. Occasionally, flat creatures with gill slits that looked like stab wounds, would hover over the sandy bed and slowly move away when Frank tried to kick them. Frank was relieved to find familiar ecosystems in other realms.

He stood to look about over the branches of the trees. The mangrove forest around him extended to the horizon in all directions but one. Above him was a sunless sky that sat hot and heavy like a bronze dome. Bat-like birds flew above and through the trees, which were infested with all manner of insects, spiders and giant winged arthropods. Pale, flakey-skinned snakes slithered quietly along branches and across the surface of the water. To Frank, this place was eerily like the jungles of Okinawa on a bad day and moving through it brought bitter memories and an ominous sense that worse was to come.

Pink Guy was nowhere to be seen. Frank didn't want to bring attention to himself so calling for him was out of the question. The logical thing was to move in the only direction that didn't lead to more mangroves. In that line, above the forest was a cluster of golden, rather picturesque foothills which skirted an enormous pointed mountain. It rose up and almost touched the rusty sky. The water he was wading through was never deeper than his waist so his only real challenge was avoiding the fauna, half of which scattered in fear as he approached and half of which moved toward him in the hope of enjoying a warm meal.

The last region of the mangrove was ankle deep so Frank made quick progress toward the amber fields. Just short of the shoreline he stopped and listened carefully. An odd sound could be heard from nearby but then ceased. Frank waited patiently, listening and peering. He could see nothing. He had hoped that it might be Pink Guy. The sound came again, like a beast prancing on the spot in the muddy waters. Frank moved more closely toward it, trying to keep his sodden footsteps as quiet as possible. Again the sound came, wild and moist, through the low lying trees. It was near now, a ferocious and juicy sound, and Frank felt a fresh nausea rise up within him.

Peering through a leafy scrub on his left, he saw a white creature with a bulbous yellow head devouring the intestines of a still-conscious beast kicking in the shallow waters. Though the creature seemed skittish, it didn't notice Frank watching him from behind. He moved around in a large circle to come into the creature's view and when he saw Frank he jumped and let out a hideous cry. "I'm a lemon!" It was an apt introduction. This creature looked like a warty lemon atop a thin radish. Frank kept his distance as the two sized each other up.

"I'm a lemon!" the creature yelled again. Frank quickly assumed that debating might not be this thing's strong point.
"I'm Frank," Frank called back with a friendly wave.
"I'm a lemon!" he heard again.
"Yeah, I got that," said Frank before quietly mumbling, "I'm in the land of morons."
"I'm a lemon! I'm a lemon!" it called again, slowly approaching Frank.
"Well, you know what they say about when you get stuck with a lemon..." Frank chuckled.
"I'm a lemon! I'm a lemon!" He was becoming more agitated as he spoke, his voice rising with each profession. Frank began to sense that this creature might actually be a complex soul imprisoned in its lemony shell. As he drew nearer, Frank got a better look at his counterpart. He had an enormous yellow head, like a lemon on its side. Some lemons have a beautiful symmetry to them. This one did not. It was bulgy and lopsided and covered with pox and warts. Pure ugly. And the unattractiveness of the head was not helped by its eyes, which were vacuous and black, or the entrails of the organism dangling from the corners of its mouth. Whatever intelligence may have been buried within, it held an overall countenance of retardation.

"I'm looking for Pink Guy," Frank said. The citrusy organism just stood there looking at him, utterly confused. "Pink Guy," Frank continued in slow speech. "Ah, a pink humanoid who is actually a rankenfile. Looks... pink. And sort of like... a guy."
"I'm a lemon!"
"Yeah," Frank said before mumbling, "this could take a while". He took a few steps toward Lemon Man. "Listen carefully, I don't have all millennium. I'm looking for Pin..." Taking his approach as a threat, Lemon Man immediately set upon him with a flurry

52

of blows and a maniacal ripping with layers of razor sharp teeth. "Lemon! Lemon! Lemon!" was all Frank could hear screaming at him as his head was buried in the ground. He rolled back over to defend himself, kicking and occasionally punching, but the Lemon Man was too quick and too powerful. Again and again Frank received the hard end of a warty lemon in the face; over and over it was pounded into his mouth, his eyes and for good measure, his groin, all to the accompanying sound of an animal in great distress. Frank was done. He had nothing left to fight this creature off.

As the brown skies above him were about to dim to gray, he saw another white shape drop from a tree above him onto the Lemon Man. The new white creature planted itself firmly on Lemon Man's shoulders and began to shout and holler as the Lemon Man tried eagerly to throw the creature from him. The two of them formed a singular staggering, screaming beast, the white and yellow one on the bottom, bucking and convulsing in terrible distress, and the white and green one on the top holding on for dear life and calling out in an entirely different dialect. "Nyeees!" he called in a most triumphant but still cautious manner. "Nyess!" Frank sat up with an acute desire to have his eyesight and hearing checked. He had no idea what to make of this flurry of white and yellow and green, and this cacophony of 'lemons' and 'nyesses'.

Eventually the Lemon Man was able to free himself from the green and white creature and ran off sour and sore. Frank's savior watched him flee before turning to Frank and helping him up. An odd-looking entity, he appeared unnervingly like a humanoid salamander. His body was slimy and white, while his head took a green amphibious form. Frank opened his mouth to thank him for coming to his rescue but was cut off with a face palm. Immediately, the creature then produced - seemingly from nowhere - a recorder, placed it firmly in his left nostril and began to play a rousing rendition of an ancient tune.

53

"Ah, a cultured man!" said Frank when he had finished the tune. "I guess you're here to help me and not eat me?" He was beginning to calm down from his beating.

"Nyeess."

"I'll take that as a 'yes'."

"Nyess."

"Listen, I wonder if you can help me. (That was beautiful by the way. I wonder if you could play a few oom-pah-pah tunes for me later on.)" The Salamander Man looked perplexed but continued to give his attention. "I'm looking for Pink Guy," continued Frank. "You haven't by any chance seen him?"

"Nyes," he replied, shaking his head. Frank was beginning to speak this guy's language.

"Well, would you mind helping me look for him? I don't know my way around here and I'd hate to come across Lemon Man again on my own."

"Nyeeeesss." Frank somehow understood this to mean, 'Lemon Man is not a bad guy. You just scared the shit out of him, that's all'.

The two of them walked out of the waters and along the dry shoreline, between the muddy banks of the mangrove to their left, and the hazy fields to their right. "I'm Frank, by the way," said Frank, checking his cranium and his testicles for injuries. It was an odd series of gestures to accompany an introduction.

"Nyyeess."

He was going to explain where he'd come from and why but stopped, realising this would be an impossible task, if not a risky one, given the turn of events so far.

They hadn't walked much further when they heard, off in the distance, the faint sound of a caterwaul. They hastened toward it and as they drew nearer they could hear just how intense the howling was. Some creature was in terrible agony and Frank could only hope it was Lemon Man. The screaming came from a cluster of trees in front of a large rock formation. Frank ran toward it with Salamander Man galloping right behind him. Approaching it, Frank was able to see what he had been hearing and it filled him with horror. They had found Pink Guy. Still kicking and screaming, he had been noosed from the highest branch of a tree. Only this clearly wasn't the common hanging of a common land. Shadows passed in and out of his eyes and nose and ears and mouth and with each entering and exiting he shivered in pain and fright. Not an orifice was left untouched, nor a fear left unstoked. The rope choked the breath out of him as the shadows violated his spirit. Pink Guy completely lost his coloring.

Salamander Man was up the tree in a flash and produced - again seemingly from nowhere - a knife with which he cut the rope. Frank caught him as he fell, lay him on the ground and removed the noose from him. It took some time for Pink Guy to regain his composure.
Salamander Man reproduced his recorder and began to play a soothing tune which cut through the stilling air. As he did, the shadows retreated and a spirit of calm returned.

"What took you so long?" he eventually asked Frank.
"Um, well, Lemon Man. That's what."
"Ah, Lemon Man," said Pink Guy with a knowing nod. He was familiar with the lemon folk. "He can be a real pain in the ass." He turned and saw Frank's new friend. "Hey, Salamander Man," he said cheering up. "Haven't seen you for a while."
"Is this guy safe?" Frank asked Pink Guy, pointing to Salamander Man.
"Absolutely. Trust me on this. I can sense it." Indeed Pink Guy's ability to sense the good and evil in creatures was one of his defining traits, and a reason that he had been chosen to bring revelation to Frank.

"Nyeess!" Immediately Salamander Man had his recorder in his hand, shoved it into his left nostril again and began playing his favorite tune. It was beautiful. For a short while there, everything felt right with the omniverse and Frank was happy.

"Okay," Frank said. "What do we do now?"
"We lay low," Pink Guy returned. He was back to full cognition now. "We have to stay here until your chromosomes are fully replenished and then we look at getting you an audience with a higher power. I suggest we make for the woods along the foothills and use their cover." Everyone was in agreement, so they forged a track through the long grass of the fields and didn't stop till they were in the shade of the trees and sipping water from a pond.

Frank reclined by the still waters. "Now this is more like it! I've had quite enough of lemons and nooses and being groped by embryos." Pink Guy was tempted to ask about the embryos but knew better than that. "Don't be fooled, Frank," he said. Frank looked at him. "It's in the quiet oases that the greatest perils lie. Always be vigilant, Frank. Always be on the watch."
"What, are you clinically depressive, or something, Pink Guy?" He'd forgotten that Pink Guy, just a few moments ago, had been hanging from a tree and tormented by demons. "Can't you let a guy enjoy a quiet moment?"
"Enjoy it while you can, Frank," Pink Guy said, but there was more than a hint of resignation in his voice.

Before he finished speaking, there was a loud rustle from a shrub behind him and a brown creature sprang out and cried "Be all!" Frank jumped up and immediately spooned Pink Guy. "Who is this and what does he want?" Frank whispered in his ear in a way that was much more creepy than concerned. The creature in front of them was another humanoid, brown from head to foot, except for an enormous black afro on his head, black sunglasses and a huge set of white choppers in his mouth. He looked very happy to see these three visitors. "The by up for jump and happy!" he said.

"I'm sorry," said Frank, sitting up and releasing Pink Guy. "My filter's playing up. Could you say that again?"

"Ah!" he said with a chuckle, "If without or a buckle so likely!" he said, before breaking into a tremendous cackle. Clearly, he was having a wonderful time. "Can't up the heath for soil!" he added, ribbing Salamander Man in the chest.

"Nyeess!" said Salamander Man.

"What is this guy talking about?" asked Frank.

"He's a balderdash," said Pink Guy. "A rankenfile of small intellect but enormous charm." The creature stood there beaming. "But no-one has any idea what they are going on about."

"A balderdash?" said Frank.

"So the last!" said the brown one. He was thrilled.

"Does he have a name?"

"Don't know," said Pink Guy. "But even if he does, we wouldn't understand what he was telling us. I suspect he can understand us but we can't follow him."

"Far too the lucky but cheese and excited!"

"Nyes, nyes," Salamander Man chirped in.

"You understand Balderdash?" Frank asked him. He was starting to enjoy this communion.

"Nyess!"

"Ah, so you're both retards." He turned to the newest entity in their troupe. "Brown Guy, ah, Turd Man, ah, sir, do you have a name?" Frank asked.

"Ha ha ha!" The Brown one replied. "A pus bucket to enflamed!" No creature had ever looked prouder of himself.

Salamander Man turned to Frank. "Nyess!"

"What did he say, Frank?" asked Pink Guy.

"He said his name is Negi Generation 4."

57

"I have to admit," said Pink Guy, reflecting to Frank. "I never would have guessed that."

"Kind of odd for a name, don't you think?" he whispered back to Pink Guy. "How do you say your name again?" he asked Negi Generation 4. "In your language. I want to speak your lingo."

"Blonde muscles of under and coughing," he said. He was bouncing on the balls of his feet and pissing himself with joy.

"Negi Generation 4," Salamander Man confirmed in his language.

"Ah, but that's not, er, what he said before." Frank was genuinely baffled.

"Hence, a balderdash," said Pink Guy, reclining back down beside the pond.

They spent the rest of the afternoon catching their supper, and the evening roasting it over an open flame. Frank recalled stories of Okinawa, slightly embellished for the telling, which Pink Guy occasionally interrupted with calls of cock and bull. Salamander Man played his flute whenever there was a lull in the conversation, which was rare because Negi Generation 4 talked virtually non-stop, pausing only to laugh at his own, rather fabulous eccentricities. Indeed Negi Generation's delightful chuckling was the last thing Frank heard before falling into the most pleasant sleep he'd had since childhood.

When he woke in the morning, the sky above him was a pale yellow and the higher foliage around him moved with the gentlest of breezes. The others were still sleeping by the remains of a fire that continued to smolder, and a few small creatures were docilely picking at what was left of their meal from the night before. Yet all around them, on the floor of the forest, on the canopies of the shrubs and the branches of the trees, sat ever so delicately, a sea of translucent spheres ranging in size from grape to watermelon. Despite the frivolity of the previous night and the peace he had found in the present company, Frank was gripped with alarm at the sight of these bubble-like apparitions.

He rapped Pink Guy on the foot. On waking, he immediately sat bolt upright and stared at the phenomena, deeply troubled by it. His movement caused the others to wake and soon they were looking in bewilderment at this sea of enormous suds surrounding them. All were disturbed by it except for Negi Generation 4. He promptly strutted over to one and picked it up. "A sty and with the jolly be!" With that, he opened his mouth wide and threw it in. He swallowed, his eyes sparkled, and then he let out a hearty burp.

"What did he say Salamander Man?" Frank asked.

Salamander Man, not sure if he had heard correctly, stuttered out his answer. "He said, 'breakfast is served'."

"Ha ha ha!" cackled the brown one before picking up one of the larger bubbles and sucking it slowly out of shape and into his mouth. "Ah!" he cried. "Far the frisk!"

"He said..." began Salamander Man.

"...Yeah, we get it," said Frank, cutting him off. He ventured over and lifted one of the opaque spheres from a leaf, sniffed it, and then popped it into his mouth. "Hey," he said after some savouring, "that's pretty good. Sort of like a sticky strawberry gel but with a touch of honey." His licked his teeth and gums. "Not bad at all."

The others all promptly tucked into the servings on offer and enjoyed every moment of it. It was only Pink Guy, apparently, who had a moment of angst with the meal, having the misfortune to suck in a bubble that he said tasted rather like dog faeces. He added very quickly that he had never actually tried dog faeces but that if he had, that is the taste sensation that he would very much have expected. His other circular jellies (as he called them) were very much to his liking, especially the largest one he consumed which he said reminded him of caramel ice cream. They feasted on these treats until they could feast no more, which was rather timely because as the dome above them heated to a burnt gold color, the bubbles melted into the ground, sustaining the plant life, until none remained at all.

The days passed like this, yet it was unclear to any of them how long the days were and how many days or months or years they had been there. They simply existed, as though in their own ageless sphere. Frank asked Pink Guy why this was so. "Time is relative in the omniverses, differing from realm to realm and from dimension to dimension, affected also by the total number of chromosomes present in any region," he said. "When the peace lords gathered, for instance, there was such a massive abundance of chromosomes that time in that realm dominated the time in any other realm. It's not that time moved more quickly or slowly, but simply that it was dominant over the time specs of other realms and dimensions. By contrast, in realms where chromosomes were in scant supply, time was inferior to that of just about any other realm about it." In this environment, Frank had no idea how much his own chromosomes had been multiplying. "So you can grow chromosomes faster," Pink Guy continued, "in regions where time is dominant but you do so at your own risk because there are a greater number of higher tier entities there. The strong get stronger," he said by way of conclusion.

It was an uncharacteristically warm morning, possibly a Thursday in other realms, when Negi Generation 4 strolled over to Frank, slapped him on the back and with an enormous guffaw said, "Tonsils go by the stave to fry and why not!" Absolutely clueless as to what he had just said, Frank returned the slap on the back and laughed along hard with him. "So the donkey and kindly the nuts!" he said trying to speak the Negi's language. At that very moment, the balderdash suddenly fell to the ground as rigid as a pole on an icy day. Frank wondered what on earth it was that he had said to make him stiffen like that. "All I said was…" but he could no longer remember what it was that he had said.

"Go up the mountain!" Negi said.

Shocked, Frank, Pink Guy and Salamander Man gathered around him. "I understood him," Frank said, perplexed. "He said, 'Go up the mountain'."

"Go up the mountain," the Negi repeated in the same mechanical voice.

"Negi!" shouted Pink Guy slapping Negi in the face as hard as he could. "Snap out of it! Snap out of it!"

"What's wrong?!" Frank asked him. He grabbed him by the shoulders and began to shake him violently. "C'mon, Negi. Snap out of it, son!"

Negi Generation 4 lay completely seized up on the ground. "Go up the mountain," he said again. The three other entities stared at each other. Suddenly an entirely different vibe possessed them. Laughter, peace and levity were replaced with somberness, fear and gravity.

"Go up the mountain," came the same cold command. Negi began to convulse. It was just a quiver at first, but it grew quickly into fully fledged convulsions till he looked like a fish flopping about on dry land. With the spasms came a torrent of the same directives. "Go up the mountain! Go up the mountain! Go up the mountain!..." He was screeching like a possessed man. And then he stopped. At first the others felt quite sure he was dead. There was no movement, no breathing, no life. They slowly squatted around him and prepared to give him a solemn farewell.

Frank was about to poke him in the cheek to see if it could elicit any response, but before he could, Negi Generation 4 sat up on his elbows, flashed his smile and declared, "Moons to blue and milky when the stirrups!" He broke into his familiar cackle and jumped up on his feet. He looked curiously at his three companions. "Pacing neither with oil or not?"

"He wants to know why you're all staring at him," Salamander Man translated. It was clear to the others that Negi had no idea what had just transpired.

Frank paused before answering. "We're just looking at a very handsome fellow," he said.

"Book off for under the grouse!" he replied bouncing on his toes again. "Oh, the yet!"

"Absolutely, my friend! Just what I was going to say!" Frank encouraged him.

Yet the command that had been incessantly repeated during Negi's missing minutes was not lost on Frank, Pink Guy or Salamander Man. Their discussion on the matter was a mere formality. They knew they had to ascend the mountain. They just had no idea why. Negi couldn't understand why the three were so determined to make the climb, but as long as they were all together, he was happy enough.

The day was still young when they started off. None of them had gone up the mountain before so they were complete novices when it came to its terrain. Yet the mountain was, for the most part, even and without treacherousness. As such, they made good progress. The morning events continued to weigh on their minds so there was little discussion between them as they climbed. Negi Generation 4 picked up on this and he, too, remained uncharacteristically quiet. Walking in single file and with their eyes fixed toward the summit, none of them noticed the swarm of creatures coming out of the swamplands and mudflats and woodlands following them up the slopes.

It was Pink Guy who first sensed their presence. "We're being followed," he said, without turning around to see them. They all paused and sat on a ledge to rest and looked back down the mountain. There, while still at a considerable distance, was a multitude of creatures, great and small. Predominantly brute beasts but also some other rankenfiles and possibly some from the higher tiers, their numbers couldn't be counted; they covered the foothills like pebbles on a beach. They stopped when the four rankenfiles stopped, and continued when they continued. They retreated when the rankenfiles turned toward them, and advanced irresistibly when they turned away.

Sitting on a gentle rocky ledge surveying the distant mangroves below, Pink Guy explained this happening to the others.
"It's you, Frank." All three looked at the Okinawan. "They sense it," he continued. "They sense, Frank, that your chromosomes are multiplying at unprecedented rates. They can feel it. It's rare that entities not of this realm pass through here, but they have never sensed from anyone what they are sensing from you."

This seemed so ridiculous to Frank that he was ready to dismiss it outright. But he had no other explanation for what was happening, so kept his thoughts to himself for the time being. More creatures began emerging from the trees and grasslands. "The more I see what's happening in and around you, Frank, the more I worry," Pink Guy said. "And the more we need to take care," he added with caution. "You are what this world might consider royalty."
"Too minty and the under of out," Negi said, in a much more sullen voice than they were used to hearing.
"If we stay together, we'll all be fine," Pink Guy assured them. He was lying. He looked out over the landscape. "The tiers are changing," he recalled in a still voice. "We should move on."

On turning back to face the mountain, they were startled to see a hideous creature just a stone's throw from them. A reptilian humanoid, he was a fearful sight. His head was singed, a rusty distortion of what it had once been and its torso and upper limbs were burned beyond usefulness. Scorched flesh hung and dripped from its body in large chunks. But its most terrible trauma was to

63

the lower half of its body, a charred mess of staggering legs, exposed organs and twisted tail. He stumbled toward them. "Come with me," he moaned. None of them moved. "Come with me," he said again, gesturing with what was perhaps his only functioning limb. The wind picked up as he spoke and blew his stench toward them.

It was Negi who took the first step. "No!" called Pink Guy, and Negi stepped back in line with the others. "He's condemned. He's soon to be one of the Wretched and he wants us to save him. But we can't. If we go with him we risk being condemned ourselves. Have nothing to do with him." Pink Guy turned and headed up the mountain at a brisk pace, with the others all following in like manner, leaving the condemned creature to his morbid fate.

At this point they were more than half way up the mountain and the summit came into view. Yet as it did, the gusts of wind grew stronger, the sky began to gray (a phenomena they had never seen in that place before) and clouds began to form (also something they had never previously seen there). They pressed on. The higher they climbed, the fiercer the winds became, the thicker the clouds were and the blacker the sky grew. Each of them were aware, if not terrified, of the ominous implications of this atmosphere yet they each knew, without doubt, they had to scale the summit. Frank hoped that somehow in reaching the top, they would have satisfied some cosmic requirement and everything would return to normal. Pink Guy suspected something entirely more nefarious. Salamander Man and Negi Generation simply had the feeling that they were way out of their depth.

By the time they reached the summit it was completely shrouded in dark clouds. The wind blew in flurries, peels of thunder began to echo about them and a smell of burning filled the air. Atmospheric conditions aside, there was a creepiness which none of them could source yet which they all sensed vividly, a sulphuric stench which sickened them. It caused them to pull apart and observe each other with a hint of suspicion. Time stood still there on the mountain top; an eerie emptiness in the midst of a storm.

But that was it. The four entities looked at one another, unsure what to make of it all. They had satisfied the mystic command through Negi Generation 4 to go up the mountain, and they had experienced some highly unusual phenomena on the mountain top, but there seemed to be little more to it than that.
"What do we do now?" Salamander Man eventually asked.
"Do we just go back down?" It was more of a suggestion than a question from Frank. No-one responded. They continued to wait, looking about them and wandering on the spot like kids lost in a canyon.

Pink Guy was about to suggest they return to the foothills when a swirl of dark clouds lowered before them on the very pinnacle of the mountain, not a tree length from them. The clouds slowed to a majestic stillness before parting to reveal a dark figure descending on a cushion of gray clouds that delivered him like a royal visitation. In the parting mountain top air, they could see without any restriction, the manifestation before them and it was one of fearful ugliness. Every aspect of his presence, from his physical appearance to his spiritual disposition, proclaimed a sickening hideousness. Before him, leashed with heavy chains, were two small but ferocious minions. They lashed out indiscriminately, clawing and leaping, snarling and drooling and hungry for blood. As the cloud settled on the ground, the central creature squirmed and then rolled forth into a crouch position. Then it moved toward them.

The four climbers could sense nothing but outright fear. Frank felt a stabbing pain down the side of his neck. His face turned a ghostly shade of gray and though it was cool, he began to sweat uncontrollably. The creature moved in awkward tics, slowly at first, but occasionally in bursts, and in a line that would normally be associated with the stagger of a drunkard. Crablike, it approached them, and though they drew back, it was upon them, right before them and within them. Terror seized each of them and they were unable to move. Though their spirits within them tried to flee, their feet remained locked firmly to the ground. All the creatures that had been following them up the mountain had no such impositions placed upon them and scattered as soon as they saw the presence.

It was Pink Guy who first uttered the words: "Lord Chin Chin". The whole sky lit up as he said it in one enormous lightning bolt that seemed to forget to flash back off again. The light from it revealed his appearance in its fullness, not least of all his eyes which were stitched together, yet seemed to be looking in all directions at once. His faced twitched again as he looked up at Frank with a mixture of longing and detestation. "O Chin Chin ga dai suki da yo." The words gave Frank a tingling paralysis in his spine. The peace lord's face twitched again as he considered Frank. "O Chin Chin," he repeated.

There was a curious, perhaps mystical, connection between Frank and Lord Chin Chin that neither of them could identify and that disturbed both. But it did mean that Frank could understand Chin Chin's language without any misconceptions. Where the other three only heard "O Chin Chin ga dai suki da yo" repeatedly, Frank heard a language, ancient and complex, powerful and innate, and he responded in kind.

"I have come for you," Frank heard the dark lord speak. His voice had a piercing authority and a childish whine. Initially Frank remained speechless, horrified to his core but as Chin Chin repeated his claim, Frank found his voice.
"What do you want with me?" he asked.

"You dare speak to me without me asking you to?" He looked incensed at this. "Have you no respect for higher powers? Have you no idea who I am and what I am capable of?"

"What do you want with me?" Frank asked again.

The dark lord convulsed with rage at this. There were more peels of thunder and rain pelted against Frank's face. "You speak when I tell you to speak!" The words came out like exorcised spirits.

His face suddenly jerked as though receiving a fresh inspiration. "You don't fear me," he said, sickened by the thought of it. "Oh, you're afraid of me but you don't fear me." He looked up at Frank who, to the relief of the others, commanded his full attention. "Fear comes from knowledge," he said giving Frank an education. "Knowledge of good and evil. Knowledge of one's true place in this life. And knowledge that I... am... GOD!" The last word spewed out, and as he said it, it reverberated around the mountain. With it, he cast his arm powerfully toward Negi Generation 4, instantly decapitating him and knocking his lifeless body down the slopes of the mountain.

Pink Guy and Salamander Man reeled back in horror at the sight of this. Never in their lives had they seen such wanton disregard for innocent life.

Frank watched the body slide down the rock face before shrugging. I quite liked him, Frank thought. What a shame.

"Do I have your fear now?" Chin Chin asked him. Frank remained in silent terror.

"I came here to kill you, Frank." He paused for effect. "I don't like you. I despise you. I have in my very soul an intense desire to hurt you. I want you to feel all the pain of the omniverses. I want you to suffer like no-one else has ever suffered before. I want your name to become synonymous with unspeakable pain." Frank already felt halfway there.

"But I won't, Frank." If it were possible, there was a slight softening in his voice. "I have other plans for you." Frank gave Chin Chin his full attention. (The other two had no idea what he was saying.) "You have an impressive rate of increase in your chromosomes, Frank. And the rate is increasing. This makes you useful. So I will give you the honor of allowing you to make a deal with me. I will return you back to your human world and allow you to live - and relatively free of pain - and in return you will give me your chromosomes. What sayest thou? Which do you choose, Frank? Eternal suffering of the highest order or an obscure life without excessive chromosomes?" His face ticked again as if it functioned as punctuation.

Though eternal suffering of the highest order was clearly not the choice to make, Frank lamented the miserable option that the other choice left him. And so with sad resignation he said, "I'll give you my chromosomes."
"I want to hear it again," the dark lord said.
" I will give you my chromosomes," Frank repeated.
"Very well. When I leave here it will be with your chromosomes. And I will be transporting you to a secret place far from here where you can replenish your chromosomes in relative peace and quiet and where I can find you anytime I want. Is that understood?"
"Yes," Frank said solemnly.
"After I have left, go back down the mountain, your transport will be complete before you get to the bottom."

With that, the dark lord Chin Chin crawled back to the pinnacle of the mountain and curled into a ball. The wind picked up once again, thunder and lightning cracked and hail stones the size of limes fell all about them. Dark clouds slowly enveloped him and then he was gone. Very quickly, the clouds dissipated, the weather cleared and the sky returned to its golden glow. The three remaining rankenfiles came together, observed Negi Generation

4's remains for a while, and then headed back down the mountain.

Physically, the trek down was somehow more difficult than the one up. Psychologically and spiritually, they were all changed entities for the mountaintop experience, and as they descended, Frank shared with Pink Guy the conversation he had had with Chin Chin. When he had finished, Pink Guy stopped and looked at Frank with a hint of relief on his face. "I wonder..." his voice trailed off there.

"What?" asked Frank.

"I can't be sure..." He thought some more. Frank waited as a gust of wind blew between them. "But I suspect that Chin Chin might not be God," he said.

"You could have fooled me," Frank returned.

"Oh, he's powerful. He can control atmospheric conditions and he can take life. But he's not God."

"How can you be so sure?"

"What he does is the work of a peace lord. God..." Pink Guy paused to find the right words... "wouldn't need your chromosomes."

Frank wasn't sure whether to be relieved or more anxious at hearing this. Yet the more he thought about it the more it made sense. The further down the mountain they travailed, the better they all felt, until halfway down, when a spirit of utter levity came upon them all. Salamander Man produced his recorder and began to play a spritely tune. Pink Guy actually began to skip along as he played. As they drew nearer to the foothills, just above a series of steep cliffs, there was a sudden and very powerful earthquake. The whole mountain seemed to bend and start cracking.

Holding on to a sharp rock ledge for dear life, Frank's forearm was cut from wrist to elbow and then the three of them were tossed from their thin ledge and fell bouncing and flopping down the cliffs. They landed together in a circle of blood, broken and cut and bleeding and torn, groaning and moaning and screaming and cussing. Egg size rocks, and boulders the size of large dinosaurs, fell on them till they were buried under a small mountain that rose from the foothills like an altar to a deity. When the dust had settled, there was nothing left alive in that land higher than a brute beast.

Chapter 6

It is a truth universally acknowledged, that a bunch of guys caught under heavy debris are in a lot of trouble. All Frank was aware of, upon waking up, was the sound of sirens and the thick dust which clogged his nostrils. He was pressed down, trapped under a load of wreckage and flesh, and disturbed by a series of grunts and primal whines. He pushed several layers of plasterboard and broken pieces of concrete from him, removed Pink Guy's knee from his groin and Salamander Man's recorder from between his thighs, stood and dusted himself off. "Where the hell are we?" he said. His companions slowly rose from the ruins, complaining of aches and pains, and surveyed their new landscape. They could see little of it.

Everywhere they looked was concrete. Concrete flooring, concrete walls and concrete pylons. The only thing that wasn't entirely concrete was the ceiling, which now had a gaping hole in it. It was dark. A lack of windows and a quiet air, still choking with the dust of an explosion, gave them little to see. Clearly, they were in the basement of some sort of building but beyond that, they had no idea where they were or what lay around the corner. Sirens continued to blare periodically and there was a distant sound of bustle.

"Pink Guy," said Frank. "Do you have any idea where Chin Chin has sent us?"
Pink Guy replied with a long demented groan.
"Yeah, I know buddy. I'm feeling it, too."
Frank's pink friend let out another painfully twisted cry, this time tinged with frustration.
"Pink Guy!" said Frank. "This is no time to be playing Lemon Man." He began to shake him by the shoulders. "I need you buddy. Where are we? What's going on here?"

Pink Guy shrugged and repeated his sorry whining.

"Looks like those rocks might have hit you harder in the head than I thought," Frank said, more to himself than to the others. "Salamander Man, you got it together?" His froggy friend nodded in an impeded way, slowly placed his recorder deep into his left nostril and began to play a slightly gloomy tune. It was clear to Frank that in this realm at least, he would be the leader of his clan.

"Come on," he said and led the others across the cold dusty floor to a staircase at the end of the building. They ascended a few flights before stepping out into bright sunshine. It took a while for their eyes to adjust to the brightness but when they did, they were amazed at all the sights and sounds and activity of the place. It was buzzing with life and this gave the three travelers a feeling of excitement and a sense of anxiety. Street after street lined with apartment buildings and shopping complexes spread out in every direction around them. Yellow taxis, trucks and other vehicles thundered up and down the streets completely ignoring the emergency vehicles which rushed from time to time one way or another with their lights flashing and sirens wailing. And then there were the sidewalks. Filled with mere mortals walking, pacing, jogging, sleeping, chatting, spitting and kissing; they were white, yellow, green, blue, black; they were bald and fair and dreadlocked and curly, spiked and slicked and tied and shaved; they were obese and emaciated and fit and flabby, tall and short and crooked and straight; they interacted with each other in a myriad of languages and they avoided each other in a most practiced manner. He had never seen such a bastion of individuality. Brimming with life, of sorts, it was as though every mere mortal of every walk and breath, from every corner of the omniverse, had gathered together in one place.

"Where on earth is this?" Frank wondered aloud. After assessing the passing pedestrians for a while, Frank ventured to ask. A

72

white middle-aged man dressed casually in an orange shirt and cream colored pants walked toward him. He carried a small dog and a gentle demeanor so Frank approached him. "Excuse me sir, I was wondering if you would be so kind as to tell me where I am?"

"Fuck off faggot!" came the terse reply. The man never lifted his eyes from the pavement, brushed by Frank, and continued on his way. Frank was stunned by this violent exchange and wondered what on earth he had done to arouse the man's animosity. It was nothing, of course. "I do believe," he declared to the others, "that we are in New York."

"Bwmmermmergh," Pink Guy muttered. Though still speaking absolute gibberish, he was somehow becoming comprehensible to Frank.

"Me, too. I thought he was going to send us to Okinawa." He thought about that for a while before adding, "Lying fuck".

Pink Guy grunted at him again, explaining to Frank that, technically, Chin Chin wasn't lying as Okinawa and New York were in the same realm. But the vast difference in landscapes led Pink Guy to question Frank's ability to navigate the place.

"Not really," Frank replied. "It's a far cry from Okinawa - a different kind of jungle - but I think I can get us around. I mean, people are people right? It'll be fine. I'll take it from here. Salamander Man, you'd better put your recorder away for now. We don't want to draw too much attention to ourselves." With that, the Pink Guy, the Salamander Man and Frank, with the filthy, never-washed blue shirt, made their way through the streets of New York City.

Frank determined that the first thing they needed to do was find accommodation but, being an academic genius, he had no idea how to go about it. Clearly academic excellence in radiobiology would not necessarily translate into wisdom on the streets of this town. He decided to try his luck and just keep asking people.

Surely, he reasoned, someone amongst all these people would be willing to point him in the right direction. He found a young, well-groomed man sitting at a bus stop seemingly with time on his hands. Frank approached him cautiously yet gaily.

"Excuse me, sir. My friends and I are looking for accommodation. Would you be able to let us know how to secure a premises in this realm?"

"No home?" the man dryly enquired.

"Er, no. We, er, just arrived you see, from er, another place." Pink Guy and Salamander Man braced for recriminations.

"You know why you don't have a home?" he said, rousing from his mellow posture.

Frank just looked at him curiously. "Because I don't have a job?"

"Because there is no God, man. Yeah, you heard me. There is no God." Frank continued to stare at the man, unsure where to take the conversation from this point. "What kind of God, man," he started to yell, "would create people and leave them without a home?!" Clearly he was incensed by this. "All over the world, every day, there are people starving and homeless and sick, man, sick as a dog and what does God do about it? Nothing! Nothing, man! And you know why?!"

"Because Chin Chin really couldn't care less about mere mortals," he wanted to say. "Er, no," he replied.

"Because there is no God! There is no God, man. God is just a made-up character. A figment of people's imagination. The great boogey man in the sky."

"Ah, okay Mr. Atheist," Frank responded, backing away. "I was just after some information, not a debate." He turned to walk away. "How do you know for sure, anyway?" he said under his breath.

"Because there is no God man. There is no justice. No redemption. It's all mind control."

"Just don't go up the mountain," Frank called almost out of ear range.

"Say what?"
"Don't go up the mountain!"

"Clearly a wounded soul," Frank said, turning to his pink and green friends as they walked away.
"Nyees," Salamander Man agreed. A young, black woman screamed when she caught sight of them and ran to the other side of the road.
"Wonder what she saw?" Frank mused. Pink Guy shrugged.

The afternoon sun cast long shadows down the busy streets and withdrew its heat from the city sidewalks. Frank pondered who to approach next. A feather-haired madam with a tanned leathery face carried a mouse-sized dog in her arms and crossed in front of them to greet a fruiterer as though he were a long lost relative. Two men in tight black leather shorts paraded arm in arm across from them, and stopped at a small window to consider buying coffee beans. A rotund Latino man, with a very serious expression on his face and a pair of headphones clamped across his cranium, power-walked right through them as though they had no right at all to be where he was walking. Looking dazed and confused, an old white man with a huge mustache and a hideous wig meandered nearby wondering where to eat for dinner and whether he should run for President again this year. An enormous cockroach scurried across in front of them and disappeared down a drain. They all seemed at home here.

After two misfires with males, Frank felt sure that he could procure a better response from the females of the city. He found one sitting on the steps of an old theater as though waiting for a friend to come, or a homeless visitor to bowl up and ask questions. His confidence was high. "Excuse me," he began.
"Yeah?" she returned.

Well, that was sure a lot better than the 'fuck you' I got earlier he thought with a smile. "My friends and I are looking for accommodation and..."

"Oh, fuck you," she said with a pained expression. "You men are all the same. What, did you think I was going to just invite you back to my place and have you stay? Where the fuck do you get off? I ought to put your balls in a sling, you sad, creepy, little motherfucking pig molester."

"I didn't want to go back to your place..." Frank tried to get out, but she would have nothing of it.

"Just piss off will you, you misogynistic little pissant, before I call the cops."

Frank tried reason. "I only wanted to ask you a question."

"Oh yeah. That's how it always starts. You men are all the same. It starts with a question and it ends in some back alley with your hand up my crotch while munching on a chicken tortilla and texting your mates." She stabbed her hand into her bag and pulled out a small can of mace. "Now just back off!" she yelled, thrusting it toward him. "Back off! No means no!"

Frank slowly stepped away as one would from an escaped lion. "Now hold on, I don't even find you attractive enough to sleep with. I mean, you're built like a Super Mario bullet. I'd never want to go home with you." Her eyes widened with rage. His comrades were way ahead of him, already a block away and still running. He caught up with them eventually and thanked them for their staying power. "This is going to be a lot harder than I thought," he said, as though that would rally them. "Clearly the people here are not like the locals in Okinawa." He reflected on that. "A perfect stranger would roll out a futon, give you a meal, a bath and a goodnight rubdown, I tell you." Pink guy looked aroused. "We might have to try a new strategy."

"Nyeess."

"Franku."

"What if we go where most of the people are and let them come to us!" Frank thought aloud. Salamander Man thought this was worth a try. Pink Guy thought it was the stupidest idea he'd ever heard (and across the realms and dimensions he'd heard many) but didn't have the heart to say so.

They followed the lights and general flow of people heading downtown, continuing to observe all the sights and sounds and smells which still remained utterly foreign to them. A young woman with short hair and facial piercings came up to them and greeted them.

"Well, hello," Frank said.

"Are you guys locals or just visiting New York?" she asked.

"We're visitors... er, who hope to become locals," Frank explained. Pink Guy and Salamander Man were impressed with this answer.

"Are you interested in supporting the war against factory farms and freeing all animals from slavery and suffering?"

"What?" For a moment there, Frank was unsure what language this lady was speaking.

"We're encouraging people to change to a vegan diet for the sake of animal welfare and global sustainability."

"Animal welfare?"

"Every year in the United States, nine billion chickens are killed for human consumption. Doesn't that disturb you?"

"Well, not as much as eating them alive," Frank replied.

"No, I'm being serious."

"Me, too. Have you ever eaten a chicken alive? I tried once in Okinawa. It didn't end well. Blood and feathers everywhere and I almost got my eye pecked out. I'm all for killing them first."

"What the fuck? What planet are you from, man?" she asked with utter disdain.

"Do you really want to know?" Frank asked her.

"No. No, I don't," she said, and air pushed him away.

"Does anyone in this place not have a rabid opinion about something?" Frank yelled to his friends and anyone else who might have been passing by. "Seriously, the Okinawan jungle on a bad day was better than this place." They pressed on toward the thick sea of humanity ahead of them, passing a man at a counter whining incessantly that the price he was charged was $1.89 more than the advertised price, a hot dog vender who was incapable of counting change correctly, a Wall street banker in a tailored suit walking as though there was no-one on the street but him, and a drug dealer passing his ware in a pizza box to his clients. To Frank and his boys, there was little difference between them all. In their passion for self and success, they had become one and the same: rats scurrying back and forth to create a world from which the ultimate prize was escape.

They rounded a corner and stood before the largest man-made space they had ever seen. Enormous buildings stared down at them from the peripheries decorated with flashing lights and moving billboards. News reports ran across digital screens and music blared from all directions. Shops rimmed the ground floor of the area, selling everything from miniature statues of liberty to flesh-colored aliens that glow in the dark. And between it all was the most colorful parade of humanity that any of them had ever seen. Tourists, locals, hawkers, characters wearing costumes, characters wearing nothing at all, freaks and oddballs, it was hard to tell where one end of the spectrum ended and another started. The three walked into the middle of it all bewildered, bemused and besotted.

Even in this neverland of individuality, it didn't take long for them to gain attention.
"Excuse me?" came a lady's voice. "My kids would like to have a photo with you." She slipped a couple of dollars into Frank's hand and the two kids stood in front of them and smiled for the camera before any of them had any idea what was going on.

"Hey man, me next." It was a tall, dreadlocked man with a Rastafarian beret. He leaned on Frank, took a photo then slipped a bill in his top pocket. "Thanks man," he said departing. Immediately a young woman stepped forward. "Me and my friend," she said.

"Well sure!" Frank replied. He was beginning to enjoy this.

"No, not you," she said matter-of-factly. "Just the pink one. Just the pink one." Pink Guy brushed Frank to the side and stepped forward with tremendous pride. The women took their photos, paid Frank the money and rushed off again. Next it was Salamander Man, then Pink Guy again, then Salamander Man. Sometimes it was all three but usually the other two. Frank didn't care. All he could see was the money coming in.

Pink Guy and Salamander Man got into the spirit and began to work the money. Pink Guy would break into dance and spin and pose to the rapturous applause of onlookers before a short queue of photo takers would form again in front of him. Salamander Man was not to be outdone. He produced his recorder from nowhere, thrust it into his nostril and began to play a tune while dancing on the spot like a leprechaun. Within an hour they had enough to buy themselves a fine meal for dinner.

Frank recalled seeing a Japanese bar and bistro named Kyushu Kuisine on their way to the square. "It's not quite Okinawa," he explained to his friends, "but I don't think we're going to get anything closer than Kyushu." Retracing their steps, they found it easily, descended a dark staircase and entered a world that was vaguely familiar to Frank. Adorned with rice paper screens that opened onto blank walls, rising sun flags and posters of Japanese beer girls, it was a taste of Japan, sort of, in the heart of New York City. They were greeted with the customary '*Irasshaimase!*' although to Frank it sounded more like 'It's a shame to say!'. The place was full. True to New York, there were people of every color, size, language and odor gathered there, drinking and eating and having a merry time. At the end of the bar, holding an audience with tales of his homeland, was an odd-looking Japanese man wearing brown tortoise shell glasses, a Hawaiian shirt and a safari hat, speaking with bad breath in a voice that was aggravatingly loud.

Frank and his friends took a seat nearby. "So I said to them," he was saying, "'why don't you try some octopus balls?' And they said, 'We didn't even know that octopuses had balls' and I said, 'They sure do and let me tell you my friend, they are enormous ha ha ha. The size of golf balls and they come in packs of six'." The small crowd around him were enthralled by his storytelling. "I once ate twenty-four in a row," he said. "I almost inked myself ha ha ha!" There was hearty laughing all around. "Now as I'm sure my compatriot friend here will tell you," he said gesturing toward Frank, "there is no place on earth that produces more delicious octopus balls than the streets of southern Osaka. Right, my friend?"

"Okinawa," Frank replied. "Okinawa actually has better takoyaki than Osaka." The Japanese safari man laughed with a hint of embarrassment. "You must be a little confused, my friend. Okinawa has the *goya chanpuru*, Osaka has the octopus balls."
"Have you tried Okinawa's takoyaki?" Suddenly there was silence around the bar. It was a showdown and a tension rippled across the bistro. "Osaka's are good and they have the name, but there is a stand just off the beach in Onna-son in Okinawa. Their balls are equal to those of Osaka but they top them off with green *furikake* and shaved fish that is second to none. I tell you, Safari Man, their takoyaki is superior." There was an awkward silence before the safari man spoke again. "Ha ha ha! Looks like we'll all have to go to Okinawa then!" and the whole bistro returned to levity.

The safari man took a seat at Frank's table and introduced himself. "Good to meet a fellow expat," he said. "My name's... oh just call me Safari Man. I like that better."

"Frank," said Frank. "Pink Guy, Salamander Man," he added pointing to the others.

"I know," said Safari Man. There was a suspicious silence for a moment. He leaned in. "I'm a rankenfile, too," he whispered.

"How did you recognize me?"

Safari Man pointed to Pink Guy and Salamander Man. "What else could they be?!" he belted out in an audible voice again. "Ha ha ha!" Pink Guy looked perturbed at the idea that he stood out so much. "What brings you to New York?" he asked again, in a quieter voice.

"Chin Chin."

"SSShhhhh!" Safari Man pressed his hand hard against Frank's mouth. "Don't say the name. He knows this realm well. He could be listening." They spoke in lowered tones for the rest of the evening at the end of the bar. "Are you on the run?"

"We were cast here by the dark lord. He found me in another realm. He knows what even I have only recently come to know. My chromosomes are multiplying."

"Wow, Franku!" Safari Man jumped up at this, startled and excited. "It's you!" he said. "It's you! There have been rumors. But no-one knew if they were true. But they are! And it's you!"

Salamander Man began to play a tune on his recorder.

"Not now, Salamander Man." He sullenly put it away. "The dark lord gave me a choice: provide him with a lifetime supply of my chromosomes or spend eternity in the deepest, darkest abyss."

"New York?"

"No, I gave him my chromosomes. I'm here so he can find me again when my chromosomes have increased. But I don't know how long that will take in this realm. In the meantime, I'm trapped here.

Safari Man leaned across the table and whispered in his ear. "Come and stay with me, you and you friends. There are ways, Franku. Ways to increase your chromosomes here. You can defy the dark lord and escape, Franku. Gain your freedom. There are ways that he doesn't know about. Come with me and I'll show you. Frank turned to his friends. "What did I tell you? If you go where the people are, they will come to you." Pink Guy grunted his annoyance.

Their new friend lived in a small, one bedroom apartment in Brownsville, Brooklyn. He offered Frank a futon in his room, leaving the other two to sleep on the sofa or the floor. They all gratefully accepted. As Safari Man started passing around drinks, the real conversation began.
"What year is this, Safari Man?"
"2017."
"2017?! That takoyaki stand in Onna-son is surely gone now."
"So I was right after all, Franku! Ha ha ha. It is Osaka with the best balls."

"I hate this place," Frank said. "I hate it with a passion." The sound of gunshots could be heard outside in the distance. "I was born at a time when the Americans were destroying us - nuking the flesh off our bones and, after the surrender, terrorising us and shooting the innocent." Vivid memories of Sergeant Benson came to him and he began to sweat and tremble. "They were monsters. I hate all they were and all they stood for and now - look around, Safari Man - it's only worse. Look what has become of them! They are an immoral people filled with poor discipline, rudeness, greed, gluttony, perverseness, stupidity and pornography. And they're so angry."
"Ha ha ha, er, actually, er, I don't mind the porn to be honest. It's...er... it's..well, just a bit, you know. But you're right, Franku. A perverse people!"

There were more gunshots followed by screaming, car tires screeching and more gunfire.

"This culture is so self-centred and self-righteous. It makes me sick. How can you stand it here?" There was silence between them for a while. "Of all the realms I've been to, Safari Man," Frank said dejected, "I think this one confuses me the most."

Pink Guy and Salamander Man were exhausted after their first day in New York, and soon fell asleep on the sofa to the sounds of police sirens, knife fights and neighbors making wild love. Frank and Safari Man continued their conversation in the other room.

"You said something about increasing chromosomes?" Frank asked.

"Yours are already multiplying, Franku, but you can speed up the process. And the more you get, I'm betting the faster they multiply, It's exponential ha ha ha!" He leaned in as though to whisper a secret of cosmic repercussions. "You could outwit Chin Chin. Get out of here before he comes back."

"How, Safari Man?"

His Hawaiian-shirted friend leaned back out. "You can win them!" he said opening his arms wide. This was pronounced in a voice that was way too loud and Pink Guy and Salamander Man turned in their sleep in the next room as he said it. He looked so pleased to be revealing this to his new friend, one who he sensed was vastly superior to him even though they were on equal tiers.

"How?"

"Illegal crawfish racing!"

It was a common, yet unexplained phenomena, that that those who found themselves stranded in foreign dimensions were quickly drawn to one another. Whether this was a cosmic working beyond their means or a natural gravitation of the like-minded was unclear but small gatherings of them would assemble and, with little or no hope of escape, bet chromosomes. The mechanisms for such betting were almost endless yet for some reason illegal crawfish racing just happened to be Safari Man's favorite kind.

Frank's response took Safari Man by surprise. "Why is crawfish racing illegal?"
"Oh, Franku, it's not the racing itself, it's the betting. Only we won't only be betting for money - that's just the cover - we'll be betting for chromosomes and the idiot mortals won't even know what we're doing!" He was delighted with this in a 'toying with the cosmos' sort of way. It was like a kid at the electric company finding a screwdriver in daddy's toolbox, sticking it into a fuse box and bringing the whole grid to a halt. "Leave it to me, Franku. I'll bring in the shady characters, you just wait here. We'll have you bursting with chromosomes in no time ha ha ha."

Frank woke in the morning after a night of deep throat snoring and heavy salivation. Safari Man was nowhere to be found. Pink Guy and Salamander Man were squatting on the sofa squealing and grunting and 'Nyessing'. They were spinning a tangerine on the floor. Frank was left to wonder if he'd woken up in a sheltered workshop. Without so much as looking in a mirror, Frank left the apartment and began to walk the streets of this metropolis. He felt different doing it. Edgier. Angrier. Filthier. It was as though the very ether of this place was infecting him, polluting his DNA and retarding his mind. There was something weird about this city. As he walked by a vomiting woman, stepped over an addict and under a statue of Roosevelt heralding the wonders of the free world, he sensed that this might not actually be the real New York. It felt as though it was more like a fabricated, alternate version of the real thing. Yet his own senses were being so frustrated he could no longer be sure of what he was thinking or feeling.

He turned into a large park hoping that nature would restore some peace to his mind, if not bring full rejuvenation. He was disappointed. The grass, shrubs and trees gently bent and bowed in the breezes that blew across the ponds, the birds sang to each other in rounds and the squirrels playfully quarreled over nuts and berries before returning to their drays and resting from their escapades. But all that life, teeming and tumbling and leaping and laughing, seemed to be overcome by something else, quenched by a great melancholy, tormented by a ringing anxiety. He headed back to the apartment not only without the cheer or carefreeness that eluded him when he left, but now completely without hope as well.

He barked at his friends upon entering and they scrambled out of the way. Safari Man had still not returned so Frank entered the bedroom, closed the door, sat on the bed and clutched his head in a deep despair. "This isn't the earth I wished for," he muttered. He stood and paced the room before sitting again, then stood and paced and sat again. This routine went on for hours. He began talking to the wall, gesturing toward it as he did so and occasionally screaming. He was going out of his mind. Pink Guy and Salamander man, too scared to intervene, remained curled up on the sofa in fetal positions, waiting for Safari Man to return and offer help.

In a moment of lucidity, Frank grabbed a video camera from one of Safari Man's drawers, sat it on a tripod and began to record his ramblings. He thought he was dying (brain cancer, he suspected) and had to document his deterioration. Little of it made sense. Most of it was incoherent filth yet it provided him with a means of self-analysis and escape.

"Ha ha ha! Franku!" called Safari Man, swinging the front door wide open. He was taken aback to see the other two curled up and sucking their thumbs. Pink Guy pointed toward the bedroom door and began to tremble slightly. Safari Man burst into the bedroom in the same freewheeling fashion. "Ha ha ha! Franku!" He took one look into Frank's bloodshot eyes and said the only thing that would come into his mind: "Ha ha ha! Franku!" Frank turned and looked at him with a surly expression. Safari Man was not to be deterred. "Wow! Franku!" he continued in his excitable tone. "You look like you've just gone ten rounds with one of those midgets on roids, ha ha ha!" He spoke in Japanese but Frank had no trouble understanding him. "I think you need a drink, Franku." With a stiff drink and Safari Man's ineffable good cheer, Frank returned to a less disturbed state and invited Pink Guy and Salamander Man to join him and Safari Man for dinner.

"It's set," Safari Man announced thirty minutes later while wiping his greasy mouth with the back of his hand. The three newcomers all looked at him. "The illegal crawfish racing event! Ha ha ha! It's all set! It's good to go! It's ready and steady. Next Saturday. In the park. Ha ha ha! It'll be great!"
"How do you know that? Who's coming that will make this event so great?"

"I've got a few old friends lined up."
"Do tell."
"Well two of them are amongst this city's finest black gentlemen."
"When were they released?"
"Just yesterday ha ha ha."
"Excellent. What were they in for?"
"One was in for assault. It was no big deal. He survived. But ha ha ha, he's a tough cookie. He went fifteen rounds in the ring with Mike Tyson."
"That is impressive."
"Unfortunately it was during training and he was unconscious for fourteen of the rounds."
"You're kidding me?"

"Tyson simply used him as a punching bag. But hey Papa Franku, he was still in the ring with Tyson for fifteen rounds!"

"Fair enough. Who's the other?"

"A low-life who makes the other low-lifes look like shining arcs of kindness and charity."

"What's his specialty?"

"He was arrested for molesting a dead elephant seal, but was released on a technicality (the elephant seal was not yet dead) and was then rearrested for stage diving at a nun's funeral."

"I like him already."

"But otherwise a really nice guy. As I said, he's only just been released. He's up for anything."

"Excellent. Who else?"

"An old Latino friend of mine. Always good for a flutter over chromosomes."

"When was he released?"

"Ah, ha ha ha. He's never been caught!"

"Sounds like a smart cookie."

"Wouldn't know if his head was being seared with an iron. He once broke his leg in half purely to see if he could set it again by himself. He now walks with a permanent limp. Easy pickings."

"Perfect. Anyone else?"

"Anyone else? Of course, my friend, of course! This next guy is a legend. You're gonna love him. Just love him. All three foot two of him."

"What?"

"He's a leprechaun. Alpha Centurion. Escaped from the circus just last Wednesday. Not a clue when it comes to gambling chromosomes. Not a clue ha ha ha. Ripe for the picking, my friend."

"Do we want the chromosomes of a leprechaun?"

"They work. And they're better than the chromosomes of a vegan."

"Good point."

"I must say, Safari Man, you've done a stellar job."

"Not done yet, Papa Franku. I have also arranged for Drone to come."

"Let me guess. Drone is the product of an incestuous relationship and has spent the last fifteen years roaming the wilderness and howling at the moon?"

"Not quite. Drone is a drone. A flying camera."

"How are we supposed to get chromosomes from a flying voyeur cam?"

"We don't. But it comes in useful for controlling those who do have chromosomes."

Frank enjoyed hearing of the fruits of Safari Man's labors but remained unconvinced that the event would produce anything of real value. "Safari Man, I just don't see how this is going to work. How can we even be sure of winning, let alone obtaining any chromosomes from the losers? And I do mean 'losers'."

"Franku! It's set! It's rigged. Our crawfish can't lose!"

"How can you be sure of that?"

"Because our crawfish are actually mice disguised as crawfish! Brilliant, huh?!"

"I like your style, Safari Man." Frank was starting to really enjoy this camaraderie.

"But I just can't see how we're going to get many chromosomes from a bunch of misfits like that. I'm mean, why would humans be gambling for chromosomes at all?"

"Ah! my friend," said Safari Man rubbing his hands together. "These guys are not, you see, actually human!"

"They're not?!"

"Of course not! Ha ha ha. They're humanoid. They're tiered as mere mortals but they are not actually human. They're something entirely different. And what makes them such easy pickings is their desperation to become rankenfiles. They'll literally gamble their souls away trying to jump tiers but most of them actually have the intellect of beasts and the morals of sewer rats. They're nothing. Take my word for it, Franku. You will score at least two million chromosomes from this event alone."

"Are you serious? Two million chromosomes?"

"I guarantee it."

"How do you guarantee the procuring of chromosomes?"

"Papa Franku, I bet you my apartment that you will win over two million chromosomes from illegal crawfish racing. That's how sure I am."

There was little more for Frank to do than agree. "Ah, done," he said.

"But there is a small catch, Franku."

"I knew it."

"Lord Chin Chin will no doubt have his minions keeping an eye on you. Once he finds out you're involved in illegal crawfish racing, it's all over."

"So what's the point of all this then?"

"Papa Franku. It means you go in disguise! Ha ha ha!"

Frank loved this idea. "Yes! I could dress up as a flute playing, folk dancing goblin! Or maybe an obese, bearded lady with haemorrhoids; or how about one of those cute, large-breasted, mini-skirted, boggle-eyed girls in Japanese anime!" He was getting really excited as he said this. Safari Man, Pink Guy and Salamander Man looked at him with a hint of disgust.

"What's happened to you?" asked Pink Guy.

Safari Man broke the moment of tension. "Ha ha ha! I was thinking you could wear a World War One flying cap, some weird sunglasses and a *happi* coat and call yourself 'Kamikaze Failure

Frank'. Chin Chin and his minions will be after someone who looks intelligent. It's the perfect disguise! Ha ha ha!" This was met with boisterous laughter, back slapping and the raucous passing of wind. They celebrated Safari Man's plan until late into the evening, singing and dancing and passing out from excessive alcohol consumption.

That Saturday evening they returned to the apartment in ragged excitement. The plan, though not without its oversights, had gone splendidly. Each of the characters had turned up and on time, except for Alpha Centurion who always liked to make a late entrance. The betting was fierce and the stakes grew high. While Frank was not able to fool all of the entrants with his micey crawfish, by the time they realized, it was too late and he had absconded with all the money.

Yet not all had gone to plan. While Frank raked in all the money, Alpha Centurion, crafty little fellow that he is, stole all the chromosomes and set off across the park at full speed. Fortunately, Alpha Centurion at full speed is no faster than a sea cucumber on dry land and Frank was armed with Drone, who rounded him up in no time. Frank cut a deal with Alpha. He would swap all the monetary takings of the day for all the chromosomes that Alpha had taken during the illegal crawfish racing event. The runt, having lost his job with the banning of dwarf throwing, was in agreement and the swap was made. Alpha Centurion provided Frank with all the chromosomes (allowing him to keep one thousand as a goodwill gesture) and Frank, having quickly learned the ethics of this town, handed over half the money taken that day. His little friend had no idea and was wholly pleased with the outcome. He was so pleased, in fact, that he followed Frank back to his apartment and joined in their evening festivities. Their little friend endeared himself to them so much in fact that they allowed him to stay and join their growing posse of unlikely rankenfiles. The fact that Alpha Centurion had nowhere else to stay was lost on them, possible due to the excessive alcohol that they had consumed.

"There is one more matter to be settled before we retire for the evening," Frank said with a flushed face. He turned to Safari Man. "I believe we had a little wager going ourselves."
Safari Man replied in the only way he knew how. "Ha ha ha." Only this chortle was noticeably less jovial than those he had previously released.
"You bet, Safari Man, that I would make at least two million chromosomes from the illegal crawfish racing."
Safari Man looked decidedly uncomfortable. "Papa Franku..."
"Unfortunately, I was only able to get 1,999,000 chromosomes. A solid amount but clearly not the required amount." He looked at Safari Man with a wholly unconvincing look of sorrow. "I'm afraid I will have to take the keys to your apartment."
"But Frank!" cried Alpha Centurion. "You gave..."
"Shut up, you little butt plug!" he snapped. "I gave you your fair share of the money. Are you one of those people who comes back for more after a deal is made?"
Alpha Centurion, despite being a consummate potty-mouth himself, was not used to being scolded like that. He waddled over to the cupboard, climbed in and closed the door. Safari Man morbidly handed over the keys of his apartment to Frank who received them graciously. They were now his.

"Safari Man," said Frank. "I like you. You're like a brother to me." He turned to all of them. "You're all like brothers to me. We are family. The keys to this apartment are mine. But the apartment is for all of us. We will share it equally and fairly until I tell you to get the fuck out. What do you say?" Enormously buoyed by these words, they all came in for a group hug. Even Alpha Centurion fell out of the cupboard and came over to join them. They sang and danced and picked the lint from their navels until deep in the night.

Chapter 7

In a hole in the ground there lived a negi. And a rather nasty, dirty, wet hole it was too, filled with the ends of worms and an oozy smell, unlike those dry, warm, sandy holes with divans to sit on and smorgasbords to eat from: it was a negi-hole, and that primarily means misery. Negis were roots who tended not to have names as such, but rather went by groupings and numbers. This particular negi's identification was 'Negi Generation 1'. The '1' suggests that he was the first in his particular grouping (the 'Generations' as this group were known). He was directly related to Negi Generation 4 (who was his nephew, in fact) who had earlier come to a grisly demise in a foreign land. All of the Generation Negis had come to know of it and most of the other negi groupings knew of it, too. Much was said of his wandering off like that to distant realms and dimensions, so poorly prepared and ill-equipped, and of the dark lord who had not only dismembered him but (it was widely believed) also orchestrated the whole sorry affair from beginning to end.

Negi Generation 1 rose from his soggy hole one dim morning and made his way, for reasons which entirely eluded him, to the top of a nearby hill. There he fossicked and picked about, wandering this way and that, but staying at the top of the hill and wondering what to eat for breakfast. There was a purpose in the air that morning, a calling as it were, yet he could not put his finger on it in any precise sort of way. He just knew he needed to be on the top of that hill looking out over the fields below.

Though their worlds were soon to come together, at this point in our story, Frank and his friends remained in New York City, sleeping heavily after a night of merriment. It was Safari Man who brought the dawn.
"Psst!"

Frank turned in his bed with a head pain that was so bad he felt as though he had been struck with an anvil .

"Psst!" Safari Man said again.

"What?" he croaked.

"We have to go now." Frank wasn't used to Safari Man whispering. It gave a freaky 'alternate universe' feel to his waking.

"Why?" he asked. "And what is that awful smell?"

"Ah, ha ha ha," he whispered again. "Probably your breath, Franku. But no time for that now. We have to go. We have the chromosomes and I suspect Chin Chin knows that you have them.

"Why would you suspect that?"

"It's the air. The smell in the air. There is a tinge of sulfur in the air and that often means that he is on his way. We can't waste any time. We must go now."

Frank roused Pink Guy, Salamander Man, Alpha Centurion and Drone and the six of them, still scratching their heads and backs and pimply buttocks, silently filed out of the apartment and down onto the street. None of them, save for Safari Man, had bathed for epochs. Pink Guy groaned at Frank.

"We don't want to make a mess of the apartment, Pink Guy. You know how messy these transports can be. We might need the apartment to come back to at a later time." He turned to Safari Man. "Where to?"

Safari Man ran off toward the subway.

They were a sight early in the morning. A Japanese man wearing a safari hat and a Hawaiian shirt muttering 'ha ha ha', followed by a German/Japanese man wearing a badly stained blue shirt, sunglasses and a WWII flying cap, followed by a pink guy holding a ukulele and running with a hobble, followed by a green salamander-looking entity twisting his nipples as he ran, followed by a drone in flight, followed by a shirtless runt speaking purely in cuss words as his friends moved further and further ahead of him down the street.

93

Even in the early hours of the morning, the city was bustling. There were no public places that maintained any sense of privacy. Safari Man looked about him, increasingly frustrated and anxious. "We have to go," he kept muttering. "We have to go. He could be here any moment." The others followed closely behind him and shared his growing nervousness. "Underground. We have to go underground."

"Plenty of people in the subway already," Frank assured him.

"Not the subway. Underground. Underground. Here," he said, moving to the edge of a side street right outside a Planned Parenthood Center. "This manhole. This will take us underground. I have the coordinates. We'll make the move down there." The only problem was, none of them could remove the cover. "We need something to stick into the openings to use as leverage," Frank instructed. They looked about but saw nothing that could be used.

Spurred on by Safari Man's nervous whining, Frank turned to Salamander Man. "Your recorder, my friend. We can use your recorder to lift the lid off the manhole." Salamander adamantly shook his head. "Nyeeesssss!" he insisted. "Nyyessss," he said again, assuring Frank that the cover would only break his recorder and then they would have neither the protection of being underground nor the comfort of his music. "It's a risk we have to take, Salamander Man. Chin Chin could be here at any moment. Please." With the forlornness of one handing over a child, he placed his recorder in Frank's hands. And with that instrument alone they succeeded in lifting the cover off the manhole and, with many hands helping, were able to return the recorder more or less intact to Salamander Man's possession. The beauty of that moment was not lost on any of them. They paused to reflect on it before suddenly jumping down the hole.

Safari Man led the way. He was followed by Alpha Centurion, then Salamander Man and Drone, Pink Guy and finally Frank. Yet just as Pink Guy climbed in, a passing patrol car pulled over with the customary screech of tires and squeal of a siren. A fat white officer jumped out and ran over to the opening just as Frank was disappearing down it.

"What the hell is going on down there?" he bellowed. His pistol was drawn. Frank, now loaded with chromosomes, just managed to pull the cover back in place before jumping to the bottom of the hole. He could hear more officers gathering around and calling for back up to come and remove the cover.

It was with great disappointment that each of them realized, one by one, that they had not entered an electrical manhole, nor a manhole for telephone lines or gasworks. They had entered a sewer tunnel. And though the cracks in the pipes were small, the stench they released was intolerable and as they moved along the tunnel, the pipes crumbled away to nothing and they found themselves wading through fetid, ankle-deep waters of urine and faeces. Each of them were caused to vomit at least once. It became clear that the risk of disease from this hole in the ground was greater than any risk they might face from a bullet.

"Now, Franku," Safari Man said.
"You've got the coordinates?"
"I think so."
"I hate it when people say 'I think so'. We're not going on a holiday, you know. I don't want to end up in some hellhole on the other side of the omniverse."
"I have the coordinates," he said but his voice was wholly unconvincing.
They huddled together, all six of them. Despite the squalid environment, Alpha Centurion had never known such affection and found the intimacy very comforting. "This is nice," he said. The others looked at him with tremendous concern. Then

ignoring him, Frank removed a small piece of broken glass that he kept in his pocket, made a gash at the base of his left palm and moved around his five tightly gripped friends, sprinkling a circle of blood into the foul waters now at their knees. Safari Man began to recite the co-ordinates. Frank continued circling his friends and dripping the life source around them.

Pink Guy groaned.
"Sulfur?" Frank asked. "You smell sulfur? Over this stench you're able to smell sulfur?"
"Yes, that is definitely sulfur," said Safari Man. "When you eat as much ass as me you learn to smell what you want to smell." Then a tear dropped from his eye.
"If you ever need to talk, Safari Man, I'm here," Frank counseled warmly.
"Thanks. My dad can be a real dick sometimes."

Safari Man began to call out the co-ordinates with greater speed and fervor.
"I smell it, too, Frank!" shouted Alpha Centurion. "It's overpowering the reek of the sewer! Chin Chin must be close!" He began to wail as he said this. Frank circled a little more quickly and Safari Man began to call the co-ordinates with a fresh desperation. Even Frank now, as he worked his way around and around the group, could distinctly detect the sulfurous odor. Pink Guy and Salamander Man began to shout and scream. Alpha Centurion muzzled hard into Pink Guy's thighs. "Come on, Safari Man!" yelled Frank. The sulfur was so pungent now there was no longer any scent of bodily waste. Safari Man started calling the co-ordinates so zealously it became unclear what language he was speaking.

At that moment, three things happened simultaneously. The ground dropped beneath them; a flashlight shone from one direction; and a small orange flame appeared at some distance in the other direction, licking and flicking in an ominous manner. The ground they were standing on dropped again. The five friends found themselves standing up to their necks in the thick malodorous soup (except for Alpha Centurion who was clinging to Salamander Man, and Drone who was hovering above). They stuck together tightly. The flashlight slowly drew nearer. "NYPD!" came the call. From the other side, the orange flame took form, silently morphing from the outline of one creature into another.

The ground dropped again and all six of them were under water. Though they became frantic in their inability to breathe, they remained tightly held to each other. They kicked and bucked in the filthy solution, desperate for air and repulsed to their core as the torrent of effluent flushed about them. It was Alpha Centurion who gave in first. He inhaled and took a full measure of the soiled waters into his lungs. There was a moment of tremendous shock and then the life was gone from him. This experience was then quickly shared by Salamander Man. Pink Guy held on for longer but it was of no benefit. He opened his mouth and the brown river flowed in. He convulsed for a few short seconds before falling lifeless and taking Drone with him. Frank looked over at Safari Man who was smiling back with two thumbs up. He was swishing the stuff around in his mouth and gargling and giggling. "When you've eaten as much ass as I have you learn to taste what you want to taste. Right now I can imagine tasting cheap soil." "How is that any better?" asked Frank.

A tremendous explosion then collapsed the tunnel and punched a hole right through to the road above. It shattered the Planned Parenthood Centre and left glass and debris all over the remains of the street. "Hmm…" said Frank as everything began falling in upon him. "'Planned…Parenthood'? Seems like a nice place." Two policemen were caught in the explosion, one killed and the other critically wounded. The wounded policeman, a black man, fell in on top of Frank. Frank, seeing he had a hand in his pocket, began to beat him furiously. Other police on the scene began to deal with the fallout, help the injured and cordon off the area. The officer who had seen Frank enter the manhole provided his description to a sketch artist and soon Kamikaze Frank's mug appeared on all news bulletins as one wanted in connection to a terrorist attack.

Frank looked up through the fetid waters and wreckage to see a huge menacing orange flame hover above him. He gave a mighty gasp and felt the pulpy waste flood into his mouth, swirl around his teeth and tongue, and fill his lungs. He vomited but it was returned, washed straight back into him with the tide of filth. His last recollection was of a flaming hand reaching down through the waters toward him but not before the dark covers closed above him.

~

Negi Generation 1 stood on the peak of a large hill, moist from heavy rainfall and lush with green foliage. He peered out over the landscape. Aside from the greenery which dotted the countryside in hilly clumps, it was a decidedly gray and brown outlook, the sort that would immediately make one want to go back to bed and curl up for the day under blankets, if indeed one were fortunate enough to have a bed and some blankets. Negi Generation 1 didn't so he remained on the top of the hill pondering what mysterious force had led him up there.

Before the overcast sky had lightened, he noticed the muddy ground under his feet becoming more sodden and slippery, as though affected by a great deluge. Only there was no deluge. There was nothing in the air but a cool and gentle breeze. Underneath him though, in a circle about five meters from side to side, the ground continued to soften and liquify. He tried to step out from it but only slipped before sinking into it. Panic set in as he was swallowed deep into the mire. He grasped for his life, digging and clawing at the softening clay but to no avail. The more he struggled the more he was sucked further down until his feet found support in a mesh of branches and sprigs beneath him. These stoked his relief (in keeping him from sinking further) and his curiosity for he could feel the branches moving, wriggling and twisting. They were rising up from under him and as they rose, so did he. The boughs, he began to make out, were colored - pink and blue and red and green and white and brown - and they soon found voice, initially with the moans of a tree bending under the force of a hurricane, then with the screams of one in utter torment, but eventually in utterances that distinctly resembled intelligent language.

"Get the fuck off me!"
"Get your foot out of my mouth."
"I hate you, you clod."
"You are disgusting."
"No, you are disgusting."
"Agh, I can still feel it between my teeth!"
This was followed by incessant spitting, deep and prolonged burping and the odd vomit. Rather suddenly, the blue one turned to Negi Generation 1, who was still lying in mud with his legs over the bare chest of a froggy looking character, and said, "Who the hell are you?"

"Iha amhi Negihoo Generationhe 1ho."
"What?"
The little white and brown-topped creature repeated his introduction. He stood before Frank with a rather cute and harmless demeanour, a slight lean in his posture and an apparent readiness to bow at any moment before his visitors.
"I think I understood that," Frank said, more to himself than to anyone else. You're Negi Generation 1?"

"Yesha!" he said with a cautious grin.

"Any relation to Negi Generation 4?"

The old negi's face dropped. "Yeshi."

"He was a good negi," said Frank. "I miss the little fella."

"Indeedhoo hehe washo goodha. Hehi hadhoo ahe badho speechha impedimenthi thoughhoo. Madehe himho veryha hardhi tohoo understandhe."

"You're not kidding."

"Butho heha washi allhoo hearthe. Aho trueha neggerhi. Youhoo musthe beho Frankha."

"How did you know?"

"Youhi havehoo becomehe knownho acrossha thehi omniverseshoo, Frankhe. Theho powersha arehi shiftinghoo andhe thereho isha muchhi talkhoo concerninghe youho."

Frank's friends were still a writhing, screaming mess on the ground, clawing at and striking one another and calling each other all manner of names and verbs.

"What'sha wronghi withhoo themhe?"

"It hasn't been an easy passage."

Indeed it hadn't. Death by faeces turned out to be the least of their issues. Safari Man's co-ordinates had taken them to another realm; a dark, hellish corner of the omniverse haunted by fallen mere mortals, those of the very worst ilk who had betrayed their kind and brought unspeakable misery to others. Below that of lawyers and dictators and even internet spammers, this inferno was kept especially for the most vile and depraved of all humankind. Dark, cringy and plaguy, this hell had been reserved exclusively for atheists, feminists and vegans and was infinitely worse than even Hitler's bastion of hell, which appeared like an uppity girls' juvenile detention centre by comparison. The torment experienced by Frank and his companions in that place brought personality-changing trauma and they were furious with Safari Man for making such an appalling blunder. Trapped there, their only means of escape turned out to be through a series of

100

murky underground streams which brought them up to where they now lay. Though released from its infernal clutches, the virulence of that place remained within them, eating away at their souls and their solidarity.

It was Negi Generation 1 who restored their fellowship by assuring them that Safari Man had made no such mistake. The 'maximumha infernohi', as he referred to it, was well known (and feared) by those in Negiland. For reasons that none of them knew, both the hell they had passed through and the land they had now arrived in, had shared coordinates despite being completely separate realms. Possibly the interconnecting streams were to blame yet, Negi Generation 1 explained, there was never any interaction between the two realms as the Negis were always too afraid of the maximumha infernohi and the inhabitants there were either unaware of, or disinterested in, any entity belonging to this particular realm.

Upon hearing this, the other members of the band removed their fists and feet and blades from Safari Man's face and rib cage and testicles and the whole lot of them stood, a bit sore and sorry, before Frank and Negi Generation 1. "Weha musthi behoo carefulhe," their new Negi friend told them. "Theho darkha lordhi Chin Chinhoo hashe sentho outha ahi messagehoo thathe aho highha chromosomehi manhoo ishe runningho aroundha withhi hishoo possehe. That'sho youha, Frankhi. Andhoo ahe largeho bountyha hashe beenhoo puthe onho yourha headhi."
"How much?" Safari Man asked, his interest piqued.
"How could you even think of asking that?" Pink Guy put to him. He was fully eloquent in this realm.
"Nice to have you back, Pink Guy. What happened to you in New York?"
"I can't say. But it was awful. Like being a fully functioning person trapped in a wholly retarded shell. Very frustrating."

"Wehoo musthe beho quietha," Negi 1 cautioned. "Lookhi downhoo therehe." Drone took flight to observe. Below them, spread across the landscape as far as their eyes could see was a field of negis, impossibly large and surprisingly uniform, with their white necks and brown heads protruding from the ground and lolling about as the gentle breezes blew across them. They were all asleep, as though in a trance, yet, warned Negi Generation 1, if awoken, they would turn vicious and without any hesitation rise and attack. The negis spread out before them were not of the Generation clan. The Generations, who made their home in the moist hillsides to the south, were rankenfile-friendly and indebted to Frank for his tutelage of Negi Generation 4 (despite his unfortunate demise). The other negi clans, primarily of the plains, had no such allegiances and with an unparalleled fear of Chin Chin and a handsome bounty dangled in front of them, would think nothing of lopping off the heads of these harvesters.

Negi Generation 1 gestured for silence before leading them single file along a low mountain ridge which rimmed the field of negis. Their mood was somber. They still carried the trauma of the recent transport and one got the feeling that Safari Man, though excused for any misdirection, had not been wholly forgiven by all in the party. The stench of the sewer, the desiccation of their skin and the flecks of excrement still between their teeth kept them all irritable. Furthermore they were hungry. They traipsed along, occasionally tripping on roots rising above the ground or the uneven surface of the terrain; sometimes giving each other a less-than-friendly poke or shove for good measure.

Negi Generation 1 picked up on their tetchiness and led them deep into the vegetation on the hilltop. There, he pushed them all under the cover of a thick fern-like plant where they were to hide in silence until he returned. They watched him through the fronds of the plant, this demure little fellow gingerly making his way a short distance through the greenery before stopping at the base of a tall branchless tree. Then in a most practised manner, he hopped onto the trunk and began to climb up to the top where he waited without a hint of motion. Time passed but, in this land also, it was virtually impossible to determine what period of time it might have been. Pink Guy, however, did notice that the clouds above them had almost moved from one side of the horizon to the other before Negi Generation made his move.

It happened following a soft rustle which came from a shrub just under Negi 1's tree. A second quiver saw a susquian, a reptilian bird slightly larger than a wild turkey, come strutting out into the open and this set Negi Generation 1 into action. One moment he was a languid little vegetable clinging to the top of a tree, the next he was a demoniac in flight. He dropped from his position and landed right on top of the creature. It never had a chance. Negi was a whirlwind of razor sharp teeth, claws and cacodemonic screaming. The posse sat, still hidden, with their eyes and mouths wide open in shock, each thinking exactly the same thing: if one negi was capable of such savagery, what would become of them if a whole field of negis were activated against them? The job done, Negi bundled up his catch and dragged it over to where his new friends were waiting. He stood before them, now calm, genteel and seemingly half the size he was a moment ago and with a hint of glee said, "Lunchho!" He dug a pit in the ground, threw the bird in along with some coal (which was plentiful in that region), lit it, covered it with leaves and in no time they were eating the most delicious barbecued meat they'd had in a long, long time.

Negi said, "This is a rare delicacy in my land. However, it's not as good as faggot."
"What?" said Frank, spitting out his food.
"Faggot."
"Is that a speech impediment thing?"

"What do you mean speech impediment? You've never seen a nice juicy faggot before?"

Frank refused to comment any further.

He was keen to take a little nap following the meal, something the others were happy to join him in but Negi Generation 1 assured them that they had to move on and away from the mass of negis littering the landscape below. They followed him back to the ridge, again in single file (and in much better spirits with fuller stomachs and friendlier words) where they proceeded to march in careful silence with the lush vegetation to their left and the enormous expanse of negis below them to their right.

They hadn't gone far when Pink Guy let go with a fart that was so loud it sounded like he was starting up a chainsaw. It reverberated across the fields below as though played through a bullhorn. The seven of them stood motionless on that ridge, in a frozen fear, and watched as hundreds of thousands of negis below slowly awakened and came to life. It was a serene scene at first as the negis stretched and turned in their burrows, bending backwards and forwards in a gentle rhythmic fashion. In no time at all though, they turned decidedly hostile. Their faces, just moments earlier calm and sleepy, became agitated and gnashed with a ferocity they had rarely seen. The negis ripped themselves out of their beds, turned and faced the characters on the hill and with a spine-chilling war cry, rushed as one toward them with nothing but leaks in their hands and death and destruction on their negiminds.

It was the sheer sound of the coming onslaught that instilled a deep fear in Frank and his friends. A hideous, high pitched scream, it filled the skies and penetrated their bones, sending them running in all directions. As their enemies drew nearer, the posse could see in more detail than they cared for, the very face of feral. With shards of glass for teeth and icicles for eyes, the negis advanced at a rapid pace, wielding leaks like mad men and tossing their heads about like laundry in a typhoon. The friends' flustering about was the very antithesis of any sort of organized response and only spurred the negis on to greater violence. Yet it soon brought out the primal savage in each of them (except for Safari Man who soiled himself).

Frank scared himself with a newfound aggression and began to punch and kick while producing sounds from his mouth that he had previously only heard from animals in agony. Utilising a good sized branch he found lying nearby, he discovered it worked superbly as a mace and with it he beat the negis black and brown. Wielding it, he found he could wipe out scores of the veggies in a single sweep. He found a new thrill in hearing their war cries turn to screams or, better still, their bodies rip in half as he clubbed right through them. He picked a negi up and snapped his neck before letting out a hideous cackle. It aroused in him an aggression that had been lying dormant for many years. Provocations of the Indonesian military and Sergeant Benson flashed across his mind. He poured out his vengeance, a wrath he never knew he harbored, on the hapless negis and they paid dearly for their assault.

Finding skills within him he had never previously known, Pink Guy, too, came alive. Drawing on the break dancing he picked up in New York, he proceeded to spin and kick, and thrust and chop all to the accompaniment of haunting Kung Fu howls. Despite the brutality of the battle and the enormous loss of negi life around him, there was a poetry to the way Pink Guy fought and there were moments when he almost succumbed to the attacks of the negis because he was so absorbed in the beauty of his own movements. Furthermore, he found his ukulele to be a most effective weapon, not only in the way it could knock the whole face off a negi, but in the beautiful sounds the strings made when it did so.

Alpha Centurion was in his element. Not only could he put his finely tuned miniature physique to work, but he could also finally give his unsavory vocabulary a solid work out in an appropriate context. With his natural height restriction he was perfectly placed to strike long and hard directly into the testicles of the negis. This turned out to be a particularly sensitive spot for them and many began to withdraw from the runt when they saw how much agony and damage he was capable of inflicting in such a short space of time.

Taking his position in the air where the negis had neither the height nor the brains to reach him, Drone was king. He was able to wreak losses upon the negis on a far greater scale than any of the others and with little threat to his own safety. Occasionally one of the negis would try to throw a leak at him. As ferocious as they were, they were hopeless shots and Drone was never in danger. He soon found himself actually enjoying the battle.

Salamander Man's tactics were wholly different. A musician at heart, not a fighter, he began to play a soothing lullaby on his recorder. Frank very nearly clubbed him with his mace for this until he saw the effect it had on the negi. All within hearing range would stop running, drop their leaks and become completely docile, swaying gently before falling to their knees and drooling. What followed was the physical result of a spiritual phenomena. The souls of the negis began to leave them. They rose up, a translucent version of their physical frame, into the air before disappearing altogether. Demons then attacked the negi souls and violently raped them mid-air. They begged for help as every one of their orifices was filled with demonic genitalia. What remained on the ground were the soulless shells of what once were negis. They remained motionless husks. Salamander Man leisurely walked through the throngs of negi, playing his tune, leaving a trail of gentle destruction in his wake.

The big disappointment amongst the posse was Safari Man who turned, ran and hid in a small cave, rolling a large stone up to its mouth. He waited out the battle in a cool darkness. Never having engaged in battle beyond karaoke before, he was thoroughly intimidated by the whole affair and simply fell to pieces. His own cowardice shamed him enormously, yet not quite enough to offer support to his friends whom he knew were engaged in a battle to the death. He sat in the cold black tomb and wailed incessantly.

Despite the tremendous valour and prowess displayed by Frank and his friends and the enormous damage they inflicted on the negis of the field, the enemy kept coming in ever-greater numbers and with ever-mounting hostility. Frank began to see the futility of this battle and was unable keep his heart from turning. The more he looked about, the more desperate their situation appeared and the more dispirited he became. He looked for his friends to see if there were some way they could regroup and escape. He needn't have bothered.

At that moment reinforcements came in their thousands. For his part, Negi Generation 1 was a formidable presence, showing the form against the negis of the field that had so traumatized his friends earlier in the day. Clearly, the Generations from the south were a larger and fiercer breed than their cousins to the north. Yet Negi Generation 1 had withdrawn from battle early on and the posse assumed he had simply deserted them or been killed in action. On the contrary, he had departed to secure a greater force and they arrived with a cry that left the negis of the plain sounding like the air coming out of a balloon. Leading them, Negi Generation 1 came screaming in on the back of a susquian, carrying an enormous clock as their standard. He left it by a clearing before leading his clan into the fray with a rousing battle cry.

With the arrival of the Generations, the battle took on epic proportions. While the negis of the south were larger and fiercer, the negis of the plain retained formidable numbers and multitudes of them continued to rise and advance, surrounding the Generations as they had Frank and his allies, and inflicted heavy casualties on the Generations. Negis of both clans were being set upon, sliced up and butchered in most unholy manner. In scale and in savagery, it was by far the greatest battle in negi history.

One of the Generations had the most enormous phallus and with each swing of it he could kill hundreds of negis from the north. This monster was known amongst his own people as a hero and his name was "Negi Negris the Mandingo". He was worshiped by all the Generations for generations to come.

Even for Frank, who didn't have a merciful bone in his body, the scene was disturbing and it troubled him to see the extent of the death and destruction unfolding all around him. He was still chromosome rich and saw no alternative but to use his genetic muscle to bring an end to the atrocities. Though he lacked teaching and experience in the matter, his innate intuitions took over. He fought his way over to the large clock that Negi Generation 1 had carried into the battle and when it was within reach, he grabbed it and held it high above his head. With an almighty bellow he yelled "It's time to stop!" and thrust the clock hard into the soil at his feet. His words echoed out across the plains and the valleys, and power emanating through the clock altered the very fabric of time that they were in. A weird atmospheric distortion overwhelmed them and every living creature in the land fell to the ground. For the rankenfiles, it was momentary and they soon roused themselves, though weakened and achy. They observed all the devastation around them. The Generations of the south, slightly more robust than their cousins to the north, survived the ordeal but only just. It took days (even weeks for some) to recover and even then they were not quite as valiant or as resourceful as they had been before the incident. For the negis of the south, chromosome weak and genetically deficient, the impact of the diffusion was permanent. As one, they fell silent, dropped to the ground and ceased to breath. The landscape was littered with them as far as the eye could see.

The posse slowly regrouped, though there was little said between them for a long time. This had been a baptism for them, one in which they discovered new possibilities within themselves, new strengths and most of all a renewed camaraderie, one in which they now knew implicitly, they had gained the full trust of each other. They were a formidable unit now. Although they remained physically weak at that time, they were spiritually strong and they felt a delight in the bond they now shared. The exception to this, of course, was Safari Man. He remained in his cave unaware of anything that had expired in the course of the battle and indeed unaware that combat had even ceased. The others had no idea what had happened to him but after a cursory search, decided with sad reluctance to press on without him. The decision to do so didn't go unchallenged.

"We can't just leave him behind." It was Salamander Man.
"What choice do we have?" Pink Guy pressed. "He is almost certainly dead and in the event that he abandoned us in our hour of need, *should* he continue with us? They muttered backwards and forwards on the matter for some time until Frank, who had wandered off a little, returned with an artifact in his hand. He held it out to his friends for them all to plainly see. He held Safari Man's glasses, shattered and twisted.
"He is surely gone," Frank said sullenly. "My brothers, he is gone. So should we be."
At this point they had two great needs: time and coordinates. The clock maneuver had so exhausted Frank of his chromosomes that he needed time to replenish and in this chromosome-weak world, there was no telling how long that would take. They also needed fresh coordinates because none of them knew where to go from

here. The primary dilemma for them was that Chin Chin would soon trace them to this place and they would have neither the strength to face him, nor the chance to escape.

They were in agreement that finding a quiet, secluded hamlet was their priority and Negi Generation 1, who had now joined their troupe, led them westward along the ridge of the hills toward the pink and orange clouds which hung over a region which he knew would meet their needs. Their spirits picked up as they made their way and Salamander Man began to play a merry tune on his recorder. Pink Guy revealed some amusing secrets of the omniverses like the fact that mastoids (mortal-tiered creatures with hideously huge noses) of the realm CX5P4200 reproduce asexually through laughter, and Frank told exaggerated stories of Okinawa and jokes of which the punchline invariably involved Sergeant Benson's demise. The others, trundling along in single file, laughed along and enjoyed the cessation of hostilities - now known as the Great Negi War - in a way that only those who had known battle could. They made good progress and by the end of the day were several landscapes away from their point of origin.

None of them were aware of the change in the color of the clouds behind them or the gentle swirling motion that turned the skies into a whirlpool. Above the battleground, now eerily silent and empty, the heavens darkened and the wind whipped up into a chilly gale. Icy rain started to fall and the beasts in those hills which had survived the violence of the day, scattered with a new-found fear. Lightning cracked and the atmosphere parted, delivering a new entity to that environment. It was preceded by two minions, chained at the neck, thrashing and lashing at anything within reach. Gargoylian in appearance, they were wrapped in a wrinkled, gray leathery skin like infants prematurely aged. Razor sharp teeth protruded from their mouths, lacerating their own lips as they snarled and snapped, their drool a mix of saliva and their own blood. The prime entity set his feet on the ground immediately behind them and looked around at the devastation of the landscape, the razed vegetation, the negi corpses that littered the land, the clock still half-buried in the ground, and was both intrigued and not a little concerned at the might which could have wrought this.

Safari Man remained in his hideout, still wailing in anguish over his profound cowardice and loss of friendship. He sat in total darkness until the rock which he had leveraged up to the entrance of the cave suddenly moved. He looked up with unbridled fear and trepidation. The rock moved again, dislodging enough to allow light to pour into the cavern. A third time the rock moved only this time it was flung with a mighty force to the very back of the chamber. Though he could see nothing of it yet, Safari Man was horrified at the power which had blown a boulder clear across the cavern and he reeled back into one of the tiny recesses of that place.

Then it came. At first it was almost pleasant, like that of thermal underground pools but quickly turned acrid like the pungent rubbery smell of the subway escalators in New York. Then the odor became thoroughly toxic, burning his nostrils and lungs and he began to choke and gag. A dark presence entered, ominous and fearsome, moving slowly but with unstoppable momentum, and turned to the little Japanese man. He looked down on him with eyes of detestation and contempt. Safari Man soiled himself again.

It spoke with the voice of immortality. "Oh chin chin ga dai suki da yo." A stench filled the cavern as he said it. Safari Man was well versed in the language of the dark lord and heard it as though it were his own tongue. "You are now mine," he said.
"Chin Chin, I had nothing to do with what's been going on out there," the Japanese man squeaked with a quivering voice.
"So you're a traitor and a coward."

111

"Well," Safari Man struggled for words. "A coward, yes. 'Traitor' is a strong word and I can't say that…"

"It wasn't a question, you pathetic little rodent. It was an identity that you will wear for the rest of your sad little existence." He sniffed about like a bear in heat. "Where is Frank?"

"I don't know. I haven't seen him."

Instantly, Safari Man found himself face down in mud at Chin Chin's feet.

"Try again."

"He was here. There was a battle. But I fled. I couldn't take it. I hid myself in this cave. And now they must have gone but I swear I have no idea where."

"They left you behind."

"Ah, yes. Ha ha ha," he muttered, standing to his feet again.

"They must despise you. I don't blame them. Who wouldn't?"

Safari Man retreated and slumped against the wall of the cave. It was over for him and he knew it. He was beyond fear now and had nothing left to lose and no tears left to cry so he spoke directly, almost disrespectfully, to the dark power before him. "Why do you want to kill Frank?"

"Kill Frank? I don't want to kill Frank. I want to harvest him. I want to rein him in." The air in the cave grew frosty and mean as he spoke. "He will come in handy in time. But he's useless to me right now."

Safari Man, still loyal to Frank in his heart, spoke on. "How so? He's just another rankenfile."

"You want to play me?" He was incensed. "You know he's chromosome rich and evolving all the time. That clock move was something. I've rarely come across such power. I felt it reverberate across the omniverses." He spoke in a way that approached awe. "But it wiped out most of his chromosomes. I need to give him more time to replenish. But it will take forever in this realm. So I will have to make a few adjustments to my agenda."

"What is your agenda?"

Once again Safari Man found himself face down in the mud in front of Chin Chin, only this time, the dark lord rested his foot heavily on Safari Man's head. "My agenda," he breathed "is none of your business". He let Safari Man breathe again. "Except to say that I will be taking you on a short pleasure cruise with me." He then laughed an awful screeching laugh that was eerily similar to the cries of the Wretched in the dark sea. "Pleasure for me, that is."

~

Negi Generation 1 led the posse onto a clearing of level ground at the foot of a small hill by a gently flowing freshwater stream. This part of the realm appeared uninhabited so, though they were away from the thicker vegetation and somewhat exposed, they were at ease and began to prepare for the night. Without the aid of any clear leadership, each made their own contribution and their efforts produced a surprisingly unified and very pleasant result. Negi Generation 1 returned from foraging in the hills with another susquian and several mitostrons (large avianesque rodents about the size of a young capybara) to eat. With the aid of Drone, Pink Guy found a large number of edible plants and berries. Alpha Centurion prepared a roaring fire for the barbecue. Frank sat off at a distance and looked up into the sky. He could sense that something was off before he was able to observe the unnatural hues and behaviors of the clouds in the distance. He watched them turn and discolor and he pondered them, sometimes fearfully, sometimes with an intrigue that bordered audacity. Salamander Man squatted on a rock in the middle of the stream and played his recorder, pausing only to caress his nipples for a moment before playing on. Pink Guy joined him later on his ukulele. It created a calming atmosphere at the end of a very traumatic day.

They feasted and fooled about and farted until the sky grew completely dark and the only light they could see by was the fire which Alpha Centurion continued to stoke (with nutty little giggles) well beyond what was needed. It was Pink Guy who first felt the chill which he initially mistook for a natural drop in temperature. Frank caught it shortly after and the two of them locked eyes. They turned toward the hill to vaguely make out an enormous dark creature quietly descending from the vegetation. As it drew nearer the fire they could make out its form and tier.

Alpha Centurion had no such knowledge. When he saw it he jumped a mile in the air. "What the fuck is that?!" he shrieked. Before them stood one of the ugliest creatures to roam the omniverses. A hideous-looking bug with umpteen long spindly legs on each side of its torso, it was essentially a *gejigeji* the size of a bus yet with a mortal face. "How do you squash a bug that size?" Centurion asked. "You can't," Pink Guy responded. "It's not a beast, it's a chimpilla and its name is Gitzon." He approached his superior defiantly. "What do you want here?" It struck Pink Guy hard, knocking him head over heels into the stream. "Put a leash on your friends," it said to Frank in a waspish voice. "Unless you want to see them permanently ruined." The others all immediately fell in line behind Frank.

"As much as I'd love to stay and play with you all," it said sneering, "I'm only here on business." It spoke with a wicked raspiness and its face scrunched up as it spoke, as though forming words required tremendous and painful effort. "Stand over there," it said to Frank, smacking him off his feet to a spot on the other side of the fire. "Thank you." It turned and faced the remaining members of the brotherhood. "The dark lord has decided that he would prefer to have you in other realms."

"What other realms?" Salamander Man asked in deep distress.

"Oh, she speaks?" Gitzon said. "Then you will go first." It reached up and over with one of its long gangly legs, picked up Salamander Man and dropped him into the centre of the fire which was still roaring with activity. "Noooo!" Alpha Centurion called. Suddenly the mischievousness of making such a conflagration overcame him and he buried his face in his hands, guilt-ridden to the core, and howled. The horror of this sound was only surpassed by that of Salamander Man who screamed an agonising 'Nyeees!" for a few short moments before disappearing altogether when Gitzon spoke into the fire a language that was unintelligible to any of them.

Immediately, Drone took flight and raced away but he was no match for the speed and dexterity of the chimpilla who grabbed him in another skeletal leg and flung him hard into the heart of the fire. It uttered once again into the flame and Drone was gone. This left Alpha Centurion and Negi Generation 1. "You," it grumbled to Negi, "piss off".

Negi was caught completely off guard by these words. "What?"

"You don't know what 'piss off' means? Perhaps you'd rather be with your friends in the fire? We don't need you. You're dead weight. Piss off to whatever sorry little hole in the ground you came from and never come back here again." Negi Generation 1 looked at Frank and with welling eyes, wished him all the best. He then took flight with his little white legs spinning as fast as they could go, and his brown negi hair sprouts flailing about, and disappeared into the darkness.

The chimpilla wrapped itself around Alpha Centurion and began to prod him with its knuckley feet and feel him out with its antennas. "You're cute," it whispered in deep, amorous tones. It salivated as it said it. Centurion was a ball of screaming terror, taboo words and thrash, and this only served to excite the chimpilla even more. It put an antenna deep into Centurion's throat before placing it in its own. "I like the taste of your tonsils," it said with the hint of a smile. "I'll bet you taste good all over." Alpha Centurion, rediscovering the fight in himself, began to bite at the joints of Gitzon's legs in between screams. This had little effect other than to further endear himself to the chimpilla.

"I thought you were here on business." Frank spoke with the same tone of defiance that Pink Guy had. The creature looked over at Frank with revulsion. It picked up Alpha Centurion and tossed him into the centre of the flames without so much as even looking in that direction. With a brief shrill from the runt and another burst of unintelligible words from Gitzon, Alpha Centurion was gone. "You want to do business, let's do business." It began to slither towards Frank as it spoke and its words now came with spittle and hiss. "Just know that if it were up to me I'd have sliced you into pieces and had you for dinner before the eggs were ready."
"Well, it's a good thing we don't have any eggs."
It pressed its ornery face up to Frank's. "I hate you so much." The words seeped out. "I want to damn you. I want to make you one of the Wretched."
"Remind me to never let this guy near a public high school," Frank said to himself.
It looked ready to strike Frank again. "But I'm only here with a message. I'm confined to the message. Tomorrow you will be given co-ordinates. Go where they take you and don't ask questions. It is a high chromosome realm. There you will replenish and the dark lord will harvest your chromosomes in his good time. With that, I must leave." As it slithered away Frank heard it mutter, "but I will damage you."

Frank dropped and sat up against a flat topped rock. He was shaking. There was no longer any sound other than the crackle of the fire, and no light save that coming from the flames. Beyond him, out there, there was no longer anything. Sight, sound,

116

presence all ceased to exist. He was alone. And it petrified him. He took his mind back to the start of the day - whatever period of time that was - when Safari Man woke him in New York. Back then, he had a warm bed, friends and respite from the madness of the omniverses. Now, he had nothing but fear and an antipathy to life. He lay down but was far too worked up to sleep. And the night seemed to drag on for aeons. At some point he drifted off but unease was never far from him.

He was woken in the dim light of an overcast morning by the sound of an almighty thud. The impact it made shook the ground and Frank sat up startled and looked about him. There were no further movements or sounds. The fire had desisted to a large heap of embers. A very gentle breeze blew over the wispy shoots coming from the ground, and the stream they had camped by produced a very lazy flow that meandered around the rocks. Frank continued to look about him. He surveyed the vegetation on the hilltop, the empty plains that stretched out in the opposite direction and the tedious gray of the sky. Nothing. He roused himself and made his way to the still waters. There he washed his face, his arms and hands, and drank freely.

He waded downstream a little before making his way back to the campsite. The scenery was less familiar to him in the morning light. The terrain appeared sandier and less stepped than it had in the twilight hours. A large pale branch up ahead had gone completely unnoticed in the evening preparations. The flora was more sparse and less lush than he had remembered. Suddenly he thought it prudent to gather firewood to keep the fire alive as it's much easier to kindle a fire than start one. As he was about to step around the pale bough, it struck him with alarm that it wasn't a branch fallen from a nearby tree. It was Negi Generation 1. His body had been mutilated and he lay lifeless on the ground. It was clear to Frank, from the sound that woke him and the damage to the corpse, that he had been dropped (or thrown) from a very great height. Most disturbing of all were the lacerations all over his body. He studied them fastidiously. The coordinates of Frank's next realm had been carved into Negi Generation 1's flesh. He fell back horrified, making primal sounds from the back of his throat. Just when he thought he could no longer be scared, a new horror would befall him and he would learn the meaning of fear all over again.

It took him a while to regain his composure. He had a dreaded sense that by following these co-ordinates he was simply moving from one nightmare to another more treacherous one. But what choice did he have? He took a moment to consider his options but there was simply no choice that worked. Inevitably, he succumbed.

He grabbed a small, sharp stick from the bank of the stream and, driven by anger, thrust it into his forearm far deeper than he needed to for the task. Blood shot out and Frank began to create the crimson circle that was beginning to define his life, on the ground around him. In an utterly morbid and detached voice, he repeated the co-ordinates that had been cut into Negi's body. The response was rapid. He fell into a trance, collapsed onto the ground and began convulsing. His field of vision narrowed and all he could recall seeing were the tendrils of a small tree growing over the stream reaching out to him. They touched his face, gently and affectionately at first, but gradually more menacingly and forcefully, till its clutches were tugging at his features and pulling at his hair. As though anaesthetized, Frank could say or do nothing in response. He was screaming inside but his body seemed incapable of responding. The entity wrapped more and more entrails around his face, ripping at his flesh and gauging at his eyes. At the moment of his ultimate suffering, Frank found his voice. "I'm sorry!" he screamed. "I'm sorry. I couldn't help it!"

Chapter 8

The sky above the port was the color of television, tuned to a dead channel. A curious rectangle of it opened above him, framed by four ominously dark walls. Dirty gray clouds blew quickly from one side of the picture to the other, and the call of seabirds, hungry and fearless, echoed across the skies. He lay in a pile of filth and putrid shallow waters with his face, neck and torso covered in what felt like strands of seaweed. Removing it from his face he could see it was cold instant ramen, buckets of it all over him, and the refuse that he lay among was primarily rotting and fetid foods, spiced with battery acids and human waste.

He stood quickly and brushed most of the refuse from him, and looked out over the walls of the vessel that held him.
"What hell am I in now?" he muttered to himself. On three sides he saw nothing but dry empty fields, sparsely covered in grasses, surrounded by waterways. He would automatically have assumed he was on an island but behind him, up against which the lid of the container rested, was a medium sized building, and beyond that, a number of other buildings and structures stood in clusters. The birds continued to hover above and call out their threats. The wind blew in salty gusts.

Frank jumped from the dumpster and removed most of the remaining dross from his blue shirt, his hair and his nose. He turned to observe the building behind him and from the clanging sounds, smells of soy and miso, and the angry, throaty dialogues coming from within, he discerned he was behind the kitchen of an Asian restaurant. Long having abandoned trust in people, he set off in the opposite direction for the respite of the waters which surrounded the fields.

119

He had barely left the smells of the kitchen when the back door swung open aggressively and a red creature with a 'warning: do not touch' countenance staggered out. The two locked eyes for a moment before they instantly broke into a sprint: Frank for the safety of the waters and this new nemesis in pursuit. Frank turned mid-stride to observe his attacker. A creepy, corpulent character, tomato-red all over except for the dark-framed glasses which sat pressed into the fat recesses of his face, he ran with astonishing speed given the girth he carried and the clumsy, uncoordinated stride in his gallop. Before Frank was even halfway to the shoreline, the red beast was upon him, diving from several body lengths away and landing right on his shoulders. He set upon Frank, dragging him to the ground as predators do their prey. The Okinawan crumpled beneath him. He began to scream and thrash about, kicking and swinging for his life but he couldn't overcome the power of the red one.

"Frank!" he said, pressing Frank's shoulders to the ground. "Frank!" Frank stopped struggling.
"How do you know my name? What do you want with me?"
"Come with me. Quickly." He stood and pulled Frank from the ground so violently it almost pulled his arm off. He looked around momentarily before darting off toward an apartment complex to the west of the restaurant, the collar of Frank's shirt firmly in his grip and Frank stumbling and tripping in his effort to keep up.

On arrival, they stood with their backs to the wall of the complex. "You do not want to be seen here," the red one said in a half-whisper. "Too many people know you."
"They do?"
"It's not safe. Everyone wants a piece of you." He looked about again before tugging Frank into a corridor. "This way." He led Frank into an elevator and immediately put his hand over the security camera which was staring down from the front corner.

120

Their ride stopped at the sixth floor. The red creature cussed and hid Frank in the front left corner of the elevator. As the doors opened, a young couple moved to step in but were blocked by a grotesque red figure. "Stay out if you want to live," he said in a deep, accented voice. The couple had no hesitation in withdrawing back into the foyer. The doors closed again and the elevator continued to the twenty-first floor. Once again, Frank was thrust along, this time to a door at the end of a long corridor. The red one knocked firmly twice and then once, and then the door was quickly opened.

With the door closed behind them, the red guy visibly relaxed and guided Frank into a small, barely furnished room. The curtains were closed, giving the room a heavy, leaden feel. He shut the door behind him but continued to speak in a low voice.

"My name is Red Dick. I was sent by the dark lord to help facilitate the replenishment of your chromosomes."

"What's in it for you?" Frank asked bitter and weary of being accosted and dragged from place to place like a commodity.

"Reprieve from the sea of the Wretched." There was fear in his eyes.

"What is this place? Am I back on earth?"

"No, this is Godore. After its creation it was conquered by a peace lord several million chromosomes ago, who modelled a new existence and environment on that of the earth. It's a failed experiment. Over time it has become nothing but a hovel for mutants and deviants, yet it remains chromosome rich and that is why lord Chin Chin has sent you here. The dark lord himself will be here within days to harvest you and if we don't deliver then we're both damned."

"How can I possibly replenish my chromosomes in a couple of days? What sort of fertilizer do you use here (although by the smell of things I'm starting to guess)."

"On your own, you can't. That's why I was sent to you. You're going to win your chromosomes, Frank. It's been set."

Frank was extremely wary. Recollections of deceitful crawfish (though they were his own) and thieving little runts came to mind. "How do I win them?"

"It's easy, Frank. You win them just by eating."

Frank relaxed a little on hearing this. "Well, I am pretty hungry you know. It's been awhile since I've had a decent feed and all that transporting makes a guy ravenous."

"Good boy." He patted Frank on the back. "In that room," he said pointing out the door, "are a bunch of demented fruitcakes. They have been especially chosen for this task. They couldn't find their way out of a bath, not that they'd probably ever had one. But they are chromosome freaks and ready for the taking. Just eat whatever is put in front of you and we will both live to see another day."

With that introduction, he opened the door and led Frank into a large open area which functioned as a living room, and introduced him to the kind folk there. Initially, Frank was on the defensive and ready to be accosted, if not violated, but he needn't have worried. Those present had either no knowledge of Frank and his ability to cross tiers or were without care even if they did know. They sat about like drunken seamen, each placidly acknowledging Frank as he was introduced to them.

"Frank," began Red Dick, "This is Trash." A tall, lean man, bare-breasted and heavy-haired, swayed gingerly in his seat before Frank. He raised a finger in Frank's direction in acknowledgment but never removed his gaze from the floor. "He is a rare species in that he actually falls between mere mortal and brute beast. He has the appearance of a mortal but the intelligence and constitution of a beast yet for some reason believes himself to be a chimpilla. Try not to provoke him by taking his food or poking him with sharp objects."

"I'll try not to."

"Over here," he said, pointing to a creature that was clearly a sad, genetic mutation of some kind of deer, "is Jingle Balls". The organism sat back in his chair with his knees behind his ears, exposing his subtleties and rocking gently to an imaginary rhythm. Jingle Balls was as near to a vegetable as a functioning mortal could be, yet he was chromosome rich and ripe for the picking. "Very nice to meet you," Frank said politely. For a second he was moved to shake the mutant's hand but that temptation passed very quickly at a second look of his tender regions. He turned to the next entity in the room.

There, sprawled across a sofa like a king, reclined a young demigod of a man wearing nothing but a pair of rainbow-colored briefs. Herculean in stature and resplendent in appearance with his Roman features and lush blonde hair, unbeknownst to him he was the prize of the event. A chromosomal colossus, he alone could power a city for a decade and still have something left over and was, as such, Red Dick's prime reason for the gathering. He stood to face Frank and, looking down at the hapless rankenfile, introduced himself in a rich, creamy voice. "Prometheus," he said before repeating it again in a slightly deeper tone - "Prometheus" - to evoke Frank's fullest admiration. He then broke into a series of very impressive flexes. Frank was actually aroused by this and couldn't resist reaching over and giving one of his pecs a little squeeze. This was a foolish thing to do (he quickly learned) as the demigod smashed an open hand across his face, knocking out a tooth and cutting his tongue. As he lay on the ground cupping his mouth and feeling the blood run through his fingers, Prometheus picked up the garbage bin from the kitchen and slammed it down hard across Frank's back. He then returned in a stately fashion to the sofa where he continued to sprawl as if sunbathing. The other characters in the room had no reaction to this violence as though it were as normal a part of their day as smelling fingers.

It was Red Dick who broke the ice. "Well then, shall we start?" He wheeled a table in from the kitchen upon which five plates sat in a circle. On each plate jiggled a large green mass of what Frank initially thought was the phlegm of a deep sea creature. As it turned out, that would have been preferable. The substance, Red Dick announced, was wasabi, an organic radish grown inside the bowels of horses. The members of this club all gathered around the table and considered the challenge before them. Prometheus did this by rubbing his chin. Jingle Balls played with himself. Trash began some deep nasal picking. Frank dabbed at his lip with a tissue. "Gentlemen," Red Dick continued, "the rules are simple. Whoever orally consumes their plate of wasabi first shall be the winner and receive the chromosomes of the others, as well as their personal services, if he so desires, for the period of a thousand chromosomes."

They each indicated their agreement by standing behind their plate, with Red Dick taking the fifth position behind his plate. "Start when the cane toad hits the wall," he said holding up one of the amphibians by a leg. After a short pause for dramatic effect, he hurled the creature hard against the wall behind him and when they heard the unmistakable splat, they began their task.

Red Dick's strategy was a good one. Prometheus, for all his muscle, was predictably weak when it came to certain spices and Jingle Balls, like Red Dick himself, was hopeless with the green paste. They were all immediately reduced to quivering, teary masses and withdrew from the competition shortly after starting. Frank on the other hand, having been raised on a spicy Okinawan diet, was able to soldier through and make good, if not painful, progress. His primary hindrance was the sting the wasabi made on his cut tongue. The real problem, however, was Trash. Unbeknownst to Red Dick, Trash, being an indeterminate species and physiologically a beast, was immune to isothyocyanates which meant he could eat wasabi like he was eating ice cream. As such, the young afro'd creature finished off his plate in record time and stood in bewilderment wondering what all the fuss was about. Having received all the chromosomes due to him, he wiped his fingers on his pants and walked out the door.

Frank now had to attend to a bleeding nose, while drinking milk to ease his throbbing throat and dab at his lip at the same time. None of these, of course, were his principle concern. Chin Chin would be arriving in a matter of days to collect his chromosomes and without them, Red Dick and Frank would almost certainly end up in the deep end of the Wretched sea. Red Dick began to run around the apartment in a psychotic rage.

"Calm down," Frank said, becoming a bit unstable himself. "We have to get chromosomes. We have to get a lot of chromosomes. We have to get a lot of chromosomes very quickly." He rocked back and forth in an autistic rhythm as he said this. "There's only one way. We'll have to steal them." As he said this, Red Dick stopped on the spot and looked at Frank.

"That's it," he said. "We'll have to steal them. And I know how." Frank looked at Red Dick with great expectation. "We start a new religion," the Red One said, "and have children and stupid, gullible youth make blood sacrifices to the dark lord. The blood of children is especially potent. We harvest their chromosomes from the blood sacrifices, and present them to Chin Chin when he comes. It's foolproof!"

"How long do you think this would take?"

"About a hundred years." Red Dick was completely unperturbed by this length of time.

"Or," Frank interjected, "we could just break into a children's hospital and steal all the blood samples from there." Red Dick looked at Frank with the expression of an idiot just exposed. "Or that," he conceded.

They wasted no time. That night, Frank and Red Dick did the very deed. They broke into the local children's hospital and removed every single blood sample from it. This earned them many more chromosomes than they could possibly have won from the wasabi eating competition. These surplus chromosomes Frank kept for himself, hiding them in his deepest recesses where he hoped Chin Chin, for all his powers, would never find them. Frank had never felt as powerful as he was at that time. What he was unaware of though, was that many of the chromosomes he had procured from the children's hospital were actually cancerous. They were, after all, the samples of some seriously ill children. Frank was of the belief that he had just won a great victory.

It was a sultry evening when the presence came. It turned the heavy, balmy air instantly into frigid gusts. Frank and Red Dick went out onto the balcony to watch the phenomena. They knew what was happening. The people outside twenty floors below were not so knowledgeable but they could sense the evil in the air, smell the stench percolating in the breezes and see the turmoil of the skies. They began to scatter about like ants on uppers. Red Dick started to tremble with fear and moved back inside the apartment, wedging himself in between the cushions of the sofa.

Frank was inexplicably calm. He knew who was coming and he knew the threat that he posed. He was aware of his own ultimate vulnerability. However, for the first time, he knew he had something within him that was of greater value to the omniverse than his demise. Though not defiantly, he watched the changing atmosphere with a sense of willing participation.

As though by command, the clouds thickened and lowered and amidst a swirl of wind and matter, the dark lord appeared in his own sphere of composure, alighting beside Frank on the balcony of the apartment. Together they looked out over the landscape -

126

the unnaturally colored skies over shadowed buildings and turbulent waterways, the traffic lights and neon signs now rendered dysfunctional, the people peeping out from behind curtains and the dogs howling. "Oh Chin Chin ga daisuki da yo," he spat in his twitching tones. "All this is mine." He surveyed it a little longer, proud of his work. The wind continued to moan. "You've done well," he said. "You have proven yourself capable." He continued to look out over the terrain. "Now give them to me." After a brief silence he turned and looked at Frank. Frank reached out and placed his hand on Chin Chin's wrist. They both jumped at the transaction.

"My, my. So many chromosomes." The dark lord rolled his neck with satisfaction and blinked his demented eyes several times. "But did you really think I wouldn't notice?" Suddenly the air turned acrid and Frank was pierced with fear. "You've hidden many, many more chromosomes deep within. My, my. So many chromosomes. So many. I'll take those, too." He latched onto Frank's bicep and instantly drained him of strength. Every last chromosome that Frank had taken from the children's hospital was transfused into the peace lord. Frank crumpled to the ground as the dark lord stooped down and peered into his watery eyes. "Hiding chromosomes from me?," he growled. There was a tense moment of finality between them. "Good job, Frank. That's exactly what I would have done. Perhaps there's a little of me in you." He then made a heinous throttling sound which Frank suspected was laughter.

Once more, Chin Chin wrapped his grubby, long-nailed fingers around Frank's arm. "You'll need these," he said and returned some chromosomes to Frank. "I have another little errand for you. No co-ordinates necessary. This one's express." With that he picked Frank up and hurled him from the balcony. Frank fell clutching and screaming into a deep black abyss.

He never recalled landing. Only feeling the terrain under his back. And seeing the darkness. It was total. Frank reached gingerly about to feel out his surroundings. All about him he felt rich, moist soil and fronds growing in thick bunches. He would have assumed from the texture of the soil that it was compost, except that it didn't smell. The strands were thin but robust and stood higher than he could reach in a lying position. In the blackness, he was too afraid to move so he just lay there, terrified, and listened for anything that might approach. He heard sounds. Small sounds. The sounds of distant whistles and chirps and calls and bug cries. Occasionally the wind would moan as it rolled over him. Listening to it, he was eventually lulled by it's sad rhythms before falling into a deep and exhausted sleep.

When he woke, the sun was high in a pale blue sky and he sat up startled. All about him, as far as the eye could see, were rice fields. He touched his face. It was sore and felt as though it had been lightly lacerated all over by the sheaths of the rice plants. "Welcome to the rice fields," he said to himself. He stood to see further and noticed to the north a small mountain far off in the distance. It drew him so he began to head off in that direction.

There was a tranquility and solitariness to this place that Frank actually enjoyed. It seemed so devoid of the perils of previous lands, and the climate was pleasant and calming. Though he missed his friends and felt a twinge of unease without them, there remained a respite from the fears and anxieties caused by the other realms and he walked onward with a sense of ease and adventure.

He hadn't gone far when this fantasy was completely razed. In a paddock in front of him stood what on earth would have been a farmer. He stood there gently teetering in the breeze as though remaining upright were a major achievement. Frank called to him but there was no response. He waved but there was nothing in return. Suddenly the air chilled and the sounds of the crickets and frogs were stilled. Frank drew nearer with a feeling of deep-seated alarm. The farmer wore a tattered white shirt under a pair of beige overalls. An old straw hat sat awkwardly on his head, tilted back toward his neck revealing a stony expression and grotesque empty eye sockets. The sun shining into his face revealed every dry sinew and vein lining the back of the cavities, and every wrinkle and abrasion on his face. His mouth was wide open yet moved awkwardly as though trying to speak. "Tay… Tay…Tay…," he seemed to be saying, but he was incapable of completing his utterance. As Frank watched the farmer try to speak, he saw his whole jaw detach and fall from his face, only to be left hanging by its parched skin. Slowly he raised an outstretched arm and pointed to Frank as if to announce a warning. A rasping, painful exhale came from his throat and then his arm dropped by his side and he turned away.

Frank hurried around him and continued on his way, but was shortly met by another soulless mortal. A woman dressed in rags, carrying a baby in her arms, staggered toward him. She and her child had the same vacant eyes and pale gray hue as the farmer, and the mother, her head covered with a tattered veil and a hand raised out toward Frank, began to scream out a breathless warning like a kettle on the boil and it scared Frank to death. The baby in her arms mimicked the cry and started uttering the same pained expression that the farmer had. "Tayt…Tayt," but then burst into a wail again. Frank covered his ears and ran by them yelling "Stop! Please just stop!"

The journey through the rice fields continued in the same manner throughout the day. On every stepped hilltop and descent he would encounter more of the soulless bodies, usually on their own but sometimes in groups of two of three. All had the same stolen appearance and presented the same dire gestures and warnings. Most strained so badly to utter their words that their necks broke or they simply froze as though stricken with paralysis. A few were able to complete more of their words (though their efforts produced the same horrific disfigurements) and Frank was able to piece together their warning. A certain type of chimpilla called tatums were about, yet that was all that was divulged. Their appearance, size and number remained a complete mystery. This ignorance only served to stoke the fear in Frank all the more and he continued through the fields, crouching and crawling, trying to remain as inconspicuous as possible.

He recalled Pink Guy's campfire talks on how all the rice field realms were on the very edges of the omniverses and how anyone who found themselves there would know they were in the most desolate of places. He also remembered Pink Guy's words warning of the unknown dangers lurking throughout the rice fields. He never mentioned the tatums by name but he did speak of the awful entities that inhabited these regions. Did he know that Frank would end up here? Could he see it before it happened? Was there more to Pink Guy than he knew? Could Pink Guy be a chimpilla himself or possibly even a peace lord? Frank ponded these possibilities as he ventured closer toward the mountains, skirting the soulless folk who continued to come out to him.

By evening Frank had reached the base of the mountain, and stumbled out from the edge of the rice fields onto firmer ground. Though the mountain was not a high one, its incline was steep and rocky from the rice fields and Frank set up a small camp by their periphery. The sun dropped quickly over the horizon and Frank made a small fire before the darkness was complete. The land grew eerily silent. Other than the soft crackle of the fire, there was no sound at all. Had he not just spent a long day encountering soulless beings issuing dire warnings, this might have actually been a beautiful and refreshing moment. But he had traveled too far and seen too much since leaving Okinawa to find any rest in any region. He wondered if he would ever know peace again.

As he journeyed, he had collected some small crickets and grasshoppers from the rice fields to eat in the event that nothing more appetising came his way. None did. So he prepared to barbecue them in the fire before munching on them. Yet a rustle suddenly came from the rice fields a stone's throw from where he was sitting and he put the creatures back in his pocket. Another rustle followed shortly after from his right, and then another from his left, and then another again from immediately in front. Each rustling was followed by a piercing but brief shriek. "Yeff!" Frank's fear level went through the roof. "Yeff!" a shriek echoed from another location. Within moments, the rice fields were filled with aggressive rustling sounds and the screams of "yeff!"

Frank was on his feet and *en garde*. He began to sweat profusely and grabbed a small pointed branch he had gathered for firewood in one hand and a second from the fire that burned fiercely in the other. He struggled for breath. These were surely the tatums that he had been warned about. Beyond the fire there was a darkness as black as the abyss itself. Frank could see nothing. The scampering amongst the rice plants and the shrieks of "yeff!" continued to heighten in frequency and intensity until suddenly a small but vicious looking creature darted out of the fields and stood scowling and sneering and gnashing at Frank in the glow of the campfire light. It had the body of a marsupial and the face of a raccoon with rabies. Its head was crested with a bright yellow comb. Solid black eyes, glazed and wild, sat in ringed sockets and its teeth looked like it had bitten into a bag of nails and they had all just hung there.

Immediately others appeared, at first just a few, but quickly others surfaced till there were dozens surrounding him. They all shared similar fiendish features but their combs were all of a different color. And each of them held rice sheaths in their paws, wielding them with heckles and murderous intent. One jumped toward Frank from the side and slashed a sheath across his calf and in a flash bounded back to the safety of the rice fields with a gleeful chuckle. Frank looked at the small welt that was building on his flesh. "Hey, that hurt!" he said. While dabbing at it with his finger, two more attacked from the opposite side leaving harsh red marks down the side of his other leg. "Right, that's it!" he declared, as another leapt at him in attack from directly in front. Frank shoved the sharp branch he was holding right through the creature's palate. It dangled there lifelessly as though a warning to any other who might venture toward him. The tatums hopped about insanely when they saw their kind impaled like that and began 'yeffing' in a frenzied cacophony.

A few more attempted to assail him but Frank quickly found his valour. They were easily and proficiently dealt with. The first was struck hard with the burning branch which knocked the top off its head and left it lying lifeless with an expression that would have been comical had its brain not been oozing out. Never before had Frank felt so potent. There was almost a joy to the power he was feeling. The second was met with a perfectly timed kick to the groin which sent it flying out into the night sky, screaming "yeff!" until the cry trailed off rather beautifully into the distance. This initial retaliation proved too much for the other tatums. There were a series of 'yeffs' called in a different tone and suddenly all them, except for one, bounded back off into the rice fields. That remaining one stayed firmly held under Frank's size ten foot, screaming and yeffing for all it was worth until Frank placed the sharp end of the stick in front of its ear and finished it with one thrust of his shoulder.

He picked it up, collected the other carcass which had been impaled on the same weapon and carried them both over to the fire. He roasted them, pleased in the knowledge that he would be enjoying a much more satisfying meal than the crickets and grasshoppers which he released from his pocket back into the paddies. And when the tatums were ready, he feasted on them to the faint but rather delightful sound of yeffs withdrawing off into the distance.

As he ate, Frank grew curious as to the nature of his own powers and abilities and the transformation that was continuing within him. He had never felt so powerful and had never struck at enemies so forcefully or effectively. The tatums were chimpillas yet he squashed them aside as though they were bugs. Perhaps Frank himself was no longer a rankenfile. Had he jumped another tier? Was he now a chimpilla himself? How he wished Pink Guy were with him to help him understand this.

Despite his exhaustion and his full belly, he was unable to sleep. He remained on a high, both in his victory over the tatums and in his wariness of the unknown that still lay ahead of him. He no longer considered any realm safe or peaceful. Every dimension required vigilance and care. Though the tatums were no longer a threat, something or someone else surely would be. He was wise in his appraisal.

In the early hours of the next morning, just as the glow of the sun was beginning to awaken the sky and that of the campfire embers was dying, he heard movement from the rice fields. This was not the light scampering of the tatums. This was heavy, sizeable, even cumbersome. As he peered toward the sound, he could make out depressions in the fields as it moved. The sound grew louder as it snaked toward him eventually stopping just short of the edge of the field, still partially hidden in the greenery. It lay there observing Frank. Frank slowly reached over and picked up the sharp stick with which he had inflicted his toll on the tatums. At that point the creature slithered out of the reeds and into the open.

A massive centipede-like organism, it had a bulbous head and a face that approached human likeness except for its fearful ugliness. Its individual features probably qualified as human - in terms of function at least - but they were so weirdly arranged and disproportionate in size that Frank assumed its disfigurement had to be mutational. "Man, you are one ugly sucker." Frank had no idea he had actually spoken the words until the creature replied.

"Is that any way to speak to a guest?" It spoke in a deep, polished voice, one that would normally be associated with intellectual excellence. "I've come quite some distance to accommodate you, Frank, and to expedite your passage."

"Who sent you?" Frank was on high alert and he held the branch firmly in his grip.

"I sent myself." It scratched the corner of its mouth as it spoke. "And you can put the weapon down. I loathe that sort of hostility. I come in a spirit of goodwill and assuagement."

Frank was not easily comforted. "How do you know me? How did you know I was here?"

"The omniverses sing, Frank, and there is much talk of you echoing across the ether. Indeed, it seems you have created something of a stir. Yet I suspect there is also some misinformation and misunderstandings about your present state and I have come to offer you my counsel."

It would have been easier to accept this creature's words had it not been so hideously ugly. Frank held onto his stick defiantly. "I don't want or need your help. Leave me alone."

"Frank, you have no idea what lies ahead of you. I do. You have already been warned by your pink friend of the hostilities of the rice field regions. I'm afraid even he doesn't know the half of it. I will tell you. Frank, beyond here are pains and atrocities so awful they make the realm of the Wretched look like a vacation. Believe me, you do not want to go on. Beyond this mountain are sufferings far worse than you can imagine and your growing strength is not what you think it is. You have been deceived, Frank."

"I just knocked out a whole score of chimpillas," Frank retorted. "How do you explain that?"

The creature laughed and as it did, convulsions rippled up and down its rubbery body from its head to its tail and back. "The tatums?!" It laughed again, only more heartily this time. "You may as well have been fighting potato men! They're not chimpillas! They're just vege-beasts and very poor ones at that." It laughed again in a very deep, condescending way. "That's why you were able to defeat them so easily. Your powers are not growing, Frank. If anything, out here in these nether realms, you are actually weakening. You are susceptible to almost anything that attacks and increasingly so. You cannot go on and I regret to say that it may be too late to turn back. The true powers, the dark forces are moving in this very realm as we speak. You are being surrounded, Frank. They want you gone. There is no way out for you."

"So, what are you telling me? I'm just cactus and that's it?"

"Kill yourself, Frank."

"What?"

"Kill yourself. The only way to save yourself from the terrors beyond this place is to take your own life. Take it before they do. Believe me, they will abuse you in ways you never thought possible. Take your life, Frank. Take it quickly."

Frank had been through so much already. He had seen such misery and suffering, experienced so much horror and evil that taking his life no longer seemed scary or wrong. Yet something irked him about this creature. There was something distasteful and distrusting about it. And deep inside he knew that there was something more for him, a meaning and purpose that he had to find. He didn't have the fortitude to call it hope, but it kept him from despair.

He grasped the stick in his hand and turned to head up the mountain.

"No," he said. "I'm going on."

The creature recoiled for a moment as Frank turned and walked from it. It then charged at him in a blind rage and with its front appendages knocked Frank flying against the rocks at the base of the mountain. "You dare defy me?" Its voice was now a guttural scowl. "Do you have any idea who I am?" It stood over Frank in a rage, saliva and mucus dripping from its mouth and other openings. "I am Tatorium! I am the lord of this land! I am the power you were warned about! You shall not pass! You shall not trespass my rice fields! And you shall never turn your back on me!"

Frank stood up, his face inches away from the monster's odorous face. He looked deep into its eyes. Though afraid, he didn't fear this creature and it recoiled again at Frank's stance. "Back away!" Frank called, as though commanding it , and the creature instinctively did so at first, before rallying and attacking Frank with a roar that rang out over the fields and hills. Critters great and small, near and far, scampered away at the sound of it. As the chimpilla descended on him in a wild fury, Frank thrust the point of his spear through its bottom jaw. It reeled back in pain and Frank went with it as he held fast to the branch, flying through the air, and landed on the creature's upturned belly. "Welcome to the rice fields, motherfucker!" he yelled and with one almighty thrust of his weapon, he pierced its brain with a satisfying crunch. After writhing for a few desperate moments, it lay lifeless, a twisted, coiled pile of ugliness.

Frank removed his spear - it was serving him well - and jumped with it from the belly of the beast. He surveyed the remains, stepping backwards to view it in its entirety. Though trembling with adrenaline, Frank was in awe of his own prowess. Whatever the tatums were, he had overcome them with ease. And now, he had overpowered Tatorium, surely the true chimpilla of which the soulless bodies had been warning him? Despite the chromosomes needed to repel and overpower the chimpilla, Frank still felt strong. He felt a power welling within him that he had never known before. And with it, he felt an innate desire to press on beyond this mountain. He knew there was something beyond it that the dark powers didn't want him to know or find. Emboldened by this inherent knowledge and his victories in battle, he ascended the mountain in no time.

From the summit he had an uninhibited view of the whole land, and most notably, an island which sat in the middle of a sea beyond the shores rimming the foot of the mountain. Frank made his way down under golden sunshine, through lush, grassy fields and felt a cool breeze blow off the water and through his hair. The freshness invigorated him and he hummed a tune as he strutted toward the sparkling waters.

The sand on the beach was fine and white and Frank removed his shoes and felt the grains tickle his toes. He lay back and enjoyed the warmth of the sun, high in a cloudless sky, massaging his face. Such respite was rare and he savored the moment. With half-closed eyes, he listened to the gentle breezes gust across the water and play with the leaves of the trees which dotted the shoreline.

Sitting up, he looked across the expanse to the island. It lay shrouded in a light fog that moved backwards and forwards across the landscape, revealing and concealing its features. The wind continued to move across the water from the island, picking up and carrying a soft sigh as it blew. As he listened, he began to make out words in the wind. At first he denied it but the more he listened the clearer it became. It stunned him and left him standing perplexed. It was calling his name. In a faint but deep whisper, his name rolled over the surface of the deep. 'Frank! Frank!'

There were no signs of life on the beach. Yet at a far end, a wooden raft bobbed in the shallows, tied to a post protruding from a rocky ledge. With the sun beginning its descent toward the horizon, Frank, lost no time jumping onto the raft and using the oar upon it to paddle his way toward the island.

Chapter 9

The past is a foreign country; they do things differently there. That lay behind him; the future had now arrived. It was an innate knowledge that rose up within him and he never doubted it. It sustained him on his brief crossing and brought him a disposition which he suspected might have been cheer. He sensed that by passing over this body of water he was simultaneously passing over not just time, but history; not just space, but tiers. His identity was reforming, his purpose consolidating. He could feel it in a fashion and with a certainty that he had never previously known and it exhilarated him and scared him.

The water gently lapped at the side of the raft as it twisted through the swell, occasionally spilling over the side and wetting his feet. He continued to work the oar and as he did, the island loomed into view. It was considerably bigger than it had appeared from the shore and it contained flatlands leading to a hill which rose grandly at the back. The nearer he drew, the more the mists lifted and by the time he reached the shoreline of the island, the air was crisp and clear. He alighted into cool and fresh waters and dragged the raft high up onto the sands.

Pausing to scan the landscape, he heard it again. "Frank!" The deep whisper rolled up to him like a gentle wave. It was the most inviting voice he had ever heard. He froze to catch it and when it came again he could tell it was emanating from the hill. Immediately, he set off for it. The plains he walked over were covered with a thick but soft green grass which swayed gently in the gusts blowing across it. Fat, twisted trees with thick caramel-colored bark, each producing a multitude of leaves of different colors and designs, dotted the terrain. In clusters around them, shrubs spawned flowers of the most vivid colors and shapes while neighboring bushes grew fruits of seemingly unlimited variety.

Frank noticed little, if any of this beauty, such was his determination to reach the hill before sunset, yet his spirits couldn't but be lifted by the ambience that the landscape provided.

He made good progress. With the sun ahead of him and still a fist above the pointed horizon, he stood at the base of the hill and peered up at it. Much of it appeared in silhouettes yet he could identify everything clearly. Every piece of flora on the hill seemed to be arranged around a massive tree rising from its summit, as though an audience before it, as though in celebration of it. It rose into the sky like a tower and had the girth of a grain elevator. Frank strode toward the tree. The closer he got the more he could feel its presence and its reach toward him. The grass he walked on somehow felt inexplicably connected to the tree, and in brushing his hand over the flowers as he passed them, he could feel the tree in each touch. It made no sense but he knew it was true.

It wasn't till he was a stone's throw from the tree that he could make out its essence and it struck him like a knife to the heart. He stopped dead in his tracks, eyes frozen wide like skeets, his breath stolen from within him. He could neither advance nor retreat. The tree swayed slightly, though there wasn't a hint of wind, as though to observe him. Gripped with fear, Frank continued to stare at the trunk of the tree, still unwilling to believe what he was seeing. Protruding from it, yet one with it, was the silhouetted effigy that he had seen in his nightmares long ago in Okinawa. The dark figure of unknown origin and nature, powerful and mighty, leaned toward him; fused to the tree, he could do no more than that. Just as Frank had seen in his visions, the entity was one with the tree, bare-chested with arms stretched across the trunk as though crucified on it, yet not. He was not just with the tree, he was the tree, sharing life with it, sustaining it.

The horror of the Okinawan nightmares returned to him in all their fierceness yet at the same time, this was not the nightmare. This was something different; a fulfilment of the nightmares yet not their essence. And when the entity spoke to him, it confirmed this.

"Don't be afraid." The voice was deep and sonorous and majestic. Frank didn't so much respond as obey. "Come closer." Frank stepped toward the tree till he could make out every line in the humanoid's face and see every vein that ran from the trunk into his arms. "Frank," he said. His voice carried such magnanimity that Frank was fearful and comforted at the same time.

"How do you know my name?"

"I've known you for a very long time." Frank peered into the figure's eyes. They revealed much in their paradoxes. They were gentle yet powerful, ancient yet youthful, mystic yet simple, tragic yet consoling. Frank's fear left him completely as the figure spoke on in a warm, resonant voice. "I saw you in the gutter in Indonesia. I watched you work at Soncorp. I felt your pain in dealing with the military. I heard your screams in your first passage to the frozen wasteland. I know your deepest fears and greatest longings. I know everything about you."

Frank felt a tranquil mesmerising as he listened. And when he thought he couldn't be any more amazed, the entity spoke again. "I know everything." These three words seemed implausibly absurd yet he believed them. The richness of the voice alone was convincing but it was more than that. A spirit of authority came forth with the words, leaving Frank no doubt as to their truth. Yet Frank still had no idea who this was. He didn't have a clue as to his status. And despite the calm he exuded, Frank was still unaware if this figure was ultimately benign or malevolent. He asked.

"Are you God?" The top rim of the sun set behind the earth supporting the great tree as Frank presented his question.

"I don't know."

"If you know everything, how can you not know?"

"I don't know. I just know that I don't know."

Frank thought about this. "Could you be God?"

"I'm afraid of the thought that I could be. Yet I don't want that burden. I suspect I am deity because I am all-knowing but if it were possible, could God choose to not be God?" There was a faint rustle of discontentment from the surrounding bushes and shrubs as he said this. Some of the flowers closed. "I am what I am. And you are what you are, Frank."

"What am I?"

"Yes," he stated. Frank almost understood this.

"Am I a chimpilla?"

"You are both more and less than that."

"What is your name?"

"Don't ask my name." Frank wondered for the life of him why not but honored his request. The flowers and leaf buds seemed to re-open and shiver at this response.

"How old are you?"

"I have no age. I have always been."

"What is my age?"

"Older than you know, but still young."

"Did you make my world?"

"I created your universe from nothing but only your universe."

"Are there others like you?"

"There are others who appear like me to others."

"Why are you here?"

"The rice fields on the edge of the omniverses provide... shelter."

"Shelter? Shelter from what? Shelter from whom?"

"Shelter from my identity."

This perplexed Frank and led him to a million other questions but he suspected the answers would take him no closer to his most critical enquiries. His desperation to know who he was and why he had become like this, returned to him as a roaring flame. The entity pre-empted him.

"You want to know your purpose."

"Yes, I do."

"Sit at my base and lean against me." Frank didn't hesitate to do so yet moved slowly and respectfully. As he rested his back against the bark of the trunk he felt immediately rested. It was as though a small bough were reaching inside of him and stroking his soul. Frank exhaled and softly lay his head back against the great tree and for the first time in his adult life, Frank knew peace. He had known of peace and he had longed for peace but he had never truly known it for himself and it was beautiful. Beautiful. The entity continued to speak in his lush tones.

"You must leave here, Frank." This would have devastated Frank had he not been in the cradle of serenity. Yet he failed to understand it at all. The figure spoke on. "Your purpose is not here. Nor will you find your true identity here. Your identity is inexorably tied to your purpose and both lie beyond."

"I'm scared to go on."

"You must leave here," he repeated with a tone of urgency. "Let nothing distract you or tempt you from this."

"There is so much that is macabre and evil in the other realms. And besides, I have no co-ordinates other than those given to me by higher powers, and they always lead to unimaginable horror."

"You're not trying hard enough."

If this were intended as comfort, it failed.

"I don't understand," said Frank frustrated.

"Try harder." From anyone else these words would have been torment but from the entity, they brought correction and hope. "With enough chromosomes, you can discover just about any coordinates you like."

Frank's face fell at this. "Each time I begin to amass chromosomes, Chin Chin harvests them from me. I can't escape him." The thought then came to Frank and he didn't hesitate to ask. "Is Chin Chin God?"
"If Chin Chin were God he wouldn't need your chromosomes." Frank recalled hearing this somewhere before.
"So he's a peace lord?"
"A very powerful one. But he's not your primary concern."
"He's not?" Frank felt like a small child talking to this figure. "Who is my primary concern?"

At that moment Frank sensed the answer that the entity wished to speak: "Yourself". But those were not the words he delivered. "I will share with you a mystery, Frank. Listen carefully. You are unique. Your multiplying chromosomes are a gift. They have been given to you for a reason. The chromosomes are yours. A curse be on anyone who takes them from you. But you must learn how to keep them. You must know how to hide them. Veil them. Possess them."

While still resting against the trunk of the tree, Frank turned to look into the entity's eyes. They were magnificent. "How?" he asked. The longer he spent in his presence the more infantile he understood himself to be. He also felt supremely protected.
"Translephony."
Frank looked up at him for an explanation.
"Share your chromosomes with other entities and organisms. Chromosomes should never be taken but they can be freely given and returned. Chromosomes given through translephony remain the property of the giver. They are shared to sustain, and stored to nurture others. But there is another quality it brings. It makes chromosomes untouchable to any who would endeavor to steal them."
"Translephony?" Frank said in a soft daze.

"Look around you. The trees and plants, the flowers and the grass - even the birds which have retired for the evening and feed off the plants - contain my chromosomes. I have given to all of them. I sustain this whole island. I can give and receive my chromosomes as I please. And this great tree," he said looking about him, "I have given of my chromosomes so greatly that we are now as one. We remain separate entities yet we function as one."

Frank sat in silence for a long time absorbing all this. The sky was now quite dark and its expanse was flooded with a starry host. "Can I use translephony?"
"Anyone with the gift, the purpose and the focus can employ it. The first you have. The second is forming. The third comes with practice." Frank placed his hand on the grass beside him. It was soft to touch and he desired a connection with it. But he felt no more than that.

He was tired after his long day and in the calm of the island he soon became sleepy. He moved away from the tree and lay down under its branches on a plush carpet of grass. Billows of peace rolled over and over him and the last thing he remembered was running his hands backwards and forwards delicately over the tips of the blades and feeling them tickle his palms. Sleep came over him like a warm blanket.

An almighty crash startled him awake in the pre-dawn light. He abruptly sat up and looked out, incredulous, over the hill - that great hill that had supported the indomitable tree and the entity that was one with it. There was nothing left of them but an enormous stump cut clean through. The tree had been felled and lay, with the wise and mighty humanoid, now cold and deceased still attached, at the back of the hill, all broken limbs and wilting canopy. Beside the stump sat an enormous figure, dark and silent. It looked at Frank with a murderous gaze. Swollen, blood-red eyes bulged out from a huge emerald-colored, triangular head. Its body was lean but muscular and its limbs were hairy, impossibly long and sat neatly folded in front of its torso. It reminded Frank of some of the enormous praying mantises from the Okinawan jungle. It rubbed its front appendages together in a slow, hypnotic rhythm before leaning toward Frank and opening its steely mouth with a hint of a smile.

"Fear the peace lords," it hissed, "for we are more powerful than anything you can possibly imagine." Frank was on his knees, mortified with terror. "Who are you?" The words quivered out.
"My name is Dyopatera. Remember it." Frank nodded. "Remain here on this island," it continued, "until the dark lord comes again." With that, it simply dissipated into thin air as though a hologram fading away.

Frank remained motionless. After finally experiencing such long-awaited and sweet peace, to be crushed again and swept back into a universe of desolation and death was too much for him. He broke down and wept inconsolably. When he lifted his head again the sun had peeked over the new horizon and the island was flooded with a strong but sad light. The flowers and leaf buds remained resolutely closed and the grass had a ginger tinge to it. The trees all had a wilt to them and not a birdsong could be heard anywhere on the island. Instinctively he walked up, sat on the stump and looked down over the back side of the hill. A thin rim of water separated the island from the mainland to the east, beyond which there lay he knew not what.

And then the dilemma dawned on him. Did he listen to the unsettling words of the victorious peace lord who told him to stay, or did he heed the pleasant advice of the defeated peace lord who told him to move beyond this place? It was a surprisingly easy decision for him; not because he trusted the latter, nor was it because he hated the former. It was primarily because he considered himself already a dead man and with nothing to lose he moved for whatever promised gain. He lifted himself from his seat and with an air of listlessness, strolled down the hill toward the stream running in front of the mainland. He never noticed the tiniest of hypocotyls peeping up from the centre of the stump. Neither did he see the lush, long grass which had grown around him as he slept.

The stream separating the island from the mainland was narrower and faster flowing than it had appeared from a distance. It was also teeming with fish. Frank waded into the middle of it where it came up to his knees, splashing and washing about him. The fish, so near salmon they may as well have been, were literally jumping out of the water all about him. It was only a matter of time before a big one jumped right into his hands which he caught with a sense of glee.

He carried it back to the island, all flipping and wriggling, to cook over a fire for breakfast, yet by the time his feet were out of the water, the fish was little more than a withered lancelet. His first inclination was to wonder what was wrong with the fish in this realm that they would perish so quickly out of water. He repeated the exercise and quickly caught another good-size salmon, this time keeping it under the water till he got to the water's edge but again by the time he lifted it from the swell, it was embryonic. He was about to dismiss the whole incident and move on but the words of the tree entity returned to him. Was this translephony? With the remains of the fish still in his hands, rather than taking from it, he consciously gave himself to it and was amazed to see before his eyes the fish restored to full and vibrant life. He tossed it back into the torrent and picked up the residue of the first creature. It too, with encouragement, returned to full constitution in his hands. Considering it, he took from it again and it deteriorated right before him once more.

Frank was intoxicated. He restored it to full health before throwing it full bodied onto a hastily made fire and ate it with relish. With his belly full, he turned his back on the island, crossed the stream once again and readied to venture deep into the rice fields of the eastern mainland. Before starting out though, he made one more wade into the stream, grabbed one more leaping fish and sucked from it its life source till there was nothing left of it but scales and bones. Giddy with pleasure, he discarded the remains on the ground and walked into the long, mature shoots.

The day was still young when he started out. The rice fields stretched before him in an endless run of green. The constant bleat of crickets rang like tinnitus in his ears. Distant hills broke the visual monotony but there were no impediments to keep him from making good progress. These eastern paddies seemed devoid of any advanced life forms; certainly he faced no opposition as he walked. He was pleased to be free of torment yet as the sun slowly crawled its way up the pale blue sky, it came to him anyway. Its name was Loneliness.

As field after field passed beneath his feet, he felt the tiresomeness of continuing on his own to a place of no consequence and a time without meaning. He missed his friends Salamander Man and Pink Guy, Alpha Centurion and Drone, and Negi Generation 1. He recalled all their adventures, the laughter and the fighting that only brotherhood could foster. How he longed for their company again. And the loss of the tree entity only served to exacerbate the forlornness he was feeling. The sagely words he spoke, the deep peace he afforded. Yet he recalled the words which had been given to him: "You must leave here." The words had been spoken with such potency. "Your purpose is not here." This resonated deeply with Frank. Though he had no idea where he was going, these words put a spring in his step.

"You're not trying hard enough." This confused Frank. He had no idea where to move on to and even if he did, he didn't have the coordinates to get there. Frank found this deeply troubling yet he somehow knew that the entity had spoken the truth. He needed to try harder but he was at a complete loss as to how.

The torment of frustration he felt was soon surpassed by that of loneliness which returned to him with a disturbing intensity. With each passing field, his desire for companionship increased. The higher the sun rose, the greater the desire he felt for fellowship with his old comrades. And the crickets kept singing their throbbing songs. By the time the heat of the day was at its most sapping, the sun seemed to pause directly above him and, growing delirious, he began to talk, firstly to himself, then to Pink Guy and Salamander Man as though they were walking right there by him.

"What say you, Pink Guy?" he stammered. "Are we right for direction?"

"Keep going, Captain. We're surely on the right path," he heard in reply.

"Can you concur, Salamander Man?"

"Nyes," came the answer, confirmed with the playing of a very merry tune.

"I do believe, gentlemen," Frank encouraged them, "that we shall arrive safely by nightfall." He looked to his right. "Now Pink Guy," he said, "Would you be so kind as to advise of the lifeforms that we should expect along the way? Friend or foe, don't hold back, my brother. I want to know them all!"

This conversation continued for many hours - possibly days - when Frank suddenly stopped dead and stared at an apparition off in the middle distance. There on the far side of the field they had just entered stood a thatch hut and in front of it, motionless and halting, a humanoid figure. His first understanding was to think it

149

was another of the soulless bodies he had encountered on the west side of the island yet as he drew nearer, he could see that the figure was very much alive, in full health and was female. Young and vivacious, she raised a hand and gestured with enthusiasm for him to come and join her. He turned to raise eyebrows with his companions but they were no longer with him.

Frank marched through the sheaths with a fresh vigor to see a woman of stunning organic beauty standing before him. She had an earthly mediterranean complexion, with long, dark hair, gently woven, lying over her left shoulder. She wore a sleeveless, cream-colored garment, secured at the waist with a thin brown belt. She was barefoot. "I'm so glad you came," she said, bearing a huge white smile. "So glad." She took him by the hand and led him into the hut. It was noticeably cooler inside. The interior was simply furnished with a small wooden dining table, two chairs, a short counter and sink against the nearer wall that served as a kitchen, a small primitive bathroom, and a narrow bed that lay neatly made against the further wall.

She sat Frank down and brought him a cool drink. "You must be so tired. You have come a long way. Drink up, rest well." She squatted down to remove his shoes and brought a tub of soapy water over to wash his feet. Frank had no idea who this was or why he should be the recipient of such kindness but he was far too tired to object. Her hands were soft and gentle, and as she washed his soles and caressed his toes, Frank was instantly healed of any previous torments. She looked up at him with enormous brown eyes, friendly and inviting, and smiled again. Frank couldn't help but notice the very fine and ample cleavage that was revealed, only fractionally but enough, and (simple folk that he was) he was enamoured.

"What's your name?" she asked.
He returned his vision to her eyes. "Frank."

"Frank," she repeated softly with another smile. "I like that name. It's a good name." She gently wrung the water from the cloth. "Frank."

"What's your name?" Frank asked.

"Goomba."

"What are you doing all the way out here on your own?"

"Waiting for you, of course. I knew someone would come eventually." She began to towel his feet. "I'm just glad it was you."

She removed the tub of water, washed her hands and joined him at the table with a plate of freshly baked rice cakes. He wasted no time in devouring them and she watched him do so with pleasure. She joined him and they ate in silence for a while before she spoke again.

"What are you doing out here?"

Frank waited before responding. "That's a very long story." He ate another rice cake. "How about you?"

She smiled again. "That's a very long story." They looked into each other's eyes yet Frank couldn't discern whether hers was a knowing look or one of avoidance. "Maybe we should be looking ahead rather than to the past," she said.

When he had eaten and drunk his fill, she took him by both hands and lay him down on the bed. She left him for a moment before returning with a cool, damp cloth which she folded and rested on his heated brow. He felt the sweetness of relief. She knelt by the bed, placed his elbow in the palm of her left hand and gently began to tickle his palm with the fingers of her right. Frank closed his eyes and received the gift. Tenderly she stroked his bare arm. She was unhurried in her devotion and he was wholly compliant. Occasionally she stopped tickling his arm to touch and stroke his face and neck before returning to his arm again. Frank was entranced.

Slowly, she leaned over him and drew near, and then kissed him on the mouth with the long and tender kiss of a true lover. He was all hers and he couldn't have been more grateful for it. She softly cupped his cheeks in her hands and kissed him all over his face. Frank never opened his eyes. "Stay with me," she whispered.

"I think I could be persuaded to do that," Frank returned.

"Stay with me forever."

"You must leave here!" he heard a voice bellow. Frank promptly sat up, startled and afraid.

"What's up?" she asked, surprised.

"Did you hear that?"

"What?" she asked. "You must be very tired. You're hearing things."

Frank immediately jumped up and went outside to see if anyone was there. Except for the sound of the crickets, the rice fields were eerily still. He circled the hut but there was no sign of anyone. "What, Frank?" she asked taking his hand and leading him back into the hut. "What's the matter?" Frank had no answer. "Everything's fine," she said. She cupped his face again. "Come back in and stay with me."

"I have to go," Frank said resolutely.

"What?" she giggled.

"I have to go." Frank was robotic in his delivery.

"You just got here!" she said. "I've been waiting for you. I want you to stay with me!"

He looked out over the fields. "No. I have to leave this place."

"No," she retorted. "You have to stay."

"I have to leave," he asserted.

"You don't understand," she said in a wholly different tone. "You have to stay!" She grabbed him by the wrists and pulled him toward her. "You have no choice!" Her voice dropped a whole octave as she said this. He looked deeply into her eyes, and saw flecks of blood appear in her whites.

152

"Release me!" he yelled. "My purpose is not here!"

With that, her eyes went blood red from corner to corner, her head tilted back aggressively with a loud crack and her mouth opened to preposterous proportions. Frank felt an intense heat radiate from her and then starting from her crown, her skin began to melt off and fall in daubs to the ground. He leapt back horrified, watching the flesh fall away and a whole new creature emerge. A green so dark it was almost black, an antenna'd helmet for a head, the face of a mollusk and the body of a woodlouse on steroids, it stood before him, almost twice the size of her previous incarnation, heaving and retching from the transformation. As though stuck in morph mode, it continued to produce flesh in random patches which immediately melted and dropped to the ground. The creature threw its head back and let out a piercing, ugly wail that rang out over the rice fields and silenced the crickets for miles around.

"You have to stay," it managed to utter between a collection of clicks and crunches. Elocution was clearly not its strong point. "The dark lord commands it." An enormous piece of flesh grew from its nose and hung there, swaying as the creature twitched till it finally hit the ground with a solid splat. Frank's heart was racing and it generated within him a fresh vitality and a tremendous sense of valour. He took a step toward the beast. "I will leave." The great crustacean threw its head back again and released another almighty roar which rattled the posts of the hut, yet it seemed unwilling to physically engage Frank.

He continued to observe the beast. It then made a short high-pitched squeal - a shrill burst of gas accompanied by a shiver. "What was that?" Frank asked.

"Allergies," said the creature. "From the rice fields. Liaoning, jiangsu, guangdong - they're all here. I hate it. I really do. I hate these rice fields."

"I'm sorry to hear that," Frank said in a voice approaching sympathy.

"Yeah." It seemed to appreciate Frank's concern before returning to a more menacing posture. "I still have to violently incapacitate you, you know. It's my only escape from these wretched regions." After a series of threatening gestures and sounds, which at first intimidated Frank, but soon almost amused him, it remained at a standoff.

"You chimpillas are all the same," he said. "All roar and no bite." He grabbed a chair and stepped once more toward the creature. "Bite this," he said and rammed the chair into its face, knocking it to the ground with a huge thud. Pinned to the ground on its back, its multitude of disproportionately puny legs began to scuttle in the air. "You tell your lord that I've left - if you can." With that, Frank placed his hand firmly on the creature's thorax and took from him just as he had taken from the salmon. At first, nothing appeared to happen and the giant bug wrestled and screamed with hardiness. Frank kept his hand firmly in place and suddenly the creature was stilled. Then after a pause it began to struggle again, but this time as in the throes of reduction. Noticeably it began to wither. It made a few more gagging sounds before it was permanently silenced, and continued to decompose under Frank's grip. By the time it was all done Frank was a roaring powerhouse of energy and the creature was little more than ashes and dust on the edge of the rice field. He looked out over the rice fields. "I can't believe I was about to have sex with an insect!"

Standing over the remains like an undisputed champion, his thoughts were curiously torn between his own dynamism and his desire to see his old friend Salamander Man again. Delivering one departing roar to what was left of the creature, Frank found himself yelling a series of coordinates to the sky. Though new to him, he recognized the series of letters and numbers for what they were. He grabbed a blade from the kitchen, moved out into the centre of one of the rice fields and sliced the base of his thumb. Having created a circle of blood in the middle of the field, he lay down and yelled the co-ordinates into the air. As he did, he could feel himself submerging into the mud of the rice fields. The mire encased him, covering his legs and arms, swallowing his shoulders and hips, entering his ears and finally his eyes. Far from the terror and fear that accompanied previous transports, this was strangely satisfying. He almost enjoyed it. The last thing he saw was the rice plants reaching high above him into the pleasant blue sky. When he was completely submerged and could resist no longer, he opened his mouth and took the soggy soil fully into his lungs. With that, he left the rice fields.

Chapter 10

In the late summer of that year, Frank woke by a house in a village that looked across the river and the plain to the mountains. The manner of his waking confused him because he rose from the mire of the rice fields in exactly the same way he had submerged into them. So his initial assumption was that the transport had failed and that he was still a fugitive in the rice fields realm. But on sitting up and looking out over the sheaths, he was pleasantly surprised to see a very pretty, picturesque landscape of gentle hills, scattered rice fields dotted with ancient farmhouses, the odd cow and goat lazing in the sun, and a languorous river tinkling before it all.

The atmosphere of this place, though new to him, had an air of familiarity. He trudged his way through the thick mud to one of the narrow paved roads lining the paddy. It linked up with others forming a patchwork of neat scars over the countryside, dividing the fields and linking them at the same time. With a swampy scent wafting behind his muddied shirt, he strolled down the road, by an old timber residence, toward the river, feeling rather carefree and blithe. The river was lined with trees which trickled their branches into the cool water and cast afternoon shadows over the shiftless fish.

A road, possibly considered a major artery in this part of the world, ran parallel to the river and at its junction with the road Frank was traveling down, there was a signpost pointing to the left on which was written 'Fukui'. This was exceedingly good news for Frank. Not only was he back in Japan but Fukui was, he believed, a very agreeable (if not slightly dull) part of the world to be visiting. The only thing that concerned him was whether this was indeed the true Fukui, or an alternative version of it, as the recently visited 'New York' and Godore had been.

This matter was soon established when he stumbled upon two black eggs on the bank of the stream. They were large - almost the size of turnips - and with his appetite returning, he felt that, scrambled, they would make a very fine meal. He picked them up and fingered them, smelt them and even gave them a little lick. They were still warm. Just as he was about to gather some kindling for a fire, he was doused with an enormous blob of white fluid. This was not merely a soupy liquid but contained substantial matter as well. What didn't run down his face or get caught in his hair went down the back of his shirt. And it truly reeked.

He looked up just as a huge winged creature descended in front of him.

"What da hell are you doin' with those eggs, man?"

"Oh, great," said Frank, all illusions of normality now shattered. "A talking bird."

"You better believe it. It's Percy the Pigeon, bitch. Now, I as' you a question. You gonna put those eggs back or am I gonna whip your ass?"

"Can I just have one?"

"One whippin'?"

"All right! I'll leave them! Sheesh! Jeez! I was just hungry. Just wanted a little something to nibble."

"Right. So hows about next time I's hungry I's just gonna nibble one of your nuts?"

"Point taken."

"Dumbass."

"But you didn't have to go and take a dump all over me."

"I didn't? You were about to eat my progeny, you sick shmuck. And even if you weren't, you sure as hell done some'n else that deserves a dumping."

"I didn't know they were your eggs."

"Like that matters, you low down, good fo' nothin' asswipe. So you're okay eating my brotha's kids? I really ought to peck your eyes out and then dump on you all over again."

"All right! Enough already! I'm sorry! I'm sorry!"

"Fool."

"So what is there to eat around here then?"

"Are you blind as well as stupid? There's a river right in front of you teeming wit' fish."

"Yeah. I just didn't want to eat someone else's family, you know? I don't want a big mother fish to step out from behind a tree and attack me, or anything."

Percy the Pigeon looked at him with a pained expression. "A mother fish? Step out from behind a tree? Man, yo' really messed up. Yo' sick in the fucking head."

Frank climbed down the small bank, waded into the river and then plonked himself under the cool flow. He enjoyed the feeling of being submersed in pristine waters. It tickled him all over. He couldn't remember the last time he had fully bathed and he rose to the surface utterly refreshed. Sadly, his desecration of the river had had the opposite effect on the wildlife and he lifted his head to see whole schools of fish floating sick and bloated on the surface of the water. It made for easy pickings. He gathered a few choice-looking ones and left the rest to recover in peace further down the river which is where they quickly escaped to.

When the fish were cooked and ready for consumption, Percy the Pigeon dropped back down and sat across from him by the fire. Frank looked at him curiously.

"You gonna share them fish wit' me, ain't you?" Percy asked.

"After you dumped on me?"

Percy puffed his chest up to an enormous size and gave a guttural coo. Frank took the hint. "Go on. You have that one," he said, pushing one toward him.

"Thanks man!" he said in a totally different tone. "You're not so bad after all."

"So we're somewhere near Fukui..." Frank started.
"Aha."
"And I'm guessing you're not native to this area."
"Am now. My grand daddy come here from 'merica when he were a boy an' he grew up in these hills, and then my daddy grew up in these hills till I was hatched, and then he disappeared right about the time they started serving *yakitori* in town. Damn. No shame, these people. Eatin' whatever moves in front of 'em."
"And what do you do in these parts? Seems kind of quiet."
"I keep busy." He scratched his chin with a claw. "Dumpin' mainly." Frank nodded his understanding. "I's wait for someone to be moving about and then I fly to a branch or a wire right above 'em. I do some gastric cookin', if you know what I mean, and then I let go and wham! I won't be surprised if I don't hit 'em nine times out of ten!"
"I can believe that," Frank said, picking some foreign matter from his hair.

"But what about the people? Are they mostly farmers out here?"
"A lot of 'em are farmers. Some are shop people. Others work for the agricultural council but no-one seems to know exactly what they do." He ripped a big piece of fish with his beak, threw his head back and gobbled it down. "Damn tha's good." Frank sat listening for more. "Then there's the market on Saturdays. That's when damn near eve'one comes out and sells them wares. It's really the only time the place has any life at all."
"Dumping heaven, I guess?"
"No, man. Respect. You don't dump at the market. You just don' do that. That ain't cool. The market's a sacred place."

159

"Percy, I think I might hang out here for a while. I like this place. Frank in Fukui. Fukui Frank. It has a nice ring to it, don't you think?"

"Hey, whatever roasts your rice."

"I think I'll chill here before heading off to see if I can locate my buddies. I need to find somewhere to stay. Maybe get a job for a while. Blend in with the people. Become a community man. Got any ideas?"

"You? Blend? Shit, man, all I know is to dump on people. Tha's what I do. You know, you gotta find what you do best and then you do that. I dump on people. Tha's what I do. And damn I'm good at it. You know what I'm sayin'?"

"Well, I'm quite partial to taking a dump myself, I'm just less inclined to do it on people and I can't see it endearing me to the local folk if I do. You know what I'm saying?"

"Well, why don't you go and ask the ol' farmer dude back up on the hill there? Maybe he can give you an idea."

"Where?"

Frank turned around to see the old house he had passed as he walked down the hill. On the rickety ancient verandah was an equally rickety ancient man, sitting rigid and lifeless, looking out over the fields and the river.

Frank bid adieu to Percy and made his way back up the hill toward the old farmhouse, careful not to walk under any wires. As the homestead loomed into view, the farmer's wife came out and joined him and together they sat, as still as statues on the deck. When Frank was within calling range, he waved a hand and said a friendly 'hey!' They never moved. He repeated the gesture and called in a slightly louder voice. They remained wholly detached. It was as though they were blind and deaf. On moving closer he saw the problem. They were both deceased. They sat, all mummified sinew and flesh, staring out through empty eyes with mouths frozen agape and partially exposed bones. In any other realm this would have terrified Frank to the core but here, there was an air of timeless benevolence, even among the departed. Perhaps it was the intent. The soulless bodies of the rice field realm were harbingers of horror and they targeted Frank. Here, there wasn't even a hint of hostility; just people, dead or alive, going about their business.

He took the liberty of walking around the side of the house and onto the verandah. The decking creaked and bent under him as he moved. He stood just in front and to the side of them and then made his introduction.

"Good afternoon. My name is Frank." This was met with complete silence.

"Frank," he repeated.

The two figures continued to stare, as cold as stones, out over the fields.

"Ah, I was wondering if you would be so kind as to let me know where I might be able to find a place to stay for the night."

This was met again by total indifference.

"Ah, a hotel? Motel?" A gentle breeze fluttered across the patio.

"A campsite? Even a dry hole would work. I'm not particular."

Suddenly the wife rose from her chair and beckoned him to follow. She creaked as she walked. She led him into the house toward a back room and once there, pointed to a perfectly made futon in the middle of the floor.

"Is this for me?"

"Yes," she said in a rusty voice. It clearly pained her to speak.

"I don't mean to be any trouble," Frank said. It had been a lifetime since he had needed to speak civilly to anyone. The old corpse pointed once again to the futon and then headed back to the deck. There she returned to her seat. Frank leaned against the side railing, and the three of them sat in silence and watched the sun set over the mountain beyond the river.

When darkness had descended, the old man stood and walked out into the hills. Frank watched from the deck as he moved, at times almost floating backwards and forwards through the fields. The old woman went into the kitchen and prepared a feast for her guest and when it was done, Frank sat alone at a table covered with steaming dishes and boiling pots. She then retired for the evening, leaving Frank to feast and her husband to walk the fields. Frank gorged like a pig. And when he was done, he got into the clean, warm futon and enjoyed a rare night of fat, untroubled sleep.

For the next several days, Frank stayed with the old couple and helped with the harvesting of sweet potatoes in return for their hospitality. For the old man-mummy, Frank was a godsend. With his rickety frame, bending over to dig up the crops was a nightmare, so with Frank doing the hard work and him just wheeling the barrow beside him, life was as good as it could get for a deceased person. The satisfaction was mutual. It surprised Frank how much he enjoyed toiling in the sun, soiling his hands and reaping the fruits of his labor in such a literal way. And the old lady-mummy kept cooking up feasts that were to die for. Although this realm was clearly an alternate one, Frank felt a deep affiliation and comfort with it. He felt at home here, as much or even more than he had in Okinawa.

On the first Saturday after his arrival, he accompanied the old man and his wife to the market. He wheeled an enormous cart with all the sweet potatoes they had harvested throughout the week, with the old couple stoically shuffling beside it. At the market, the town came alive, so to speak. The old couple remained as they were, as did numerous other perished folk who had similarly brought their wares. But the market also teemed with the living: mere mortals, rankenfiles from all over the omniverses, brute beasts of all kinds - they all set up shop and moved about with a sense of purpose and pleasure.

After spending the better part of the day selling sweet potatoes with the old man (the old woman had gone off to do the buying), Frank took leave to stroll through the market and see what was on offer. It was a curious and highly eclectic mix of merchandise, everything from radishes to coffee to bohemian leatherwear to T-shirts advertising the glories of foreign dimensions and realms, including - rather ironically to Frank - one welcoming people to the rice fields.

"'Sup, my man?" came a voice from behind him.

"Percy the Pigeon!" Frank was delighted to see an old friend. "What have you been up to? On second thoughts, you probably don't need to tell me. But what are you doing here at the market?"

"Sellin' my goods, man? Takin' it day by day," he said, standing in front of his stall.

"What are you selling, Percy?"

"All sol' out, my man. Busy morning! We sol' out like there's no tomorrow." He continued to move backwards and forwards in front of his stall, as though to block Frank.

"Come on, now Percy," he chuckled with a wagging finger. "What are you hiding from me?"

"Nothin' man. I's just about to pack up shop. We all sol' out."

"What have we here?!" called Frank, stepping by the bird. "Eggs! Percy the Pigeon, are you selling eggs?!"

"I can explain this, man."

"Whoa! I'd like to hear it! What about 'eating someone's progeny, *you sick shmuck*'?" Frank recited back to him. "What about 'eating my brotha's kids'?"

"Now you gotta understan'," he said with a bad stutter. "These here are hen eggs, not pigeon eggs."

"What's the difference?"

"What's the difference? What's the difference?! I ought to take you out the back, whip you wit' a rubber hose and dump on you twice for saying that. What's the difference? What's the difference between a Frank and a single cell amoeba? Probably not much. But between a pigeon and a hen, there's everything man. There's intelligence, there's smarts, there's soul." He poked Frank in the shoulder with each point. "Hens and pigeons are tiers apart. Not even close. We're talking dimensions, man. And something else. Hens are damn ugly. Don't you forget it."

"All right Percy, don't get your feathers in a flap." Frank turned and moved on. "You sick shmuck," he muttered.

"I heard that!" Percy called.

"Not you," Frank lied. "The duck they're selling over here. It looks sick."

Frank continued to nosey from one dusty stall to another, fascinated by all that was on offer and frankly quite disturbed that anyone would want to buy much of it. He stumbled upon an antique stall manned by an odd-looking character dressed in a flying cap and goggles with a long yellow scarf, a bright pink shirt tucked into a pair of safari shorts, and workman's boots. The stall sold old kettles and picture frames, model aeroplanes and spinning tops, water pumps and chairs made of bones. Yet what really caught Frank's attention was lying on the bottom of a box of what appeared to be discarded items. The box was labeled 'WORTHLESS' and was filled with mainly broken pieces of crockery and odd sandals. Yet right at the bottom, Frank saw and retrieved a recorder. At first he couldn't be sure it wasn't any old recorder but as he observed it, he could see the color distortions and the grain texture; it had the exact abrasions from lifting the manhole cover in New York; and most of all, it had the slimy aroma of his dear friend. This was, without any doubt, Salamander Man's recorder. Frank was over the moon.

"Where did you get this?" Frank asked the man. He was intimidated by Frank's intensity and took a step back. "Where did you get this?" Frank repeated, elevating his tone.

"I don't know...I don't remember...It wasn't me..." he fumbled.

"Listen buddy, I'm not after you. But this belongs to a good friend of mine and I need to find him. Now where did you get this?"

"It was brought to me. I don't get any of this stuff myself. Bounty hunters and realm scavengers bring it to me. They find it. They bring it. We trade. That's how it works. We trade."

"Who's the scavenger that brought this?" Frank pressed.

"I don't know," he whined.

"Who brought it?" Frank yelled, holding it up to his face in a threatening manner.

"I don't know, Frank, I swear I don't," the man sputtered. His voice was trembling.

"How do you know my name?"

"What? I don't know your name. Never heard of you. Who are you, again?"

Frank grabbed him by the collar and buried his nose into the man's cheek. "Start talking, dipshit, or I swear I'll end you."

The man broke down. "All right, all right, I'll tell you, I'll tell you. Just leave me alone," he wailed in a falsetto panic. He caught his breath for a moment. "Everyone knows your name, Frank. Everyone. There isn't a person here who doesn't know who you are or talk about what is happening. We don't know what's fact and what's fiction but we do know the tiers are shifting and we know that you are a part of it. As for the flute," he said pointing to the recorder, "it was given to me by a scavenger called Dr. Sack, and he lives in this very realm. Can't say if he's here now 'cause he's always traveling but his home is just a day's walk north from here." He looked Frank calmly in the eye. "Beyond the rice fields, by a lake at the foot of the twin peaks. Now please release me."

Frank wasted no time. He noticed an old bicycle standing at the back of the man's stall and quickly laid his hands on it.

"Hey! That's mine!" the man said. "It's not for sale."

"I'm not buying it," said Frank, absconding with it. Then without so much as a goodbye to the old farmer and his wife, he set off out from the market with a fresh resolve, and began pedalling his way north. The sun was bright, the roads were straight and he was cycling through rice fields. It didn't get much better than that. What's more, these rice fields appeared to be completely devoid of soulless bodies, feisty negis or seductive chimpillas. Frank began to hum a little tune as he pedalled.

By mid afternoon, the twin peaks loomed into view and the landscape gently transformed from rice fields into taiga forest, and from gently sloping topography into rolling hills. The uphill climbs were no fun but the downhill free falls made them worthwhile. Frank would coast down them, legs wide apart, wind in his groin and a 'yeeha' in his voice. It was on one of these runs that, rounding a curve, he almost ran into the largest water buffalo he'd ever seen. Huge. Unnaturally so. This thing was of prehistoric proportions. And it stood right over the middle of the road, completely blocking it. As intimidating as it looked however, it spoke in the most gentlemanly tones.

"I'm terribly sorry, old chap but I cannot let you pass."

"Ah, I don't think you understand," Frank started. "I need to find the man who bought this recorder." He held it up for the colossus to see.

"It's a magnificent instrument, sir, but I cannot let you pass."

"Why not?" Frank asked.

"There's a scavengers' convention going on and I've been employed to make sure that it remains undisturbed."

Frank walked around and put his hand up on the brute's shoulder. "That's impressive," he said giving it a bit of a squeeze. "You've been working out, huh?"

The creature looked flattered. "Well...yeah." It was weird to see such a powerful creature speak in such bashful tones.

"Hitting the steroids?" Frank pressed.

"Well, I..." It just looked embarrassed now.

"What's your name? What are you my friend?"

"My name is Tyrone, sir. I'm a rankenfile but I'm trying to work my way up to chimpilla status." He leaned in as if to whisper a deep mystery. "They say the tiers are changing." He looked around before speaking on. "One doesn't want to get left behind in these things."

"Quite right," Frank said, keeping his hand on the creature's shoulder. He was unaware that he was shrinking. Frank continued to reassure him. "A creature like you, so big, so strapping; you could really go places, you know; jump tiers. I can see you being a creature of great influence."

"Really?" he asked, with a smirk he just couldn't hide.

"Absolutely." By this point he was reduced to the size of a young cow and on finding himself now looking up at Frank, he asked in a state what was going on. "I'm just borrowing, my friend. I'm just borrowing. It's going to be okay."

By the time he fully realized his situation he was too small and too weak to resist. In the end, Frank took a ton of chromosomes from him but left just enough for him to continue living as miniature cattle. "What have you done to me?" he asked in a scared, squeaky voice.

"Less methane now, my friend. You'll be a real hit with the ladies. And I have some important work to do at the convention." Frank hopped back up on his bicycle and left the little calf to wander helplessly backwards and forwards across the road he had only very recently presided over.

A modest sized lake lay before the twin mountains, just as the man in the stall had said, and a small log cabin sat in front of the lake. Frank stopped pedalling and let his bike roll the rest of the way down the hill and right up to the edge of the property. The cabin was a humble one, rustic and splintered with a slight slant which gave it a charming old world appearance. Gray plumes of smoke puffed out from the chimney and a solitary hen clucked and scratched at the ground near the front steps. A gust of wind blew across the lake, bringing a scent of camphor from the trees.

Frank stepped onto the bottom step. "Hello?" he called. There was no answer. The hen continued to scratch and peck. He slowly clunked his way up to the top step. "Hello?" he called again. "Anyone here?" Looking up he could see the billows of smoke blowing up into the late afternoon sky. There was still not a word in reply. He made his way onto the deck, leaned on the gnarled wooden railing and looked out over the pleasant country scene.

It was then he heard a click and felt the cool end of a metal cylinder pressed up against his temple. "Get off my deck and get the hell off my property before I blow a hole in your head the size of a grapefruit!" bellowed a voice. Without a word, Frank gingerly stepped back down the stairs and out into the front yard. He turned to look at the man. He was a short, pudgy man, ageing, with long stringy brown hair and a tawny brown hat on his head. His clothes were of a color that almost matched his hat, but not quite, and were of a style that one would associate with hunting season. He never took his eyes or his aim off Frank.

"I just wanted to ask a simple question," Frank said in a kindergarten voice. The man cocked his gun and bellowed again. "I ain't warning you a second time." At that moment another gust of wind blew across the lake and over their faces. The man's expression relaxed, he lowered the gun and then broke into a soft chuckle. He looked at Frank. "Well, good afternoon there, friend. What can I be doing for you this afternoon?" Though he was pleased to be spoken to in a less bloodthirsty way, Frank looked at this guy with serious reservations. "I, ah, I," he was still nervous in this man's presence. "I was wondering if I could ask you about some of the items you have collected on your travels across the omniverses."

"Well, of course!" he said with tremendous cheer. "In fact we're holding a scavenger's convention right here as we speak."
"You are?" Frank asked. "Where is everyone?"
"Here!" he said pointing around at empty spaces and chairs. "Come on up, my friend. Come and take a seat and join us and I'll grab you a glass and you can have yourself some whiskey and we'll all talk until late in the evening about some of the treasures we've found - and some that just escaped us too." He let out a loud guffaw at the recollection of some of these. Frank took the steps two by two and stood back up on the quaint timber deck waiting to be shown inside.

Right then, another gust of wind blew across the lake. It ruffled the old hen's feathers and sent the chimney smoke off into the trees. "I thought I told you to get off my property!" came the same roar as before. Frank turned to see the old man with his rifle pointed right at his face, a centimeter from his nose. When Frank, stunned by the psyche of this man, failed to move, he pressed it firmly onto Frank's nose and pushed him all the way to the bottom of the steps. "Now go on! Get!" He was as livid as a freshly castrated bull. "I ain't warning you a second time," he said.

Making no sudden moves, Frank walked from the property and got on his bicycle. The man's steely gaze never left Frank. As he was about to pedal off, another puff of breeze blew across the lake. The old man's hair and beard waved in the wind. He looked across at Frank and called out to him. "Friend! Leaving so soon? We have much more to show you! More tales to tell! And more whiskey to drink!" He let out another series of cracker-jack laughs and gestured for Frank to come back.

Sensing there was something in the wind which disagreed with this man, not to mention the fact that he was a complete psychopath, Frank hurried back up onto the deck and bustled him inside the cabin where it was unlikely the wind could wreak any more havoc on his troubled soul. And there once inside, with the door closed and the windows shuttered, they did indeed enjoy an afternoon of treasure and tales and whiskey, with a large number of other scavengers who may or may not have actually been there. "My name's Fredrick Von Scrotumhousser," he began. "My friends call me Dr. Sack."

When the timing was right, Frank produced Salamander Man's recorder and showed it to Dr. Sack who held it lightly in his hands and gave a familiar, nostalgic nod. "I do remember this, I do!" he said. "Not worth much you know. There are thousands of these all over the omniverses and this one's in poor condition. I could take it back off your hands for a few hundred chromosomes."
"Who sold it to you?" Frank asked, ignoring his proposition. "This is very important to me."
"A reptilian fellow, if I remember correctly. Rather odd looking. White body, green head. Bulgy eyes. And he had this rather odd and disturbing habit of rubbing his nipples every once in a while. Rather odd, I must say."

"That's him!" said Frank with great delight. "Was he alone?"
"Not at all. A rather ragtag band, I remember now. Yes, it's coming back to me. He was with a pink guy and some pathetic little drooling runt . And they kept a drone buzzing above them for some reason, too. Rather odd, really."

"That's them!" Frank said. "That's them!"

"That's who?" Dr. Sack asked.

"Some friends of mine," Frank said. "I have to go there immediately. I need the co-ordinates. Give me the coordinates. They're Dimension 46y34p29e, Realm 6.2, right?"

Dr. Sack looked stunned. "Yes, that's right. How did you know?"

Frank looked stunned. "Didn't you just tell me?

"No."

"I don't know how I knew. I just knew." They looked at each other like deer in headlights for a while before Frank headed for the door. "Thank you for your hospitality," he said. "Please don't bother seeing me out."

"Not at all. Not at all. Of course I will see you out."

"No really," Frank said. "I insist. I've got it from here. Thank you again and I'll see you all when I see you. Oh, and thanks for the whiskey. That was some quality stuff."

Frank closed the door behind him and hurriedly made his way down the stairs. Dr. Sack came out onto the deck and waved goodbye to his friend. The sun was just about to dip beneath the horizon. "Do come back again," he said with a hint of melancholy in his voice. Right then, the wind blew over once again from the lake. The left side of Dr. Sack' face twitched. He looked down at the decking under his feet and then back up. In an instant he had his gun back in his hands and was yelling at Frank, all savagery and frothing madness. "Hey!" he called. "Hey! I thought I told you to get off my land!" He was really livid now. There was a rage in his voice that frightened even the trees. He cocked his gun and took aim at Frank. Frank ran for his bicycle and stepped on the hen in the process. He was an easy target for the gunman. Just as Dr. Sack was squeezing the trigger, he was suddenly doused in a thick, soupy lather. "What the hell?" he bellowed. "What the hell?"

As he scooped the secretion from his eyes he was shocked to see a large gray bird standing in front of him. "I's Percy the Pigeon, you turd-faced imbecile. No-one takes a shot at my friends."

"Percy!" said Frank.

Percy and Dr. Sack stood there sizing each other up. "Frank, you get going now," Percy said without taking his eyes off Dr. Sack. Frank hopped on his bicycle and raced up the hill away from the house, in the direction he had come from. "And don't even think about pointing that thing at me," he said to Dr. Sack, "or me and my family will make this area our home and we will dump on you morning and night till this house ain't nothin' but a mountain of pigeon poop." Dr. Sack thought about the prospects of that and turned in a huff, marched inside and slammed the door. Percy turned to the hen. "Damn ugly."

Frank lost no time leaving Dr. Sack's property once and for all and quickly rode up and over the hill that led back into the sparse woodlands. The trees were nothing but dark silhouettes on the landscape now. There, still wandering the road like a lost lamb, was Tyrone, the formerly magnificent bull. He bleated to Frank in a trembling, pathetic voice. "What have you done to me? What have you done?" Frank was not one to feel sorry for anyone but in this case he was willing to make an exception. He rested his hand on the young calf's shoulder and assured him everything would be all right. It was very calming for the young squeak. And as Frank kindly spoke to him about the dangers of taking on security work for complete and utter psychopaths, he began to return to him the chromosomes he had borrowed.

Within a few short minutes Tyrone was standing way above Frank and was already half the size of his formerly magnificent self. Frank removed his hand at that point and wished him all the best. Tyrone looked at himself. "I'm sure I was bigger than this," he said in a deeper voice, not sure at all about it. "I think you still have some of my chromosomes."

"I don't think so," Frank said. "That was about it. Besides, you really were a little on the bulky side before."

"Do you think so?"

"Absolutely. And we both know where that leads."

"Heart disease?"

"Erectile dysfunction. And believe me brother, you don't want that."

"Well, I sure appreciate that. Thank you."

"Not at all. You keep well now." With that Frank cycled off, still with a feeling of great anticipation, to find a quiet place to make his transport.

He chose a secluded grassland and scoured the area for an object to start his work. This wasn't easy in the dark but he found the broken femur bone of a young mammal, with a very sharp point at one end, and this became his weapon of choice. He held it to the base of his hand to commence proceedings. Suddenly a large figure overhead blocked the light of the moon and dropped down in front of him giving him the shock of his life.

"You ain't leavin', are ya?" The voice conveyed genuine disappointment.

"Percy, I've got to go and get my friends."

"But I's your friend, ain't I?"

"Yeah, Percy, you are my friend. But I have to..."

"Then take me, too. Take me wit' you, Frank."

"I can't do that Percy. I don't know what lies ahead. There are some pretty awful realms out there, believe me. Why would you want to leave a place like this? Besides, I need to keep all the chromosomes I can get."

Percy looked deeply disappointed at this.

"Can I at least watch you leave?"

"Sure, buddy. Whatever preens your pinions."

Frank lay on a thick rug of grass and looked up at the diamond sky stretched out above him. He was very comfortable. "Hey Percy. Say goodbye to the old farmer and his wife for me."

"Sure thing."

With one smooth movement, Frank sliced his palm and, still in a lying position, swung his arm around him to create the circle of life. He called the co-ordinates calmly into the night sky and felt the dew moisten the back of his shirt. He didn't need to repeat the address. This was an innate knowledge now. He just lay back and felt himself sink into the moist terrain. Just as he was withdrawing into the earth, Percy the Pigeon leapt at him.

"Frank! Take me, too!"

Chapter 11

The cold passed reluctantly from the earth, and the retiring fogs revealed a world of cool, dark waters. Frank stood knee deep and gazed about him. The mists slowly shifted backwards and forwards, filling and emptying spaces; at times opening to reveal still waters all the way to the horizon, at other times wrapping him in a thick blanket of vapor.
Above him was a white canopy of smoky ether. Beneath him only waterlogged sands.

There was not a sound. It was only when he walked that the soft swish of swirling waters broke the silence. Without any sense of direction, he moved, pausing momentarily when the fogs lifted to listen for anything - any voice, any birdsong or call of the wild, even the moaning of wind; but there was nothing. It was during one of these pauses that he noticed a black feather clinging to the sleeve of his shirt, and then he remembered the final moment of his last passage. Percy the Pigeon had so desperately tried to join him but failed by a whisker - or a feather as it turned out. Frank affectionately curled the feather and put it in his pocket as a reminder of his brief time in Fukui. He would remember it fondly.

This trudge, however, seemed to go on for an eternity. Of all the places he had visited, this one seemed the most desolate in terms of presence, time and chromosomes (other than the icy island where he first met Pink Guy). There was no sense of life, no sense of environment, and no sense of value or purpose. The only thing this place had, other than water, was the musty stench of emptiness and an overriding atmosphere of utter morbidness. Yet in his lonely solitude, he was unwilling to call out or bring undue attention to himself. He hated to think what might be lurking in the mists. He bided his time.

It was after he had been wading through the unchanging waters for what seemed like many weeks of earth time, that he finally heard a sound. It was a soft wail, as though coming from one in the final throes of asphyxiation. Frank headed in that direction though the mists of that region, as thick as any he had encountered in that place, kept him from seeing anything. Slowly, the groans became more audible and by the time he arrived at their source he was standing at the foot of a tall wooden pole which ascended into the clouds. As they parted, Frank, still capable of fear, was mortified to see a creature impaled at the top of the pole, lacerated, writhing in pain and struggling for breath.

It was a reptilian creature and it slowly turned its eyes to Frank. They were dark, desperate eyes full of longing for death to finally come and bring an end to its suffering. Its body occasionally quivered with pain before lying limp again in the hope that that was its final heave. It never was. Mercy was entirely absent in this place. Frank reached up and touched its foot. They locked eyes for the briefest of moments before Frank asked, "How long have you been here my friend?" The creature wheezed as though making an effort to respond but never came close to articulating a reply. With a sorry pat to the creature's foot, Frank moved on.
There were others. Some were reptilian in appearance, others were avianesque, and others still of a wholly unknown existence to Frank. All were impaled on poles and while some seemed to have finally withered and died, most were suffering excruciating agony, moving closer to a slow painful death, yet never actually tasting any relief that that finality might bring. Some were able to gasp utterances in their tortured breathing and it was through them that he was able to learn a little of this nether realm. This was, they told him, a place for the pre-Wretched. A purgatory of prolonged pain for those who had been condemned and were awaiting their final destiny in the pits of eternal damnation. Frank

could feel their pain. He could smell their agony and taste their anguish. Yet he could do nothing about it.

One of the creatures was amphibious. A sliced, bleeding salamander, occasionally twitching and groaning yet mainly hanging limp on his pole, stared down at his visitor. At first Frank was horrified to think that this might be Salamander Man but this creature was of a different shape and color and was significantly older than his good friend. Frank asked him if he knew Salamander Man.

"Nyes," came the soft reply in between gasps. Though it took time (of which they had plenty) and tremendous effort on the old Salamander's part, he was able to reveal much to Frank.

He shared liberally with Frank about his background, that of Salamander Man and the whole community of Caudata clans. Though it pained him to speak at length, he gave his all to do so. Theirs was originally a realm of harmony. All the salamanders, as well as the neighboring newts, mudpuppies, waterdogs and sirens, and even the more distant geckos and chameleons, got on well and allowed each other free passage from one area to another, if not actively encouraging others to share a meal and spend an afternoon together. Hospitality was commonplace and music was the essence of any gathering. Salamanders had extraordinary musical gifting and had assembled a very large catalogue of tunes over the years. Their musicians and composers were second to none in the caudata world and the envy of many.

"But then the tiers began to change," the old salamander wheezed. "You would know this well, Frank. But what you might not know is that the changing of the tiers, so it was thought, originated with the sirens, specifically their leader Serendeputy. He believed (with some reason) that the sirens were unlike the other more common caudatas, not for their appearance, which is quite ugly to be perfectly frank, but for their intelligence, which was evolving at an undeniably quick rate. Serendeputy made friends with higher powers and was poised to rise from his already elevated status of rankenfile to chimpilla - not by his own doing, I must stress, but by his associations. I was one of the few who opposed him. Such elevations should not be done, I told him. It was against the natural order and likely to have serious repercussions right across the omniverses. I mutinied. For that I was struck by Terminus, a peace lord of immense power and authority. He punished me and cast me into this place. I have been here for ages upon ages and will remain here till I finally perish and enter into the Sea of the Wretched." He slumped as he said this, both from the effort required to speak and from very thought of such a demise.

After an unhurried pause, he turned back to Frank. "Seamus (whom you call Salamander Man) was the finest of our musicians," he said continuing. Terminus wanted to end him, too, because of his musical capability to rouse the salamanders to a cause, but he escaped to another realm and hid there till you came along Frank. It was then we knew that there could be some purpose to it all. The shifting of the tiers, unstoppable though it had become, still held some promise." He lifted a weary finger to his left nipple and gave it a soft rub. "Nyes."

"How did you know about me?" Frank asked.

"Salamander Man told me last time he was here."

"When was that?"

"He visits me regularly, every million or so years." Frank thought about that. The old Salamander struggled to continue but Frank could piece together the rest. Salamander Man would come to stay by his old friend's side and play tunes on his recorder to soothe him. Despite his sorry condition - or perhaps because of it - he felt tremendous gratitude toward Salamander Man for his kindnesses. Indeed, just the thought of him returning to play another tune on his recorder is what sustained him through the long dark eons. There was a long pause as they both reflected on this. "But that might not help you, Frank," the old salamander added.

"Why not?"

"Because he no longer has his recorder, of course. I doubt he will come back here."

"Why would he sell his recorder? It's everything to him."

"For you, Frank. He was looking for you. He didn't have enough chromosomes to look for you and comfort an old dying caudata as well. So he chose you over me and sold his recorder for chromosomes to search for you."

Frank was moved.

"I told him to," the old fellow continued. "There is no hope for me. But for you, Frank..." His voice trailed off and he slumped once again.

Memories of New York came rolling back to Frank. He remembered Salamander Man playing his recorder and how happy it made them all; the jolly tunes which led them into long nights of dancing and merriment, the laughter and silly joking, the friendship and the farting. How he longed for those days. But he also remembered the tales that Salamander Man told him. He had told Frank of visiting an old friend every so often. He remembered that now and although it seemed to be silly nonsense at the time, it was making perfect and very sober sense now.

"So you don't know exactly if or when he will be coming back?" Frank asked.

The old salamander turned a weary eye to him. "Even if I knew for sure he was coming, I wouldn't know when. A million years? Time means nothing here." He fell again in a manner that suggested he wouldn't be reviving any time soon.

This introduced the dilemma that Frank now faced. Was he to wait a million years in this realm in the hope that Salamander Man might show up, or was he to give up on Salamander Man altogether? He considered these options very carefully and weighed all the possible outcomes in his mind. In the end, he decided in his heart that life would have little meaning or value without Salamander Man by his side. He also had faith; faith that Salamander Man would remain true to his old friend. A secondary matter, not insignificant, was that Frank was unlikely to be found in this realm, and so he felt his safety was assured as he waited. He chose to stay.

In the million years that followed, Frank fell into a dormant state. He sat chest deep in water, leaning up against the pole upon which the old salamander was hanging. Deeply entranced, he was neither aware of anything in his surroundings nor of anything within himself. His own existence was as though a distant memory or a future dream. The amniotic waters preserved him and the still air sustained him. And in this period of absence, two things happened: Frank aged; and his chromosomes, free from contaminating influences, multiplied beyond measure.

On a cool, lifeless day of endlessly shifting mists, vacant auras and soft groans - exactly like any other day in this realm - the sound of someone wading way in the distance interrupted the stillness. The sound come closer and in a direct line as though it were somehow able to navigate this place. There was a determination in its steps. On reaching the pole, the figure paused and stood patiently, silently eliciting a response.

It took some time for Frank to awaken and when he did, it was in foggy phases. When his eyes were fully opened and his cognition returned, he looked up to see a white figure, angelic in appearance, gazing down upon him. In this land of shadows, it radiated light and had an overall countenance of glory. The very atmosphere of this place seemed to come alive in the presence of this figure. Its green head bobbed to one side. It stood, slowly and purposefully rubbing its nipples with its fingers and uttered the only greeting it could under the circumstances: "Nyes." It was

Salamander Man! Frank jumped up full of excitement and joy, splashing about in the calm waters and calling out in a loud voice, "Salamander Man! Salamander Man!"

From an elevated position, however, and with his mind having progressed from its initial groggy state, Frank was disturbed to see the harrowing sight before him. Salamander Man, far from being a picture of radiance and life, was an abysmal figure. His body was lacerated all over and he was bleeding terribly. He staggered as he walked, struggling with short breaths. Yet it was his face which carried the greater tragedy. Normally mischievously spritely, he carried a countenance that was forlorn, wounded and deeply ashamed.

He looked at Frank through sad eyes and the two of them stared at each other in silence for the longest time. To ease the sadness, Frank produced Salamander Man's recorder which evoked the hint of a smile on the caudata's face. He held it lovingly in his hands, then looked up at his old friend impaled on the pole. He placed the recorder gently in his right nostril and played a slow, final tune for his old friend. The old salamander knew that this would be the last time he would hear any music, let alone the sweet sound of Salamander Man's recorder, and a large round tear fell from his eye and ran down his face. Salamander Man, too, shed tears as he played and his tune was occasionally marred by the heave of one in great sorrow. Frank stood to the side with his head bowed in a spirit of respect, and embraced the moment.

When Salamander Man was done, he gave one nipple a little rub before dropping both hands to his sides and bowing before his old friend. He and Frank then turned and left the old salamander to his dreadful fate. The two of them walked away from the watery fields of gallows, neither saying a word to the other. On they trudged through the shallow waters till they could no longer hear the soft groans of the damned, and then on they walked some more, always in silence, until there was nothing but an eerie emptiness all about them. There was so much that Frank wanted to ask Salamander Man but couldn't, and there was so much that Salamander Man wanted to avoid saying to Frank, so refrained. Frank never learned the cause of Salamander Man's condition but they understood each other and that was what made their fellowship, even in the most troubling of moments, so wonderful.

At a point where they couldn't go any further into nothingness, Salamander Man turned to Frank and in a quiet voice said, "Nyes".
"What?" Frank couldn't believe his ears.
"Nyes," he repeated.
"Are you kidding me, Salamander Man?" He could barely contain his excitement despite the salamander's sorry disposition.
"Nyes," he added.
"Back in New York?"
A small grin edged up the corner of Salamander Man's mouth. Frank was all smiles.
"All of them?!" he asked.
Salamander Man nodded.
"Then, my friend," Frank said, "It is time."

Frank stopped walking and Salamander Man drew beside him. "This place is as good as any," he said. Salamander Man agreed but expressed this without so much as a nod. Frank took him under his arm and the two of them lay back floating on the surface of the water. Frank softly called the co-ordinates into the air. This was at once intriguing for Frank and a matter of course. He no longer needed to draw blood for transport as he was so chromosome rich. He no longer needed to expose his life source to open air. And co-ordinates for the destinations of his choice simply came through menial concentration. These things were innate knowledge to him now, like his own name or the recalling of a familiar memory. When the last of the co-ordinates had left his lips, they slipped under the water and were gone.

Ochin chin ga daisuki day yo.

The voice came to him as a whisper at first, like a faint dream intended for someone else. It whispered again, this time with greater penetration,

Ochin chin ga daisuki day yo.

Frank began to stir. It was the third utterance that brought the horror to life,

Daisuki dayo,

and Frank sat bolt upright on his bed. Unlike waking up from a bad dream, Frank had woken up into one and he was terrified.

Hovering over him was a creature grotesquely familiar to him. Frank looked over the black halo that encircled his head, at his hideous, twitching body, and into the vacuum of his demented eyes. He tried to muffle any expressions of hatred for the dark lord but it simply wasn't possible. Anger and hatred and fear seeped out from him and Chin Chin seemed to feed off it all. Everything from his appearance to his speech to his very essence pushed Frank to release droplets of detestation and rage and he began to retch.

"Chin chin! Dark lord! Why have you come to torment me? Have you come to send me into the abyss?" Frank asked, paralyzed with panic.

Ochin chin.

"But I have made the sacrifices you asked for. The blood and pubic hair and nail clippings of a thousand youths were all duly provided with video evidence. I can show you right now."

Dai suki dayo.

"Why do you need extra sacrifices? Weren't those I made enough?" Frank was quivering with trepidation.

Ochin chin. Ochin chin.

"I swear I have no more. I have given you everything I had. I have no more chromosomes to give."

Daaii suki.

He placed his hand on Frank's trembling heart and wrested the remaining chromosomes from him. With that, he left abruptly, leaving Frank an empty shell on the bed.

Once the shock waves had subsided and the space time continuum had returned to normal, fear was gone and life immediately returned to normal in Frank's bedroom. That is, Frank sat on his bed and scratched his balls. He looked around to re-orientate himself. Then, very faintly at first, other activities began around the room. Initially, they started with just the lightest of movements from the cupboard door. It budged just a fraction; then a fraction more; then it peeped ajar. Finally the door swung wide open and out jumped a semi-naked little runt carrying some rosary beads.

"Alpha Centurion!" Frank exclaimed. "Good to see you, my friend! Thanks for all your support a minute ago when Chin Chin was here!"

He waddled over to Frank and sat on the bed beside him. "Good to see you too, Frank, you filthy little crapper. Good thing I wasn't here a minute ago when that dark lord was here or I would have snapped his dick in two. I would have pounded those creepy black eyes of his all the way to the back of his head. I would have reached into his chest, pulled out his still-beating heart and held it up to his face so he could see how black it is."

"Alpha Centurion, what are you talking about my lecherous little leprechaun? You were here the whole time hiding in the cupboard. You're such a pussy."

"Alpha Centurion!" Frank exclaimed. "Good to see you, my friend! Thanks for all your support a minute ago when Chin Chin was here!"

He waddled over to Frank and sat on the bed beside him. "Good to see you too, Frank, fucking tool. Good thing I wasn't here a minute ago when that dark lord was here or I would have snapped his dick in two. I would have pounded those creepy black eyes of his all the way to the back of his head. I would have reached into his chest, pulled out his still-beating heart and held it up to his face so he could see how black it is."

"Alpha Centurion, what are you talking about. I saw you hiding in the cupboard. Also, you owe me money. You came up short." The clock on the wall suddenly opened up and from it a tiny, wrinkled human stuck his head out and said, "That was a great joke, Frank. Seven out of ten!". They aggressively winked at each other. The little guy returned back into the clock, never to be heard from again.

Before the runt could respond, the bedroom door swung wide open to the sound of a series of disabled grunts and in hopped a demented looking guy, pink from head to toe. "Pink Guy! It's you! You're here, too! You made it! You just missed all the action by the way. You're a pussy, too, you know that? You and Alpha

185

Centurion are both a couple of pussies — leaving me to face Chin-Chin all on my own. It was pretty scary for a while there."

At that moment a rustling noise came up from under Frank's bed. "Come out Salamander man, I know it's you."

"Nyeessss!" came the reply as the huge humanoid salamander peeped out from under the bed.

"Salamander man, what are you doing under my bed? Have you any idea of the filth that lies under there? I tell you, there's some nasty stuff down there."

"Nyeessss!" He pulled himself fully out and immediately began to caress his nipples. He was now completely back to his normal self. All his lacerations had healed and his nipples were back to full erection. Whatever morbid woundings had previously disturbed him, he was back to his normal cheerful self again. "Nyeessss!" he cried and immediately inserted a recorder into his left nostril and broke into a rousing rendition of a tune from his glory days.

Before Alpha Centurion could start dancing to the music or Frank could compliment him on his playing or his general good looks and SICK moves, the door was kicked wide open and in strolled a strange Japanese man wearing brown spectacles, a Hawaiian shirt and a safari hat. "Wow!" he declared. "Wow, Franku!"

"Safari Man!" cried Frank, ecstatic that his whole posse was reunited once again. "I thought you were still back in…"

"No, no! Let's not go there! Suffice to say, being married to a negi was never going to work out for someone like me ha ha ha. She had no pussy. Can you imagine aggressively trying to make a dent in drywall with your dick? Not for me." He was shadowed by Drone who hovered just above his left shoulder.

Frank gestured for them all to come together. They embraced in a tight and passionate group hug, with Alpha Centurion once again burrowing with pleasure into Pink Guy's thighs. "You know I love you guys, right?" They all affirmed this. "But I want my chromosomes back." There was a lot of good-hearted complaining at this but they all knew it was the way it had to be. Frank had dispersed almost all his chromosomes amongst his posse to keep them from the dark lord, and this made them feel like kings of the world, brimming with life and power and authority and worth. As Frank embraced them all, he took back his chromosomes and a friendly murmur of discontent spread amongst them. Yet they were okay with this. They knew who Frank was and who he was becoming. They understood the honor that was theirs. They knew they were Friends of Frank, his fellow Fiends of Filth, his posse, and this was more than enough for all of them.

More so, they started to believe. They believed that Frank was much more than they had once known and would yet be much more than he now was. They had seen him overcome the dark lord, feigning fear and covering up chromosomes. And as they beheld him now they were in utter awe. He had handled the peace lord in a masterly fashion. He had just confronted the mighty Chin Chin, and here he was, not just alive and not merely unscathed, but composed, rugged and impossibly chromosome-rich. And though they believed now they were not yet willing to speak of it. Frank, the mere mortal who had shaken the omniverses by becoming a rankenfile, had in his travels, risen to the tier of the mighty chimpillas. They knew that full well. But now, Frank had ascended, he had become…it was too much for them to utter but they believed it, they owned it and they rejoiced in it.

And so it was on that softly lit autumn afternoon in New York City that Frank, Alpha Centurion, Pink Guy, Salamander Man and Safari Man and Drone came together to celebrate their triumph over Chin Chin, and to look forward to the gay and merry days which lay ahead. With the six of them now together, the circus was pretty much complete again. And there was jubilation until late into the night with everyone laughing and dancing and farting.

Yet for Frank, his deepest dilemma remained and his interest was still aroused: who was he and what was he becoming? He understood that power without purpose was corrosive. And he was now fully aware that chromosomes were not simply being added to those he already possessed but that his own chromosomes themselves were truly multiplying. Exponentially. He marveled at this yet remained greatly troubled by it. Despite increasing displays of power, he still seemed no closer to finding out why he had such power. There had to be more to this. Beyond the peace lords, there had to be a Tierless One, a Supreme Power, an Ultimate God. The Ultimate God. Frank was exhilarated and haunted by this thought. He was more determined than ever before to find Him, confront Him and demand the answers to his questions. And so his quest became all-consuming.

Chapter 12

Time is not a line but a dimension, like the dimensions of space. Though Frank woke at a time in his New York bedroom, he was also aware of his own presence in other realms. It was an odd realisation for him to stumble upon but an exciting one as well. With each multiplication of his chromosomes, it seemed, he was able to discover new things about the omniverses and about himself simultaneously. The two were becoming closer to one with each passing day. And this day introduced a dimension to him that changed not only the course of his own path, but, in time, that of the omniverses as well.

He was the first to wake that morning and he observed his still-sleeping friends with a hint of adoration. Alpha Centurion was sleeping in the cupboard (the door was open) in a position that was, curiously, very nearly upside down. The side of his head was flat on the bottom of the cupboard, his neck was at right angles against the side wall, and his body lay upright above his neck, with limbs sprawled across the side and back of the cupboard. He drooled as he slept and occasionally whispered obscenities.

Pink Guy lay across a sofa at the foot of Frank's bed. Even in slumber, his lip continued to curl in the manner of one demented. Occasionally he would softly grunt. There would be moments when his body would spasm before relaxing again for a while and then he would start to slide off the sofa. A few spasms later and he would be back up on the sofa and steamy. The whole process was endearing for Frank to watch.

Under the bed, surrounded by soiled socks and underwear and breathing in their contents, lay Salamander Man. More than any of the others, there was little difference between him sleeping and being awake. He lay on his back, a crusty sock hanging from the corner of his mouth and his nose, just an inch away from Frank's bedsprings, slowly rubbing his nipples. "Nyess," he would gently breath. "Nyesss." Drone lay beside him.

Safari Man was the only one not allowed to sleep in the same room because he kept speaking in an inappropriately loud voice and laughing in his sleep which kept all the others awake. He was banished to a room across the hall yet the doors remained opened and Frank could see his twisted Japanese friend sprawled across a futon in happy rest with his hands behind his head and an enormous erection in his underpants. Occasionally he would mumble something in Osaka dialect and then scratch his scrotum. This is what Frank had returned for. This fellowship was the fruit of his longing and he felt a rich fulfilment as he watched the dozing circus all around him.

Now, it was no secret to these friends (nor to many of his enemies) that Frank had something of a penchant for rats. Many times he had put them in a falafel wrap and served them up to Pink Guy or thrown them into the bath while Alpha Centurion was bathing. They went absolutely ballistic at Frank and were deeply concerned about his mental stability for doing such things yet Frank knew that it was episodes such as these that kept their brotherhood fresh and true.

Those tricks, however, usually contained dead rats. Frank thought it would be a special treat if he presented a living rat to them as a means of welcoming them to a new day, and he had a beautiful specimen reserved just for this occasion. He kept it in a plastic container holding some old pizza. He placed the rat gently on the ground by the tail and watched it scatter about. At first it just stood and busily sniffed the air for a while but it shortly made its way, possibly drawn by the scent of the soiled clothing, under the bed and sidled up beside Salamander Man. After contemplating him for a bit and sniffing about his navel, it moved up to his exposed nipples where it began to have a little nibble. "Nyess," said the salamander never flinching. A small smile stretched from one corner of his mouth. "Nyess."

Slightly disappointed with this response, Frank picked the rat up again by the tail and placed it gently on Pink Guy's shoulder. At first this produced no greater reaction than that of Salamander Man but after a minute or so of aimlessly wandering about the pink man's torso, and possibly becoming a little peckish for breakfast, it crawled up his side, stood on his neck and took a firm bite of his ear lobe. Pink Guy woke with a mild cry and assumed that Alpha Centurion was becoming amorous with him again. When he opened his eyes and saw the hideous rat standing over him, he screamed and instinctively brushed the rat away hard with the back of his hand. The rat sailed through the air and landed square on the face of Alpha Centurion who was just waking up from the sound of Pink Guy's scream. The little guy, still upside down, woke fully to see this filthy creature on his face, and let out a blood curdling scream with the pitch and volume of a trumpeting elephant.

The rat fell to the floor but before it could move, Alpha Centurion grabbed a bamboo kendo stick from the corner of the cupboard and began to beat the poor creature to a pulp. Despite the protests of the others in the room and Safari Man, who ran in to see why a woman was screaming, Centurion continued to pound the little rodent with a frenzy that produced unlearned languages from him. By the time he was restrained, the rat was nothing more than a pile of broken bones and seeping fluids on the rug.

Silence fell upon the room. "What have you done?" Frank asked shocked. There was more silence as Alpha Centurion's face fell and then his shoulders slumped and he dropped the stick on the floor. "You didn't have to kill it!" Frank yelled at him. He was distraught that the little runt would do such a thing. "What got into you, you little faggot?"

"What got into me?" Centurion returned. "Are you serious, Frank? What got into me? What got into you, Frank, you sick schmuck." He was livid now. "How could you do that? How could you put a rat on the face of someone who was sleeping? What's wrong with you, Frank? You've really gone too far this time. I've had it with you. Fuck you, Frank. Fuck you," he said pointing to Frank. "And fuck you, you and especially you," he said respectively to Pink Guy, Salamander Man and Safari Man.

"What did I do?" the Japanese man asked.

Alpha Centurion kept at Frank. "I'm sick of you treating me like this, Frank."

"What did I do?" Safari Man asked the others.

"I'm sorry for the rat, Frank, but you asked for it. You brought this on. This is on you."

There was another moment of silence before Frank scooped up the remains of the rodent in his bare hands. The others watched him do this. Then without giving it another thought, Frank poured his chromosomes into the rat. Just as he had done with the fish in the rice fields realm, he now did with the rat, and just as the withered fish had been fully restored, so too the rat was fully healed. It stretched its neck like it had just woken up from a long sleep, then full of energy, it jumped from Frank's hands and scampered across the floor. Pink Guy, Salamander Man, Safari Man and Alpha Centurion looked on in absolute amazement. The gravity of this moment was not lost on any of them. They looked at Frank with astonishment and with their eyes asked, "Who are you?"

The rat continued to scurry across the floor and gave a nasty bite to Alpha Centurion's big toe. "Ow! You little shit!" he said grabbing the kendo stick again. "I'm going to really finish you this time." But before he could get a swing in he was held back by his pink and green friends, who were handicapped in the matter only by their raucous laughter. The rat ran to safety under Frank's bed.

Frank was nonchalant about restoring the creature, despite its miraculous nature. To him, it was a natural happening; there was nothing supernatural to it. It was a normal extension of his being. What did surprise him though was where the episode led him. Without giving it a second thought, his placed his hands on Pink Guy and Salamander Man, spoke coordinates briefly to the air and instantly the three of them were standing in the shallows on the edge of a marsh.

Frank's two friends looked about them. They were in shock at the sudden transportation. This land had a familiar feel yet was somehow unknown to them. It took a while for its appearance to register. Salamander Man recognized it first but was taken aback by its depletion. It was as though many epochs had passed and time had worn the whole structure of the place. They stood ankle deep in water stained with red algae. Above them, the sky was singular in color, a dirty brown arching over them like a dome. Stretching out before them were grasslands, hagged and thirsty. These fed into foothills which led to a great mountain rising to a height which almost seemed to touch the sky. It was the mountain, high and once mighty towering over them which brought recollection to Pink Guy.

If they had needed any further confirmation of their location, it came with a figure rapidly approaching them from their left. Snapping and snarling rabidly, it charged toward them, a flurry of yellow and white. Pink Guy leapt like a cat before a cucumber and Salamander Man braced for battle. None came. Frank raised his hand to the creature and spoke one word to it: "Desist!" The creature slumped and stopped about twenty paces before them. They all eyed each other. The yellow and white one, despite its menacing approach, now stood small and frail in front of them. "Lemon Man?" asked Salamander Man. Lemon man nodded mournfully. He looked old and tired. He and Salamander Man approached each other and, despite past animosities, embraced as old warriors beholding the deepest respect for each other. Pink Guy, memories flooding back, kept his distance.

"Lemon Man," Frank said addressing him in stately tones. "We are going up the mountain. Would you like to join us?" The bulbous yellow-headed creature shook his head and withdrew as if scared. "It's okay, my friend," Frank said. "We're all family now."

"I'm a lemon," Lemon Man said pointing toward at the foothills of the mountain and began to tremble with fear. "I'm a lemon," he said. His voice quivered. "I'm a lemon." Pink Guy and Salamander Man surveyed the landscape and began to share Lemon Man's fear.

"Why are we going up the mountain, Frank?" Pink Guy was perfectly lucid in this realm. "Don't you remember what happened last time we went up this mountain?"

Frank didn't answer his question. "We're going up the mountain," he asserted. Lemon Man shook his head and withdrew. "You don't have to come," Frank assured him. Pink Guy and Salamander Man withdrew, too, and stood beside Lemon Man. "You two, however," Frank said to them, "must come with me."

Leaving their lemon friend behind, they quickly marched up from the shoreline, over the sparse plains and into the foothills. The high ground was covered in the long brown grasses of a cursed environment and the dry vegetation rustled loudly in the breezes. They hadn't gone far when they noticed the grasses moving all about them in a manner that was independent of the wind. Something was scuttling about them and Pink Guy and Salamander Man bunched up close behind Frank as though spooning him on the move.

As Frank stepped forward, out from between two thick tufts of weed came a huge and hideous scorpion-like creature. It flailed its pincers about and lunged backwards and forwards at Frank and his friends. Other creatures of this ilk, some bigger, some smaller came out of the grasses toward them from all directions. All of them moved with a hideous, sinister intent and threatened with clicks and rattle-like sounds. Pink Guy and Salamander Man, frozen with fear, looked to Frank for salvation. He turned his head slowly back toward them and in a calm and careful whisper said, "Run".

With that they bolted as one with frantic yelling, and dashed between the two critters in front of them. Beyond those two they continued in haste as though their very lives counted on it (which it may well have) running in between many of the other vile creatures as they approached and lunged and stabbed at Frank and his friends. More than once they were nipped and sliced but they ran like men possessed until they reached the rocky clearing at the foot of the mountain.

As the scorpions receded back into the grasses, the three friends fell exhausted and assessed their injuries. There was blood and there was bruising but with a little dabbing and rubbing and self-consolation, they recovered and were ready to proceed. "Why couldn't you just tell the scorpions to desist, like you did with Lemon Man?" asked Pink Guy. His thoughts went back to his first encounter with Frank in the frozen wasteland. There, he was the master educating Frank about 'all matters' of the omniverses. Now, quite clearly, he was the student. "Brute beasts!" said Frank. "Sometimes they just don't listen! You've just got to run." He laughed as he said this but the other two didn't think it was nearly as funny. "Come on," he said, gesturing toward the top of the mountain. "No time to lose." Pink Guy and Salamander Man still had no idea why Frank was going back up this mountain nor why he felt they should go with him. They suspected with much trepidation that this might have been leading to a showdown with Chin Chin but even then, why here? Why now? They followed closely behind Frank as they made their way up the mountain.

It grew cold as they ascended. The winds whipped up and the brown sky, though clear of cloud, darkened. Salamander Man began to shiver as he walked. Though feeling the cold, Frank began to hum a little tune. It wasn't that he was in a particularly good mood, it's just that he was free of any fear or trouble. He marched on with a purpose in his stride that was telling to the others, and they took heart in this.

The walk to the top of the mountain was longer than any of them had remembered and when they arrived at the summit they turned, tired and weary, and looked at the scenery below all about them. Though dull in color and lacking any semblance of life, the panoramic view revived them and they savored a sense of accomplishment for having reached the pinnacle. Yet it remained bitterly cold and windy and the two friends turned to Frank and asked him to explain why they had come.

He didn't answer immediately but rather, began to wander about the summit area as though looking for something. He was methodical in this. He began from the very point of the mountain and then slowly descended in concentric circles, covering every square inch of the land. Having descended about twenty-five meters he suddenly stopped and declared with a sense of delight, "There you are!" He bent over and picked up an object that was at first wholly unidentifiable to his pink and green friends. It wasn't until Frank carried the piece over to them that they realized with sad horror what it was. There, lying dry and decrepit in his hands, was the decomposed torso of Negi Generation 4. "It's still here!" Frank said with surprise. "Now, help me find his limbs."

The two friends joined him in their grim search for Negi Generation 4's remains. It didn't take long, though there was little left of his left leg and only a few bone fragments of his right arm. Pink Guy was touched that Frank would remember Negi Generation 4 so fondly and want to give him a proper burial. It was rare to see such a tender side to Frank and it strengthened the loyalty that the two friends already had for him. "Where shall we dig the grave, Frank? Here on the mountain or down on the foothills?"

"Nyess." Salamander man shared in the question.

"We're taking him."

"You want to bury him in New York?" Pink Guy asked. "Okinawa?" He thought about that some more. "Negiland!"

"We're not burying him."

There was an odd countenance to both Frank and his words which silenced the two friends. They stepped back and waited for Frank to give further instructions.

Frank dropped to his knees and arranged Negi Generation 4's remains in front of him. He then lay upon the Negi, forehead to forehead, chest to chest, hip to hip, foot to foot. He breathed in deeply once and then poured his chromosomes into the leek. This was not a singular transaction. It was a series of fillings and each one brought visible change to the color, substance and spirit of Negi Generation 4. Pink Guy and Salamander Man stood entranced by the encounter. On and on Frank poured his chromosomes, millions upon millions of them and as he did the friends could observe before their very eyes the bones reconnecting, the sinew reforming, the flesh restoring and the body reviving. Even when Negi's eyes opened and a little smirk emerged on his lips, Frank continued to lie upon him and pour into him his chromosomes. He seemed to know innately when the work was complete.

After a time, Frank rolled off Negi Generation 4 and lay upon the cold earth seemingly emptied of life. Pink Guy and Salamander Man approached him cautiously and with a sense of great concern. Yet before they could draw near, Negi Generation 4 hopped to his feet and said, "The likely for through and shazam!" He looked so happy. He gazed at the two friends with an enormous grin and, bouncing for joy on the balls of his feet, said, "Agates to the fronds!" He then doubled up in laughter.

As though lifted by the jolly sounds, Frank sat up. He seemed weak but well. He stood and walked over to the Negi. "Nice to see you old friend. Didn't think we could leave you in such disarray."
"Over for stark and by a holy nearly." Negi bowed before Frank.
"Yeah. Nice to have you back."
With the passing moments, Frank's vitality returned to him.
"Nyeess."
"Never felt better, Salamander Man. Never felt better."
"Nyess."
"No, I'm not just being polite. I really feel fantastic. I feel better than I've ever felt before." Frank stretched and turned about as he said this.
"You must have used a lot of chromosomes, Frank," Pink Guy said, concerned. "Are we okay to get back?"
Frank looked at him with a smile that was gentle yet slightly creepy. "Every chromosome I gave to our little leeky friend here has already returned to me many times over. You have no idea how pulsing with life I am right now." Pink Guy and Salamander Man were equally pleased and fearful to hear this. While Frank had grown curious as to his condition, his two friends now grew afraid. They'd never seen such turns of life or such confidence in Frank and while they were glad to be on the same team, a hint of fear entered their minds: what if they weren't on the same team?

These fears were subdued by the sheer joviality of the balderdash who began to run around from the mere thrill of being alive. Occasionally he would leap as he ran and shout "Befall!" and "Polar!" and other expressions of elation. The other three all felt better for just watching him. Frank gathered them all to him and they took one last look over the landscape before he began to call his coordinates to the wind. He held his friends tightly. His voice, though the same, sounded different now. It had the familiar gravelly timbre they knew and loved, but it now had a calmness that had always been absent from his delivery. His intoning now carried an anointing. It had the resonance of royalty.

Before Frank had completed his cantillation though, a lightning bolt came out of nowhere and hit the rocky ground beside them with an almighty crack. The four of them reeled back in fright. In an instant, a frenzied wind began to blow, thunder rumbled and hail began to pelt down. Clouds started to form and dissipate and form again, swirling and tumbling as though in rebellion, and all the while the air about them (not the sky above) began to darken and grow heavy. A deep rumbling sound then began to rise up from the ground beneath them. It seemed to come from the heart of the mountain itself. It led to a tremble which quickly grew to a most violent earthquake, rumbling and rolling and pounding and throwing the four of them about like dolls.

Though it finally settled, the tumultuous clouds only grew thicker. The thunder seemed to be roaring at them. Lightning continued to strike the ground all about them like electric whips herding cattle. The four of them huddled together and waited for the inevitable. The atmosphere then parted and gliding through on a billow of cloud descended Chin Chin, preceded by his two chained minions. They were rabid, a ball of snarl and gargoylian fury, and had to be held back by the dark lord who carried an air of cool but barely restrained hatred. He stepped off onto the rocky terrain, flinching and twitching with aggravation, and crawled toward them.

Frank immediately stood and faced his nemesis. "O Chin Chin ga daisuki dayo." The evil words slid out from the dark lord. Frank never flinched. "O Chin Chin..." the words rattled with enmity, "...dai suki." There was so much hatred in his utterance. Frank stood his ground and this only served to antagonize Chin Chin. Trembling and afraid, Negi Generation 4 came and stood beside Frank, holding on to the tail of his familiar blue shirt. Chin Chin looked at the negi, confused. He peered at him with eyes that shuddered. He looked at Frank, then back at Negi then back at Frank again. He couldn't believe what he was seeing.

"O Chin Chin!" he hissed. ["I destroyed you."] His neck convulsed hard several times. He stood there genuinely perplexed and this feeling of angst soon morphed into trepidation. He wasn't able to approach any closer to Frank and his two minions, sensing injury, moved around behind their master. Frank was steadfast but unwilling to engage; Chin Chin was too shaken to advance yet too proud to retreat. They stood there for a prolonged period: Frank, legs defiantly astride with fists on hips and his friends huddled behind him; Chin Chin a twisted ball of creepy blackness hovering on the spot with his demons behind him. The only thing that altered during that standoff was the atmospheric conditions. The thunder and lightning eased, the hail ceased and the wind calmed. These changes worked in Frank's favor. They seemed to diminish Chin Chin's control of the encounter and this emboldened Frank. Yet Chin Chin could never admit to such or relinquish any ground.

Frank fully understood the cosmic implications of this confrontation. He searched himself for the right words to speak to send this peace lord on his way. He knew this was his time. It was a defining moment not only for him but for all dimensions and tiered creatures everywhere. His words needed to be powerful, authoritative and magnanimous. He knew that what he uttered at this time would reverberate through the annals of history and ripple through the fabric of the omniverses. He stepped forward as though planting a flag on new terrain, pointed a wily finger at the dark lord and said, "Piss off".

With that, Chin Chin duly retreated into a slash in the atmosphere, it closed over him and he was gone. Negi Generation 4 stepped forward just as the window was closing and pointed his own little leeky finger at Chin Chin and shouted "Floss!" yet he couldn't be sure that the dark lord had caught his admonition or not. With the peace lord gone, the conditions quickly returned to their earlier state. What remained however, was one minion. The gateway had closed before it had entered and it remained on its own looking very silly and sheepish and somehow only half the size it was before. "Go," Frank said to it, pointing down the mountain. It immediately relieved itself and then scampered down the mountain to spend the rest of its days with a host of scorpion creatures, other unknown terrorists of the beast world, and one old Lemon.

After spending the entire episode huddled together on their buttocks, Pink Guy and Salamander Man stood and gathered themselves once again to Frank. If the resurrection of Negi Generation 4 wasn't enough of a miracle to last them a lifetime, Frank's defiance of Chin Chin certainly was. They knew what this meant. They finally understood that the tiers weren't just changing but had now unequivocally changed and that Frank was at the very heart of that change. It seemed to them that there was no longer anything beyond Frank's capabilities. Yet Pink Guy at least also knew that Frank himself was not the most stable of characters and in his heart he wondered why such power had been given to one like Frank and what would become of it. But he kept these thoughts to himself.

Frank embraced them in a huddle and once again spoke with calm conviction to the air. "Really, if that rat comes near me one more time, I will crush it completely." It was Alpha Centurion. He was ropeable.

"Wow, Franku. Alpha seems to be a little hot under the collar! Well, he would be if he weren't stark naked and had a collar ha ha ha!" Neither of them had any idea that Frank, Pink Guy and Salamander Man had been away. Frank quietly walked over and pushed Alpha Centurion back into the cupboard.

"Stay in there till you've calmed down, my friend," he said.

"Frank! Come on, Frank!" whined Centurion as Frank closed the door on him.

"Think about what you've done!"

"I'm sorry!" came the muffled cry through the door.

Frank ushered the others out the bedroom door. "I'm ready for breakfast. How about you?" They all agreed. The closet door was kicked open just as the others were stepping out the front door and the little fellow waddled quickly down the hallway. "Come on, Frank! Frank! I'm hungry, too!" The front door closed before he could get there. He opened it and chased his friends down the stairwell. "Frank!" he called. "Frank!" He raced after them and caught up to them just as he was pulling a T-shirt on. Regrettably, he had forgotten to put on any pants.

Chapter 13

Psychics can see the color of time it's blue. Everything around him was tinged that way, and nothing around him remained untouched by it. It was so divergent he couldn't properly discern if this were actuality or an alternate reality; if he were in the truth or above it. He had been to many realms and dimensions now, and had seen the most peculiar and the most heinous. But he had always been fully cognisant of their realities and his own. Until now. Now he viewed as though from outside of time and as though free from the physical constraints of the universes. His peripheral vision was lightly pixilated as though the extremes of his fields of sight were not the ends. He was intoxicated by the experience and disquieted by it.

The sapphire sky bathed everything below it in a soft blue hue turning the green leaves to aqua and the brown earth to a dark purple. It was cloudless above and around him and that only served to radiate the blueness. The leaves in the trees blew curiously in shades that were more diverse and vibrant than he had known in other realms yet were mysteriously ominous as well. The dimensions in this world - the perspectives, the depths, the lines and shapes - were strange, like his balance was slightly affected or he was hallucinatory. And somehow these oddities all seemed to come back and question whether it was his surroundings that were different or whether it was him who was different at this time.

He moved over the land as a spirit hovers over the waters, without restraint or inhibition, and he quickly recognized his locale. He had finally returned to Okinawa! Yet it was no longer quite what it had been, just as he was at this time no longer who he had been. The pristine beaches and forests remained in their purity and the ruins of the Soncorp lab in which he had spent most of his life lay undisturbed, a massive hole punched in the middle of it. The roads and schools and shopping centres and hotels were all as he remembered yet presently none of them were quite the same.

Memories trailed behind him like the tail of a kite as he soared over it all: frolicking in the surf as a young teenager with friends, finding respite in the jungles, running from the vipers, barking at Bitchiro, cowering before Sergeant Benson, the murdered Suncorp employees, the midget boxing and hooker harassment. He could also see people in real time. They were blithely going about their day posting letters, doing the shopping, attending classes, working cash registers, riding bicycles and napping in the sun. None were aware of his presence.

He soared over the island till the sun began to sink and then he set his feet on the earth by a small tavern. The otherness of this world remained. Dreamlike, he moved about, with the sensation that he was walking on sponges. He was capable of passing through solid objects and perceiving and manipulating the existence of objects beyond his immediate presence. He could sense the overflow of his chromosomes to all he came into contact with and this brought a certain harmony and affection to the whole experience.

He entered the bar through a side wall. The scene was curiously earthy with a touch of the heavenly. Rustic and friendly, dimly lit yet warm, the tavern was a like a second home to those who dwelled here. Old beer posters with stains and small tears decorated the walls and a couple of yellowing paper lanterns with calligraphy scribbled across them hung from the ceiling over the corners of the bar. Music - *enka* songs from past generations - played in the background and brought a timeless, if not sacred feel to the place. Behind the bar, an ancient mama-san leaned, her face as lined as the bark of an old tree and her hair coiffed in the manner of a bird's nest, drew heavily on a cigarette held tightly between her lips.

Though none of them had been to Okinawa before, his posse were all there, chatting and laughing, drinking and pursuing the good-natured arguments that friendships produce. Safari Man held audience at the bar as he so often did, with Pink Guy (completely lucid), Salamander Man, Alpha Centurion, Drone, Negi Generation 4 and, surprisingly, Percy the Pigeon, all sitting around as though at home. The soft illumination of the scene fostered a spirit of comfort and gentleness.

Frank watched it all with a full heart. He had never really known love but was beginning to think that, in this mob of colorful scoundrels, he just might have found it. His eyes moved from friend to friend, drawn to each as they spoke and listened and gestured and moved around. Their interactions were intensely pleasing to him. This only made it all the more crushing when another figure suddenly appeared in a back corner of the tavern. Hideous and dark, it lurked with undisguised malice. The friends all noticed it immediately and a deathly silence fell upon them. Their heads turned with horror to see a huge, ugly creature standing as tall as the roof; enormous, bulbous, red eyes bulging out from a triangular head, and long, thin contorted arms holding hands which rubbed together furiously as though making fire.

Frank recognized the creature immediately. It was the dreaded Dyopatera peace lord which had cut down the beautiful tree effigy in the rice fields realm. After all he'd been through, Frank had thought there was nothing more that could scare him. How wrong he was. With this growing affection for his friends, there came a growing fear - a real terror - that they could be damaged because of him and it cut him to the core. He called out to his friends with a raw desperation but they couldn't hear him. He raced and stood in front of them but it was as though he wasn't there. This was incomprehensible to him. He had this connection with them, not merely through friendship but through his newfound chromosomal solidarity with the omniverses. So he couldn't understand how this realm or time or apparition could be so completely outside of his influence.

The peace lord looked once at Frank and then slowly moved toward his friends. They dived for cover behind the bar, tumbling and burrowing into one another, all knees and elbows and screams and terrors. Glasses and bottles were skittled and smashed all over the bar area in the fracas. The friends had never known such fear. They lay in a squirming dog pile on the floor. Alpha Centurion pressed his face to the floor as though trying to bury his head in it. Salamander Man and Safari Man used the same tactic. Drone played dead. Percy the Pigeon and Pink Guy were on their backs looking up. They caught the full terror of its presence.

Over the top of the counter loomed the hideous figure. Twitching its head, tensing its muscles and rubbing its hands together with even greater action than before, it was a bundle of extreme torment and delight, as though it could hardly stand its own company, yet could barely contain the thrill of unleashing itself. Though its mouth remained fixed, they caught a smirk break across it. It reached down over the counter and picked up Percy as though lifting a toothpick. "You have no business being here," it said in a gravelly whisper and flung him clear across the room and hard into the back wall. One of his wings broke with a loud snap and he dropped limp to the ground. Frank was aghast but remained unseen and unheard. He was frustrated beyond measure.

Once again, the great peace lord reached down, this time raising up Pink Guy who was screaming and writhing for all he was worth. Holding him mid-air as though offering a sacrifice, the peace lord spoke to the others on the floor. "Look!" It was a weird voice; small and raspy, yet powerful and frightening. The remaining posse, terrified to their core, failed to obey and continued to burrow into the solid wooden floor. Frank called out to them, "Get out of there! Run for your lives!" The peace lord spoke again. "Look." This time the words were not merely sound waves but physical matter which seized them, spun them onto their backs and prized their eyes wide open. "Tell Frank," he wheezed to them, "to crawl back down his hole…" It stared at them with those horrifying, big, red, glassy eyes. "…or there will be suffering to come which he could never have imagined."

Those words were accompanied with one swift movement which severed Pink Guy in two. His upper half remained high in the peace lord's grip while his hips and lower limbs dropped to the ground with a thud. A steady flow of blood and other liquids gushed from his torso. The life drained promptly from Pink Guy's eyes and he slumped dead in the creature's hand. There was silence. The friends were too petrified to move or utter a sound. They just watched in disbelief, eyes wide like clocks and mouths agape. It was Frank who first screamed. "No!" he howled. "No, no, no, no, no, no, no!" He was beside himself with grief. The atmosphere in the tavern remained in stunned silence till it was broken by Alpha Centurion, who cried out in exactly the same manner as Frank had. The others soon accompanied him till the whole place was filled with loud wailing and sobbing. The peace lord looked down on them all. "Tell Frank," it said again with cold indifference. "Tell him." With that, it withdrew and dissipated into thin air.

The others all jumped up and attended hopelessly to Pink Guy's remains. They tried to place the two halves back together but they just lay there, grotesque in their bloody lifelessness and rapid discoloring. After fooling about like this for a while, they slumped against walls and counters, looked at Pink Guy's pale face, and mournfully gave up on him. The mama-san, stricken rigid with fear in a corner throughout the whole encounter, began to return to herself yet her senses were now permanently injured. She remained without speech for the rest of her life.

Safari Man took a leadership role at this point. He grabbed Pink Guy's torso and gestured for Salamander Man and Alpha Centurion to collect his lower half. They, with the others, followed Safari Man out of the tavern and struggled with the corpse over some grassy mounds and onto the beach. Not a word was spoken amongst them. Frank was there but remained undiscoverable to them. They laid Pink Guy's remains respectfully on the sand while they gathered branches for kindling. It didn't take them long to build a sizeable mound of firewood by the shoreline. They then rested Pink Guy's body on the top. Salamander Man placed five-hundred yen coins on his eyes and then stepped back. They stood together in a line, arm in arm; Alpha Centurion weeping, Salamander Man looking down at the sand, Safari Man with his eyes fixed on Pink Guy, Percy the Pigeon looking up the starry heavens and Drone hovering just off Percy's shoulder.

Safari Man gave an impromptu eulogy. "Pink Guy. You were before us; you were our instructor, our brother and our friend. You were what we aspired to be, except for being entirely pink and incomprehensible most of the time and playing your stupid ukulele all the time and…"
He was cut off by Percy, "Keep it together, man!"
Safari Man collected himself and continued. "But that was what made you you. And we loved that. And we are better people for that. May you rest in peace, brother. May you move on to pinker skies. May you discover pinker horizons. May the pink lords be with you. May the pinkness of your…"
"Come on, man, can't you just let him lie in peace?"

Safari Man threw a small flower onto the wood pile. The others all did the same. Salamander Man began to play a sad tune on his recorder which Frank recognized as one of the tunes that he had played to the dying salamander man in the watery netherworld.

They all shed a few more tears before Safari Man stepped forward once again and poured petrol all over the wood pile. He doused everything liberally: Pink Guy, the wood pile, the sand all around it, and when he finally set a match to it, the whole thing exploded like a bomb from the great war. They all were all blown back about twenty meters and singed to a crisp. Even Frank felt it through the weird ether from which he observed all this. When the conflagration died down a little, they gathered around one more time, black and cooked to the core, and bawled once again. Frank could bare it no longer and left them there.

He woke up on his face. He hated waking up on his face. It was like escaping from a near-fatal choke. But this time he wished it had been fatal. With Pink Guy gone, there seemed little left for him to live for. Life had lost whatever little meaning it had once had. He rolled over and observed his room in the dim light and through the fog of his morning brain. Alpha Centurion was sleeping in the cupboard as usual, only this time he had passed out onto the end of an umbrella which was lodged firmly in the roof of his mouth, cocking his head back and leaving his shoulders and arms slumping forward. He remained blissfully asleep. Frank rolled over and looked under his bed. Salamander Man appeared eternal to him: forever under his bed with a filthy sock hanging from the corner of his mouth while gently rubbing a nipple. Drone lay tipped on the floor beside him as though somehow injured. Negi Generation 4 lay in the middle of the floor sleeping in as perfect a star shape as it was possible for a negi to form. And across the hallway, Safari Man lay sleeping, glasses still on, with his mouth wide open and his safari hat mercifully covering his groin.

But Pink Guy was nowhere to be seen. This was Frank's great fear: that what he had just experienced in Okinawa was in fact reality and his closest confidant, Pink Guy, had been severed in two. This world he had woken up to began to cave in on him. All the fear and darkness and anxieties and evil fell upon him and he withdrew into a very deep, dark place. There he found a world of regret and self-loathing. There he met demons which ravaged his soul and cast him further down. And there, he heard the voice penetrate all the terror and the darkness and toll like a bell, "Tell Frank to crawl back down his hole or there will be suffering to come which he could never have imagined." As frightening as these words were, they were also a form of sweet relief. Perhaps if he lived a life of denial, as though he were just another guy going about his life unpretentiously, then he would be free from all this torment. Perhaps just giving up was not only the easy option but the safest one as well. Maybe surrender was the way to victory. He dwelt on this for a while before finally uttering his submission. "I will."

A soft grunt met him in response and Frank froze with fear to think that Dyopatera (or one of his lackeys) had just become incarnate in his room. He rolled over to see a flesh-colored figure looming over him. Slowly he came into focus. "Pink Guy?" Frank said. He immediately sat up. "Pink Guy?!" The darkness within Frank subsided as he jumped up and grabbed Pink Guy hard by the shoulders. "Pink Guy! Pink Guy, it's you! It's really you!" Frank was overcome with happiness. He shook Pink Guy hard just to be sure that it really was him and this was all real. This sudden glee and physical exuberance was thoroughly intimidating for Pink Guy, who tried to free himself from Frank's grip and back away. But Frank had him and wasn't letting go. He danced around the room holding onto him with Pink Guy shrieking with fear and trying to free himself.

The commotion woke the others and they roused themselves to ask Frank what was going on. Across the hall, Safari Man, still in the twilight zone, began to yell out something about sea cucumbers before a large fist came down hard on his mouth and silenced him. Frank quickly counted heads and realized that there was a new entity in the apartment. It didn't bother him too much. Anyone punching Safari Man hard in the mouth first thing in the morning couldn't be all bad, he reasoned. There was movement from the room before a large, hugely muscular and rather magnificent Adonis appeared and, completely naked save for a small pair of coral colored underpants, strode across the hallway into Frank's room. "Prometheus," he said by way of re-introduction. His voice was the same lush and deep one that made Frank momentarily consider bisexuality.

"What is going on here?" Frank asked. After all his recent travels and conquests, he had become unfamiliar with asking the questions. Pink Guy held his stomach and grunted his explanation: "IBS". He had spent most of the early morning hours suffering the most terrible stomach cramps and blasting away at the porcelain. That explained the first of the morning's mysteries. Frank looked at Prometheus for the other. "What brings you here, brother?" he asked.
"You, Frank." The voice remained rich and full-toned. "Everyone knows the tiers are changing. Some are moving up. I am," he said with tremendous pride. I believe I am now a chimpilla." He said the word chimpilla as though it were a fine wine. "But that's nothing. You, Frank, are something else. You have become a peace lord and a mighty one at that. You have stood up to Chin Chin, you have resurrected Negi - it's the talk of the omniverses - and your chromosomes continue to multiply at astronomical rates. In short, Frank," said Prometheus drawing his oration to a close, "I want in".

Frank looked first at Prometheus and then slowly around the room at each of them. He felt pity. They knew so little and they hoped for so much. The words of the peace lord rolled back and forth across his mind - crawl back down his hole - as he continued to look at each of them as they stood around him - suffering to come which he could never have imagined - and spoke to them. "I'm afraid you don't understand. I'm not who you thought I was. Yes, my chromosomes are multiplying and I was able to bring our Negi friend here back."

"Testy buzz to a guacamole," he said gratefully.

"But I only restored what had once already been. And Chin Chin backed off, but to who knows where and why and what's next?" He looked around at their still-expectant faces. "There are powers out there you can't imagine. Even amongst the peace lords there are tiers. Even those that I thought were invincible have been taken down." One by one their shoulders began to slump and their expressions began to drop. "I'm nothing compared to them. Nothing."

"Nyes." Salamander Man made a good point and the others were all in agreement. It was only a matter of chromosomes ago that Frank was a mere mortal and by all accounts, a 'nothing' to even a rankenfile. Now he had become a mighty peace lord and even if that were a 'nothing' to other peace lords now, how long would it be till he was their equal or even superior to them? It was true. Frank's chromosomal growth rate was exponential. He was peerless in this regard. Surely that's why Chin Chin wanted him dead? That's why Dyopatera wanted him buried. They feared what he would become. They feared that left any longer, Frank could become a power beyond even them.

The thought of this was enticing to Frank but the cost of achieving any such position would be higher than he could bear. Still they urged him on.

"Papa Franku, we're all with you. We're in this together, ha ha ha."

"Nyess."

"I'm not afraid of that dickless Chin Chin. I say, 'bring it on'."

"Prometheus."

"Up and with buffoon for forty!"

His friends were well-meaning and he loved them for it but they just didn't understand; they couldn't know. But he was lifted by their spirits nonetheless and they caused him to reconsider his surrendered heart.

Chapter 14

Many have undertaken to draw up an account of the things that were fulfilled in those days, just as they were handed down by those who from the first were eyewitnesses and servants of the truth. This account is based on careful investigation from those who were there, those who heard first hand, and those who now know the truth so that we may know the certainty of these things.

Frank woke from a deep sleep. Never in his life had he felt more powerful, more knowledgeable or more present. Immediately, he left his apartment where his friends all remained in deep slumber, and entered a large park. It was the thick of winter and a light covering of snow lay all around. The ponds had frozen over long ago and the wind blew bitterly cold, yet he felt none of it. He was now set apart from the elements.

He walked under one of the many bridges of the park and took pause. He had decided to leave. He had set his heart on going far, far away where he could not endanger his friends' lives and where no-one could be bothered to search for him, even if they found out where he was. He would come back and visit from time to time but he would, from this point on, exist only in the unknown realms of the omniverses until he knew with certainty his identity and his true place in the tiers. Unlike before though, he would now choose for himself where he would go and how long he would stay. This was freedom enough, even if it were to be a very lonely freedom.

In an instant, he was sitting on the warm sands of an endless desert. An enormous, bright ball of white radiation hung low above him, yet its heat was mild and its coloring soft. Beside him was a small oasis rimmed with a few trees and shrubs. There was nothing else as far as the eye could see; only endlessly rolling cream-colored dunes. Without removing any clothing, Frank waded into the waters and cooled off. It was very pleasant. And when he left the pond, he lay in the shade of one of the trees, put his hands behind his head and fell into a semi-doze. There wasn't a breath of wind. Just stillness and quiet. He began to collect his thoughts.

Even with his extraordinary chromosomal capacity, he could rarely tell how much time had passed from one event to another, and with a sun that never moved from its position in the sky, it was all the more difficult. After a lengthy period of sunning, a breeze began to blow in from the direction he was facing. At first it was rather bracing but it quickly picked up and became menacing. As Frank watched, the brilliant sun dimmed, the wind began to whip about and the sand was blown into an enormous shape-shifting vortex that spiralled up and scratched the sky. He stood unfazed as this built up all about him. Lightning began to strike and thunder boomed so repetitively it became one long, rumbling bass note. Hail began to pelt down but still Frank stood unflinching. The sky then ripped open and the dark lord Chin Chin descended from it in haste, once again with two chained minions going before him, snarling with lunatic ferocity.

The dark lord alighted from his train of billows and scampered toward Frank. "O chin chin ga dai suki dayo." He spat it out through clenched teeth, his detestation for Frank at an all-time high. "O chin chin. O chin chin." There was more spittle and indiscriminate twitching.
"This is getting boring, Chin Chin. Lightning, thunder, hail. Yeah, yeah." Frank looked about him before continuing. "I said it before and I'll say it again: piss off."
Chin Chin roared in a manner that Frank had never seen before and Frank nodded to the dark lord to indicate that he was impressed by this.

"Ochin chin," he said again. This utterance had a whole other tinge to it and Frank understood it completely. There were other peace lords, he had said, thousands of them, and they all wanted to see Frank - and his posse - skinned alive and rolled in salt for eternity. Frank and his friends would wish for death to come quickly, but it wouldn't.

Frank had seen enough. Through sheer force of will he pushed Chin Chin back and in an instant, Frank was floating through a world of clear liquid jelly. The jelly was breathable, drinkable and pleasantly warm. He moved through the substance propelled by nothing more than the flexing of his muscles. This was a fabulous world and, although annoyed very much by Chin Chin's interruptions, Frank enjoyed being able to disappear and reappear anywhere in the omniverses he pleased. This world was not dissimilar to being underwater on earth, only the matter was thicker and the life forms more vibrant and pristine. The weightless environment made the concepts of up and down non-existent and Frank suspected that there were none of the cardinal directions that governed most realms, either. In this world, the light was omnipresent and it refracted in entirely different ways from what he was used to so that visual focus came and went like shadows.

A school of lifeforms that looked like shuttlecocks with eyes came up and observed him. "Hey, little fella," Frank said to the nearest one. It pulled back and then they all moved on again. A large gray diamond-shaped creature hovered nearby. It appeared docile so Frank moved toward it but it, too, moved away. Frank noticed plant-like life forms growing from spindly branches which protruded from some rocky ledges. They were colorful and bulbous, like balloons, and were filled with a syrupy liquid. They looked delicious. Frank threw caution to the wind and bit into one. It immediately burst and its contents blew all over his face. What didn't go into his mouth and nose was absorbed by his skin, and it was wonderful. The taste was unlike anything he had experienced before, rich and strong in flavor and instantly refreshing. He felt invigorated by the experience.

His immediate surroundings then grew suddenly colder and darker and all life forms, no matter how near or distant, retreated out of sight. Frank was aware off a presence, a dark ominous power, but there was nothing around him that he could see. Still the darkness grew and he could sense evil touching him through the essence of his environment. Something wrapped around his foot and yanked him down hard. It caught him by surprise and old feelings of fear and anxiety returned to him. Frank looked below to see an enormous Octopussy creature boring into him with its eyes. It slithered its other tentacles around his body and face and pulled him down, pressing Frank's face against its own. If Frank had been able to sweat in this environment he would have been sweating profusely. His heart began to pound and real dread set in, not just for his immediate safety but for his whole plan of omniversal escape.

"We peace lords have determined that you shall die and in the most painful and prolonged manner," it said with a watery voice. It continued to slide its tentacles around Frank's waist and neck. Frank was powerless to move. Unless he could free himself from the peace lord, he would only take it with him into the next realm if he transported. "Die, Frank! Die!" it said squeezing the life out of him. "It has been determined." Frank put up fierce resistance but was completely out of his depth. It was as though his chromosomes were defective in this realm, no matter how many of them he had. "It has been determined," it said again in a liquefied voice.

All of a sudden a white and brown syrup covered the peace lord and a gray figure came out of nowhere and slashed at it. The peace lord removed two of its tentacles from Frank and turned its attention to its attacker. Again, there was more brown and white effluent cast upon the peace lord and another sharp slash drawn across it. Presently the gray figure stopped at a distance and called to the peace lord.

"It's Percy the Pigeon, bitch."
"Percy!" called Frank, delighted to see his old friend.
"You were warned once," the Octopus peace lord said to Percy in the same moist tone. "You have no business being here." It released Frank completely and shot a quiver of poisonous darts at Percy. He disappeared before they could hit him and reappeared on the other side of Frank.
"Percy, what's going on?" Frank asked. "How did you know I was here? How did you do…that?"
The octopus peace lord fired more arrows at Percy which he evaded again. The pigeon appeared right beside Frank for a moment.
"When you put my feather in your pocket, Frank, a part of me was with you. As your chromosomes multiplied, so did mine." He shot more effluent at the Octopus peace lord, dousing him in his noxious retardant.
"Percy!" Frank was so pleased to see him.
"When you became a peace lord, Frank, so did I!"

The octopus peace lord fired more arrows at Percy which he again dodged with ease.
"You've got to get out of here, man," Percy called to Frank. "There's more after you." He shot more refuse at the peace lord. "See you on the other side, Frank." The octopus peace lord retaliated with his own effluent, filling the surroundings with a thick black ink. Frank then heard the sound of more darts firing. This was followed by stillness. When the black plume dissipated, Frank was accosted by the sight of Percy pierced through the heart with one of the peace lord's poison darts. "Flee, Frank!" he

called and then collapsed. Frank turned to see the octopus peace lord hurtling toward him.

He was standing in the middle of a busy city centre. The buildings were unlike any he had seen before - many series of interlocking domes, and domes within domes of varying sizes and colors - yet the inhabitants of this land were clearly humanoid and almost certainly of the mere mortal tier. Frank was still shaking from the shock of Percy's demise and he hated himself for the loss of another friend. He was a real mix of emotions now. His feelings of power and presence remained, yet these were also dimmed by the fact that there were other greater powers out there determined to end him. His chest tightened at the thought of this and his temple pounded.

He was relieved, however, to be in this place. It would be easy for him to blend in, he reasoned, and go unnoticed. Yet no sooner had he come to a street crossing, curiously marked out with all the teeth of all kinds of creatures, than he saw Dyopatera, the peace lord, on the other side of the road. Frank could feel his soul fill with horror, starting with his stomach before rushing up to the top of his head. He froze momentarily, stricken with terror. He was now certain that he would never find escape, never be safe, never know peace. The peace lord (how he came to detest the irony of that title!) didn't hesitate to mow down every creature in front of it: men, women and children were all severed in half or decapitated in the peace lord's reach to terminate Frank.

Clouds surrounded him, covering him and buoying him. It was like he had suddenly transported right into the middle of a sea of cotton candy. It would have been quite pleasant had he not been on the run from a myriad of homicidal peace lords and just witnessed a horrific mass murder. He sank into a particularly billowy patch of the substance, hid himself from all view and collected himself for a moment. It didn't last. The whole fabric of the place ripped apart and the dark lord Chin Chin came roaring at him again in a whirlwind of rage. The shock of his sudden appearance was like a grenade going off in Frank's chest, a sensation he carried with him to the next realm.

A deserted planet, rather like the earth's moon was suddenly under his feet. He sat down in the fine dust, breathing heavily, distraught at the onslaught he was enduring. He hoped to catch his breath there but he was to have no such respite. Instantly from one direction scrambled the octopus peace lord and from another side came an entity unfamiliar to Frank. It had the head of an eagle, the body of a lion and the legs of a cockroach, and moved with greater speed and animosity than any of the others. Frank departed with no time to spare.

With each transport, his tormentors attacked with greater speed, and with each approach, his mind would turn to darkness and fury, his heart to hatred and vengeance. From realm to realm he bounced, from world to world with increasing haste and animosity, sometimes on his own, at other times mid-tussle with them. The only sad consistency was that on each arrival, the peace lords would be there, alone or in pairings, with greater resentment and hostility and with a keener desperation to cast him for eternity into the sea of the Wretched.

Suddenly he was in space. Floating without aim or purpose, but still with haunting memory. It was still and without sound. He looked about fearfully but there seemed to be nothing near or approaching, and none of the hatred that had met him in the other realms. Looking about, he recalled immediate events and once more collected his thoughts. He had escaped the octopus peace lord, but poor Percy had not. Why? Frank wondered. Why do these things happen to my friends? He had tried to escape all this and find peace and freedom but he could not escape from the wrath or condemnation of the peace lords. Their damnation seemed absolute and irreversible. Why was there such cruelty in the omniverses? he wondered. Where can I go from it? He had no answers of course and this brought upon him a deep sadness. This misery was intrinsically meshed with the fear and loathing that now defined him.

He was currently in what was essentially a realmless dimension. It was technically a realm, of course. It had co-ordinates and a locale but there was absolutely no matter by which to identify it. It was as empty as a realm could be. And there in the silence and the emptiness, Frank continued with these depressing questions. Over and over, his thoughts were with Percy and his other friends and his own future and his own identity. He lamented with enormous gravity the fate of his friends. Once again, they would have to pay the price for his ways. Just like in Okinawa. He would end up burying his friends the way he buried his co-workers. The way they buried Pink Guy in his dream. He was the source of all this death. "I really should have killed myself when I had the chance," he thought, recalling what the creature in the rice fields had told him to do.

Would they ever be safe? he wondered. Could he ever be powerful enough to protect them? Then the bigger questions tumbled. Why were the omniverses like this? Why were there tiers? Why was there evil? Why were his chromosomes multiplying? Who the hell was he?

He could have reflected on these questions for eons but his train of thought was interrupted by movement off in the distance. Observing it, he could see that, though it was a long way away, it was moving toward him. With its tail of light dragging behind, it appeared to be a comet or an asteroid or some such object but the front of it seemed to be moving, squirming, alive. It moved at a rapid rate and as it did, Frank could see the size and color of the meteor, and that its line would take it right by where he was

221

floating. He could also make out a sound emanating from the object. His first assumption was that this was another peace lord coming to expedite his demise and although he never fully put his guard down, it became clearer as the object moved toward him, that this was not the case.

As it hurtled through space, Frank was shocked and bemused to see a comet the size of a five story building sail on by, and strapped to the front of it was none other than his old mate from Soncorp, Bitchiro, still screaming his lungs out. Nothing had changed in him since Frank last saw him. As he flew by, he suddenly split apart with an agonising crack of his neck and another terrifying scream which echoed across the realms. His carcass dropped by the wayside and a new Bitchiro emerged, all slimy and bloody, still strapped to the front of the comet, howling in pain and begging someone - anyone - to have mercy on him. Though he felt little for Bitchiro, this happening illuminated the questions that Frank had been asking of the omniverses.

He was so caught up in these recurring thoughts that he almost missed the arrival of another creature. This one came silently and in the guise of one in suffering. Its look was shocking to Frank and after all he'd seen, that was really something. By appearance it was an entity covered in pulsating sacks and a complex system of moist tubings. These were spliced with bone fragments and tied up with an explosive mess of sinews and tendons. Above all this sat a ball with a mesh of vagina-like coverings, not unlike the openings of giant clams. Frank was perturbed. The creature was essentially humanoid but completely inside out.

Frank remained wary. The two floated at a distance, contemplating each other. The creature said nothing and refrained from moving for the longest time. Before long, Frank felt a weight come upon his chest. It was as though a tremendous pressure was being exerted upon him. Presently he noticed that a number of local space rocks and planets and other bodies had started swirling about them. At first he thought it was just his imagination but it soon became clear. The matter began to spiral about the two of them with increasing speed and intensity. The creature, clearly now a peace lord, remained in silence but Frank was acutely aware that these cosmic events were ordained by it.

More and more heavenly bodies were drawn in, at first meteors and comets, but soon whole solar systems and even galaxies were spinning around them. It wasn't until Frank tried to move away that he realized what was happening. He was caught in the centre of a black hole which was forming all about him. The circle of cosmic bodies grew thicker and their orbit faster. Amongst all the energy and matter and warping of time, Frank saw a familiar meteor return, with Bitchiro still pinned to it, pulled back in with his old mate still cracking and splitting and screaming and re-emerging. He was the very essence of suffering by psychosis.

The intensity of the energy was paralysing and all the while, the inside-out peace lord floated serenely, entirely in his element. Frank quickly called co-ordinates to take him away but they fell back in upon him. He called again and again with increasing desperation, but each time they returned to him. Though still increasing in chromosomes, he was unable to escape the energy of this black hole. He was dwarfed by its power. Terror seized him.

Rapidly, the matter pressed in about him with tumultuous clamor, compressing and cocooning him in a large cavern of rock. He was trapped. As the monolithic encasing sealed around him, others suddenly appeared. From nowhere, the octopus peace lord clambered over a rock and sat high and mighty above him. Rising majestically from where the mouth of the cave had been, Dyopatera ushered himself forward. It rubbed its hands together with furious disdain. From behind him, the eagle-headed peace lord strutted near and gave a piercing shrill. In front of him, never moving, floated the inside-out peace lord. Even without motion it exuded an aura of nefariousness. And finally, posturing as lord of all, the dark lord Chin Chin lowered himself on a cushion of air and stood before him.

As though heralding the performances at the end of an act, Chin Chin formally introduced each of his peace lord accomplices to Frank. "Octafacetious," he said, twitching toward the tentacled entity. Octafacetious spat ink to the floor of the cavern. "Dyopatera I believe you already know." Frank's trembling grew. "Accipitridonis," he sputtered, as the great avian peace lord fixed a steely gaze on him. "And Jonathan," he said, leaning in the direction of the silent, inverted floater.

Frank slumped to the floor of the cave. He was beyond terror now; beyond fear. Now his only emotion was abject hopelessness. He never wanted any of this. It wasn't his desire or his doing. He had no idea why he had become the one he now was and now he would never know. How he wished he could return to his childhood. He looked up at these powerful nemeses. They aligned in front of him, each one slowly moving toward him, dripping and drooling with hatred and abhorrence. They said nothing. They didn't need to. The measure of Frank's condemnation was now full and they all knew it. As he surrendered to them, a final stab of sorrow and fear overcame him. He wept.

In an instant they were granite. All of them. Frozen mounds of black quartz. And in the same instant, any semblance of evil was expelled from the cavern. Frank had no idea what to make of this. He was beyond understanding anything at this point. It was pure intrigue for him. He rose to his knees and leaned toward the figure that had been Chin Chin. He was so utterly granulitic it was as though his whole existence had never been in the first place. Frank looked from one face to another. Eyes that he could never have looked into before were now cold and impotent and lifeless. He was still bathed in sweat and his hands continued to tremble. Though the immediate threat to him was gone, he remained damaged from his battles, weary, and devoid of any passion.

A small light flickered from the mouth of the cave beyond the granite figures. Frank looked to it and it proceeded toward him. Unlike any of the presences he had recently experienced, this one was benign. Frank knew this innately. It moved slowly, effortlessly, gracefully, passing between two of the statues, and approached Frank. It was a light of untouchable serenity, beauty and power. Its presence and movements were captivating. Though it had moved nearer to Frank, it was at the same time back where it had first appeared. Yet it was a singular presence. And though it was nearer, it was no larger proportionately than it had been when more distant. It was a beautiful white light. So beautiful. And it gave off a warmth that immediately put Frank at ease.

He knew with absolute certainty who this was so his question was wholly redundant.
"Are you God?"
"I am." The voice was kind and warm and powerful and frightening all at the same time. Though ancient, it brimmed with youthfulness; and though majestic, it carried both geniality and levity. It was, more than anything else, a voice of authority.

"Francis," the voice spoke.
"Please call me Frank."
"I will call you Francis."
"Yes, sir."
"I am calling you, Francis."
Francis fell on his hands and knees. "Go away from me, God. I'm a filthy man."

225

"You think I don't know that?"

"Surely there's someone else more suited to a calling."

"This is the way it's always been. I use the weak, the infirm, the poor and the filthy to do my work."

"Really?"

"Yes. You are to go to the rejects, Francis. You are to go to the losers, the lost and the lonely; the small and the simple; the crude, the gross and the offensive."

"But God, I have so many questions. There's so much I need to know. So much I want to ask you."

"I can make time."

"Why is there so much darkness and evil out there? If you are a good and loving God, why is there so much pain and suffering? I've seen it. I've seen it and it's really bad."

"It is chosen."

"By whom?"

"By those with choice."

"I didn't choose for Sergeant Benson to beat me and kill those people."

"That's what he chose."

"So who chose for those typhoons to come through and destroy people's lives, or those earthquakes in the polar realms that wiped out whole communities?"

"Where I am, there is order. Where it is willed, I withdraw, and where I withdraw, disorder follows."

"And the Wretched?"

"The surface of the Sea of the Wretched is sealed from within."

The Great Voice continued. "Francis, how would you know good if you had never known evil? How could you know love if you'd never known hatred? How could there be peace if there had never been torment. Everything has its place and time and purpose. Even suffering."

226

"But where did all the suffering come from? Didn't you create everything?"

"There are kingdoms which are not of my Kingdom. There was once harmony in the omniverses. But some chose self over community and rebellion over harmony. So now rebellion must run its course. The foolishness of rebellion must be seen in all its folly and all its suffering. Then I will restore harmony to the omniverses again."

"So, who's in ultimate control then if there are other kingdoms?" This worried Francis.

"The omniverses are my chalice. There are many chalices in my sitting room and there are many rooms in my house. You know nothing, Francis, other than the knowledge I allow you to have. You have no chromosomes other than the ones I allow you to have. You have only ever visited and known the realms of rebellion. The realms in which people and entities rebel against me and against each other. But there are other realms, Francis, many other realms which are good and light and wonderful. But you cannot know them, Francis, not yet."

"When will I get to see them?"

"I can't say."

"You can't say? But you're the Ultimate God. If you can't say, then who can?"

"You, Francis. Some things I simply leave to others. This is one such thing. It's up to you."

"What do you mean?"

No answer came from the flame.

"Why won't you answer me?" Francis paused before a flood of questions poured out. "What's going on here? Why are you holding out on me? Why am I stuck in the dark ends of the omniverses? Why is there rebellion across them? What is my part in all this? Why have I been put through such hardship and misery?

"Enough!" The voice thundered around the stony womb. Be silent!" The command cut Francis to the heart. He stood before the flame, head bowed and eyes lowered.

"Who are you, Francis?" The great cavern had become as a cathedral and it was filled with otherness.

"Were you there when I flung the omniverses into their positions? Do you know how many omniverses and dimensions and realms there are?

Can you travel them all and record all their secrets?

Surely you know, Francis?! Do tell me!"

Where were you when matter first formed and spirit first arose?

Were you there when I hung the lights in the Dravidious realms?

Have you even seen their splendor?

Have you considered how they were birthed and why they shine so brightly?

Were you there when I created the fierce Ramnatharal that governs the Silus dimensions?

Were you there when I breathed into the gentle Flittingmore, with its delicate wings, and set it on its perches?

Can you count the colors in its wings?

Can you fathom the structure of its patagium?

What is it that you know, Francis?

What do you know that is hidden from me?

Where has your understanding taken you?

Share with me your wisdom!

Show me the vast riches of your knowledge."

Francis slumped before the flame. He had never felt so small and foolish in all his life.

"Do you dare question me, Francis? Are you doubting my justice? Are you putting me on trial?" Each of these questions echoed around the chamber. Not one of them fell to the ground. Francis stood still before the flame. He wouldn't move, not even to lift his head. The voice addressed him once more, rich and kind.

"I am putting you on a pilgrimage, Francis. I'm calling you into service. I have equipped you with multiplying chromosomes for the task. You can't earn your way from here and you can't go it alone. You can only prove yourself to me. Your commission starts now."

"But how can I go? I'm not ...godly. I'm a filthy man, Lord. It's all I know. I'm not worthy."
"Take off your shirt, Francis, for you are on holy ground."
Francis obeyed without hesitation and stood before the flame.

"Be still."
Suddenly a powerful wave of light burst from the flame and passed over Francis. It didn't just roll over him so much as it rolled into him, caressing his heart and restoring his mind. This wave was Peace and it relieved from Francis not merely his current fears, which had been many, but any fear he had ever had. His fears were not forgotten but they were no longer of any concern to him. They had no hold of him. And in their place was appeasement. It was as though the flame had wrapped his heart in a mantle of comfort and laid him down. Francis recalled the peace he had received from the tree effigy. What he was experiencing now was the same gift, only greater. This peace felt infinite to him. It delivered him. He found his rest.

Francis continued to watch the flame. It aroused such appeal in him. Though gentle, it emitted an impregnable strength. Another wave of light burst forth from the flame. This wave was an even more brilliant white than the first, and as it rolled through Francis he began to sob uncontrollably. It brought healing and wholeness. This wave was Forgiveness. Francis saw all the filth, all the hypocrisy, all the selfishness and hatred, all the vengeance and wrongdoing, the gossip and slander, the destructiveness, the foolishness and the theft; he saw all the good that he had left undone, the kindnesses left unextended, the care denied, and with one wipe, it was all lifted from him. He was clean and whole and he barely recognized himself for it.

Though it filled him with ease, it also presented him with challenge. It wasn't possible for him to receive this without also extending it. Memories of the Indonesian military pulling him from loved ones and gunning down innocents, Sergeant Benson's constant torments and his killing of the Soncorp employees, those who had abused him, stolen from him, hated him and hurt him. He had to forgive them all. To a man. The wounds were so deep. He had been so wronged. But he had to let go of it. He had to forgive them, proffer them wellbeing, wish them well and pronounce blessing upon them. Francis fell prostrate on the floor. His heart was ripping in two. He then released his prisoners and in so doing freed himself. "I forgive you," he said weeping. "I forgive you all."

Immediately another burst of light was emitted from the flame. This wave carried a pale yellow hue and it washed over Francis and filled him with assurance. This wave was Hope. Francis had never really known this, not in its pure form, and it took his mind beyond ease to give him expectations he had never before known or considered. Old anxieties and paranoias became fading echoes which vanished into the thin air of that cavern and were replaced with the certainty of goodness to come. He savored a deep satisfaction and allowed it to consume him.

Francis was beside himself with happiness and contentment. But like a guest who enjoys the first course without realising there was a second to come, he rose as though matters were somehow concluded. The flame moved right up to him. Francis could feel the warmth of the tongues on his face. Once more a wave of light blew out from the flame, this time a throb of orange-tinged luminosity. As it moved over him, he broke into fits of laughter. This wave was Joy and it was like a consummation for Francis. Now free of fear, guilt and hopelessness, Francis was filled with an unspeakable joy that could only be expressed in roars of laughter. It made the smutty giggles of his Okinawan days appear as churlishness. He rolled onto his back holding his sides and let his guffaws fill the cavern and echo across the realms. His laughter rang out as though it were a victory cry and, far from exhausting him, this great laughter only served to strengthen him. He lay on his back and felt the tears of joy roll down his temples. He had never known such delight.

Yet God was not done with him. Another burst of light shot out from the flame, this time with a strong blue candescence. As it washed over Francis, he jumped to his feet and stood erect before the flame as a subject stands and awaits knighthood before a sovereign. This wave was Power and it brought to Francis an equipping and an authority of which he could only ever have dreamed. Previously, as his chromosomes multiplied, he felt powerful but only as a frog feels powerful beside a flea. Now he knew what true power looked and felt like; he understood its gravity, and though it remained largely veiled to him, he knew that his power had a purpose and his might was for a reason. He felt deeply humbled.

A sixth wave came over him from the flame. This one had a green tint. It was Providence and its swell assured him that beyond his purposes and deliverances and personal healings, he would never want. He would always be provided for in every capacity, physical and spiritual, as would those who shared in his service. Francis rejoiced in this.

There was a pause and a silence before the final wave was emitted from the flame and overcame Francis. He knew to wait for it and he knew that it was the last of the favors to enfold him. A huge light - red, wild and magnificent - exploded from the centre of the flame and enveloped Francis completely. It blew him away. The previous six waves had brought unfathomable goodness, but this one brought unimaginably glory. It was Love. It was liberating, empowering, intoxicating and fierce. And it was wholly transforming. Francis, tears flowing freely, basked in it without reservation or limit.

The great voice spoke into him. "Rise, Francis. I dub you 'Francis of the Filth' for you are to go to the filth. You are to go to the cesspools, the pits, the infestations, the lowest common denominator. And I will be with you."

Frank woke in his apartment in New York and arose a new creation.

Chapter 15

He was born with a gift of laughter and a sense that the world was mad. And that was now his persona. The specifics of his calling remained obscure, yet the dimensions he now inhabited dispelled the cloud of mystery that once hung about them.

He stood in the middle of his living room though they were for the most part unaware of it. Safari Man was gambling with Alpha Centurion. Salamander Man and Negi Generation 4 were playing Scrabble which was curious as Negi was bound by no rules. Pink Guy was cooking dumplings in the kitchen with Drone. In a corner chair sat Percy the Pigeon, observing his surroundings with a knowing nod. He was the only one aware of Francis' presence though Francis remained unseen even to him.

So when he suddenly materialized right in front of them, they all leapt up to greet him (except for Safari Man, who continued with his game a little longer) and there was great joy. They huddled together and slapped backs and butts and muzzled into thighs and laughed uproariously. "Frank! Frank!" they called. They were so surprised to see him. Many months had passed in earth time since his recent encounters. "It's Francis now," he assured them. They accepted this without question (except for Safari Man who wanted a full explanation) and they asked him all about his wanderings and adventures.

They had already received a foretaste from Percy who had moved in with them shortly after Francis had left. Francis was very pleased, although not altogether surprised, to see Percy the Pigeon alive and well in his living room. "Percy told us," Alpha Centurion said, taking a seat on a shelf in the cupboard, "how you fought with the peace lords." The others all nodded in excitable agreement. "He told us about the Octopus peace lord. Man, how creepy is that?!" Salamander Man shuddered. "And how you saved Percy's life," Pink Guy added with a grunt.

"Percy is too kind," Francis said. "It was he who saved my life." Alpha Centurion looked at Percy with tremendous pride.
"It's true, man," said Percy. "What can I say? I did save Francis' bacon." He gave a proud nod. "Twice!" he added. "But then that peace lord shot me straight through the heart and the last thing I remember was telling Francis to get the hell out of there. No point messing around with that dude. He was mean."

"And the next thing you knew," said Salamander Man finishing the story for him and rolling his right nipple gently between his fingers, "Frank - sorry Frank, Francis - brings Percy back to life, just like he did with our old friend Negi here!" Negi began to bounce on the balls of his feet and clap his hands just as he always did when he was excited, which was an awful lot of the time.
"Beef to lot!" he said, before throwing his head back in laughter.

"Percy, I can't tell you how glad I am that you're here," Francis said. "I can't believe it!" He looked at Percy's chest where the dart had pierced him. "But I didn't bring you back to life." They all looked at Francis confused. "I'm sorry to say that I took your advice, Percy. I had to or that peace lord would have cut me down just as he cut you down. I got out of there just as the octopus peace lord was coming for me. I left you there, Percy. I left you for dead." There was a stunned silence around the room.

Alpha Centurion broke into a grin and wagged his finger at Francis. "Are you being modest, Francis?" The others all began to wonder the same thing.
"I wish I was," said Francis. "But I didn't bring you back to life."
"Who did then?" asked Pink Guy.

234

"I don't know." Francis looked around at their faces. "But I suspect it was..." They looked up at him with eyes so expectant, so innocent. How could he even begin to describe what he had experienced and what he now knew? How could they ever understand what had transpired between himself and the Almighty? They continued to wait for him. "I suspect it was... a friend of mine." All except for Pink Guy and Percy the Pigeon took this at face value and were relieved to know that Francis had powerful, benign friends in the omniverses. Pink Guy and Percy understood Francis to be speaking of himself in the third person. He had his purposes, they reasoned, and they were supremely content with this.

"How did you defeat the evil peace lords, Francis?" Alpha Centurion asked, taking a seat on the floor in front of Francis. He sat up straight, cross-legged, with his hands on his knees. The others gathered around. There was more than a hint of excitement amongst them. "Tell us, tell us!" they said.

For a moment, Francis was taken back to that fateful day at Soncorp when that dimension was torn apart and Frank was taken to the icy nether realm. He first met Pink Guy there. He remembered sitting, so confused and traumatized, and seeing this pink fellow and wondering what on earth was going on. He recalled the land under the great bronze sky where Salamander Man first saved him from Lemon Man and become a true friend; his horrific meeting with Chin Chin on the mountain; his first visit to New York, meeting Safari Man in the bar and Alpha Centurion while racing crawfish. How curiously they all came together, he thought. He considered Percy. By keeping a solitary feather of Percy's in his pocket, the pigeon would achieve peace lord status merely by the overflow of Francis' own chromosomes. He fell into an awe of himself.

Visions of his time in the rice field realms, his encounters with the evil peace lords there, as well as with the mysterious tree effigy, came flooding back to him; holding the salmon in the river and discovering his abilities to give and receive his chromosomes. He considered the increased frequency of his encounters with the evil peace lords. He could sense, even then, their increasing desperation to terminate him and bring to a halt his exponential multiplication of chromosomes. He remembered his first victory over a chimpilla. It made him feel so powerful. It wasn't only a physical victory - he knew that now - it was equally a metaphysical and chromosomal victory. It was a marker of his own growing power and authority. No wonder they began to fear and detest him!

And what of his latest encounters with the peace lords - rolling and tumbling and brawling across the ages and dimensions? And why? Why should such formidable and mighty peace lords be so roused to hostility against him? Rightly so, he now knew! In such a relatively short space of time, in the passing of so few chromosomes, Francis had advanced from being a mere mortal working in a lab in Okinawa, to becoming a peace lord of unsurpassable power. How could they not see him as anything but a threat? He had raised Negi from the dead! He had raised Percy to peace lord status. Had he even raised Percy from the dead without even knowing it? It was entirely possible. His chromosomes were multiplying so rapidly, even he was not fully aware of the powers and glories of which he was capable. Perhaps he had raised Percy. Perhaps his mere presence, however fleeting, had restored the power of life to his pigeon friend. It was true that Francis had never felt so strong, so unbridled, so powerful.

He considered God. What a beautiful and majestic experience that had been. What a wonderful God he was. Francis was truly in awe of such goodness, such divinity. But he did wonder why he

236

was so interested in Francis. Why didn't he leave Francis to his fate at the hands of the peace lords? Why did he intervene? Who was Francis to him that he would do so? It didn't make sense. Francis considered this some more. Why would God shower such blessing on him? For nothing? Why would he feel inclined to save Frank? Doubt was birthed at that moment.

Could it have been that even God was in awe of Francis? It made Francis wonder just how much power he had and, more importantly, what limits to his power there would be in the future. Was God merely attempting to harness Francis' powers through kindness, unlike the peace lords who failed to do this through violence? Was Francis' potential for might a threat to even God himself? As much as the thought sent a shiver down his spine, he couldn't ignore the question, nor deny the possibility.

Perhaps this great King saw himself in Francis. Perhaps he saw royalty - a rising prince with the charisma and backing to win an extraordinary number of subjects to his cause. Could this all be a process of cosmic alliances for some great battle to come in the omniverses? He could see the possibility and the value in God making Francis a vassal king under him. There would be mutual benefit, certainly, but who was to receive the greater advantage? Was this merely a scheme for God to secure Francis' loyalties and fortify his own rule? If Francis' potential were truly unlimited, he could see no other explanation for any favor extended.

Francis paused for a moment. And then from a very deep place, a monumental thought arose within him. He could feel it rising from his loins, working through his gut, flowering in his heart, bearing fruit in his mind: Was Francis a god? Was he God himself? Is this why he was so passionately hunted and courted? Was he rising irrevocably into a deity? Upon reflection, it seemed to him that this question was actually a factual statement in utero.

King Francis. Lord Francis. Francis, the Almighty God of the omniverses.

He looked down upon his subjects and answered their question. "I turned them to stone," he said. "Every one of them. They will never bother us again." Francis said this with such penetration and authority that they were afraid and overjoyed equally. He put his hands on them and shared some of his chromosomes with them.

They were ready for what lay ahead. Francis suggested they go and hunt flatchemburns in the quarry realms just for fun. At this the whole gang huddled around him for transport. He sent them off as one, intimating that he would only be a moment behind them. And when they were gone, and in that moment of stillness, he looked around the apartment and reconsidered everything. Dream, memory, alternate reality, actuality; past, present, future: it was all the same to Francis. He was Lord of them all. He was his own man. He was his own God.

The Revelation

A prologue and epilogue

The revelation of Negi, firstborn of the Negi Generations and son of the soil, given for the shedding abroad of understanding and knowledge to the hosts of every realm, age and dimension throughout the omniverses. Grace and peace.

I, Negi, was sitting under a pomegranate tree at the third watch of the day in a desolate realm, when I was visited by a brilliant light, brighter than any sun in the sky, yet gentle to the naked eye. The light moved over me till I was enveloped by it, and as it formed its sphere around me, the glory of its presence was made known to me. I fell to the ground and cried out, "Leave me! I am nothing but loam and roots!" And a voice spoke from the light, majestic and rich, and said, "Remove the soil from around your roots, for the place you are resting is holy ground." I did as I was told, but remained with my face to the ground. "Rise, Negi," came the command. "Rise and be sanctified, for you are my chosen vessel to reveal to the worlds what Was, what Is and what Is To Come." I stood and a cascade of light was poured forth upon my being till there was not a hint of defilement left upon me. And a declaration was pronounced: "Your transgressions have been atoned for."

In front of me appeared a large parchment scroll and a pen. "Write!" came the voice. "Write down the words that you hear and the visions that you see. Leave out not a single word nor a solitary shadow, and add to this not a single word nor a solitary shadow. You are to share this with the authorities and principalities of every realm, age and dimension. Leave nothing hidden, that all may be revealed. The visions that you will encounter are to echo across eternity."

At this, I fell down again before the light, unworthy of such honour, and began to shake and sob uncontrollably. A force lifted me from the ground and I sat levitated in the centre of the sphere, comforted by a sole utterance of infinite tenderness and power. It was a name, one given to me which cannot be repeated and must remain unspoken until the appointed time has come. Then the command was given to me once again: "Write".

Round one

I saw before me a young child being drawn out of a very dark abyss. The child, a boy, was delivered from the darkness into the light of a world, and placed before a beast with the face of a dragon and the heart of an angel. The beast embraced the boy. Yet no sooner had he done so than he was snatched away to a dimension of terrible darkness. The new, dark dimension was ruled by two kings. One had a red sash around his waist and a large sword by his side. He spoke kindly to the boy while holding the sword to his throat. He bore on his arm an equal-armed cross, with each arm continued at a right angle in anti-clockwise form. The other king wore a dark uniform and carried a gun by his side. He spoke harshly to the boy while holding a gun to his temple. He bore on his arm an equal-armed cross, with each arm continued at a right angle in clockwise form. That dimension became a place of outright horror for the boy.

In the vision, the boy grew instantly into adulthood where, consumed by rage and hatred, he effused the actions and utterances of the innocent evil. The negativity of his environment was a torture of the most unforgiving kind, and had a diabolical impact on his brilliant, virgin mind. He became degenerate to the core, a condition from which he never fully recovered.

I saw the boy in all his anger bathed in a violet light. The light simultaneously stimulated him and stoked his anxieties. He was unable to leave the light, though it was unclear to me whether that was by his design or another's. The light produced in him personal atrocities; microscopic afflictions which altered his very nature. The boy seemed not to notice or not to care, yet the more he subsisted in the light, the more acute his condition became.

Suddenly, the light retracted to a singular point within him, before it rapidly expanded again. It instantly vaporizing the boy, removing him from his earthy environment, and thrusting him into another time and state in the deep omniverse. There, he was confronted by a pink entity who saw in the boy divine potential. The pink one embraced the boy and led him by the hand

241

around the omniverses, training him and purging from him the influences of the kings' ideologies. At the same time, he harnessed and directed the effects of the violet light, which continued to transform the boy's constitution. The pink one saw in the boy the hallmarks of deity, hallmarks which would remain unrealised without the correct training.

In the vision I saw the dreams of the boy. He was dreaming of a white room. This was the only time I saw the boy smile. His smile was like the heavens, endless and beautiful. The white room of which he was dreaming was wonderful to the boy, because it had the two ultimate qualities he had all his life longed for and prized more than anything else: safety and distance. The white room was unsearchable and impenetrable. It was the only thing that lay beyond the omniverses.

How the boy loved the white room. He would visit it with increasing frequency. The more depressed and anxious he became in the real worlds, the more he would return to the solace of the white room. There he was free from others, free from pursuit, free from turmoil, free from pain and free from any purpose placed upon him. There, he could release his primal agonies, he could be separate from his material body, he could be himself in his purest form. He was untouchable.

At that time, three red-winged creatures flew in gyroscopic circles around the white room crying, "Blessed is the one who is allowed to enter the white room!"

The pink one then explained to the boy the meaning of the white room. He said, "In the white room, you are God." The boy's eyes widened on hearing this. The pink one continued. "In the silence of the white room, you have control. You control everything. Everything. Peace belongs to you and cannot be taken from you. Likewise, fear is unknown in the room. It can never visit you there, nor can pain. In the white room, there is only bliss. Everything in the white room is predetermined by you. You are God there. Untouchable. Intangible. Eternal."

The boy was radiant with happiness. The pink one spoke on. "But only in the white room. Once you leave the white room, you return and are subject to the laws and predeterminations of the omniverses. Do you understand?" The boy nodded. "The white room," continued to pink one, "is both useless and almighty. And access is only granted to those few who have endured the greatest pain of all: love."

In the vision I saw that love was a virtue of the lower tiers. The powers and deities of the higher tiers neither knew nor understood love. Having human qualities, the boy had known love in all its torrents of abuse, in its unrequitedness and in all its pain; and as a result, access to the white room was given to him. I saw the boy in the white room. He was so happy. So happy.

Alone with his thoughts, alone with his gentle feelings, alone. And there the boy could establish firmly the one predetermination that had always been lacking in his life: justice. In the boy's white room, justice and goodness co-existed without compromise. In the other dimensions of the omniverse, predetermination lay in the actions of those within those dimensions, and as such, was held to ransom by them.

And I saw the boy standing before a time-honoured, mahogany bench. He was being called to account. The three red-winged creatures flew above the bench crying, "Woe! Woe! Woe! Woe is the one who is unable to give an account of his life!" The creatures flew with one wing, and with the other wing they covered their eyes.

I saw an enormous gavel come thundering down on the bench, and a voice spoke from beyond it, rich, beautiful and terrifying. "49% just, 51% unjust! Into the abyss!" Darkness began to descend on the room, but before it could consume the boy a voice called out from behind him.

"He has never known love!" It was the pink one. His voice was raw and desperate. "He was raised without love! Have mercy! His evil is borne of innocence!" In a frozen twilight, a long, eerie silence followed this interjection before the pink one spoke again. "Grant me access to the white room." On hearing this, the three winged creatures flew away and hid in fear. The room

244

began to fill with billows of smoke, and when nothing more could be seen, the majestic voice called out, "Granted".

Then I saw the pink one approach the white room. He entered it radiant, yet trembling with fear. The effect was cataclysmic. In the white room where he was both God of nothing and God of everything, he endeavoured to recreate another of his kind, only more knowledgeable and more powerful. The metaphysical shift this produced allowed him to take the predeterminations of the white room into the omniverse, and by doing so, save the boy and purge the evil that he had chosen.

Yet the success of the shift was only partial. The clash between the predeterminations of the white room, and the tiers and dimensions of the omniverse, was so catastrophic that both began to fall in on each other. On and on they fell, realm after realm, dimension after dimension, predetermination after predetermination. The vision of this that I saw could barely contain the sight of it all, nor the sound. Eventually it collapsed into a small hole of eternal blackness the size of a kumquat, and there it stayed suspended in mid-air, pregnant with violence, chaos and reorder.

Stupefied, I asked what the meaning of this was. Three more winged creatures with white bodies and black heads flew across in front of me. They had the wings of a bird, the feet of a frog and the face of a bear, and together they called "Seven and ever, seven and ever more, seven and again!"

"What does it mean? " I asked them.

A fourth winged creature flew before me, this one larger and with a dappled plumage. "It means," it said, "that the omniverse will remain in darkness for seven trillion earth years. Then the ever, ever more and again will come to an end."

Immediately all four winged creatures departed with haste. The small, black hole, swirling suspended before me, then exploded. The ground I was standing on shook vigorously, and I had to cover my ears from the sound. Then I understood that the pink one had caused a Big Bang and inadvertently restarted the omniverse. And from the centre of the explosion, racing faster than the speed of light as it had been known, was the first sign of a new light.

Round two

I, Negi, was shocked by these visions, and spoke into the light which delivered them.

"Is this Big Bang the end or the beginning? "

"Be silent and wait patiently." The voice came from the light that was emanating at speed from the centre of the Big Bang. I duly waited but I can't say how long the wait was.

Then a bubble of thin light, expanding in size, moved toward me from out of the darkness. And within the bubble of light, I saw a baby in a rice field. It was utterly helpless and vulnerable to predators and disease.

"Who will protect the baby?" I asked.

"Behold!" came the reply. "The pink one shall protect the baby." And I saw the pink entity, the same one I had seen earlier in the vision, pick up the baby and hold him tightly to his breast. He ran off with the baby in his arms to raise him in safety and to train him in all righteousness.

In the vision I then saw three newts scurry through the air in front of me. Together they cried, "A few and many and only a very few! Blessed are the very few!"

"What does this mean?" I asked. "Who are the very few?"

"The few are those in the second omniverse who claim to remember the first omniverse, but can't. The many are those who neither remember, nor claim to remember the first omniverse. And the very few are those who truly can remember the first omniverse, whether they claim to or not."

"Is the baby one of the very few?"

"Write what you see," I was told.

I saw the pink one speaking with those who were of the very few. Some of them handed him precious stones, others handed him effluent. The pink one lay the precious stones on the forehead of the baby to protect it from the hatred and fear of its previous existence. But when the stones were removed from the baby's forehead, effluent remained where the stones had been. When the pink one tried to wipe the effluent from the brow of the baby, it remained as though a shadow across the mind of the infant. I was troubled by this, and asked again what it meant.

"It means that some entities will try to manipulate the pink one by claiming memory of the first omniverse, so as to corrupt his mentoring of the baby. In so doing they will bring out the innate evil in the baby, despite the precious efforts of the pink one to raise him in purity and righteousness. As the child grows, he will find the hatred and fury of his former existence seeping through into his current one. He will not know why, and he will not be able to remove the effluent from his life no matter how hard he tries. The child will grow in this wretched dichotomy of righteous knowledge and evil nature."

As soon as the voice had finished speaking I saw the babe, now a boy, grab a rabbit and dash it against rocks to its death. I cried out, "No! Don't do it! Such a thing should never be done!" but he couldn't hear me. But it wasn't the act that horrified me, it was the look on the boy's face. It was a sadistic mix of contemplation and pleasure. Then for the first time in these series of visions, the young boy spoke. He said with a voice of deep contentment, "I'm sorry, but it felt like heaven. Watching the light leave its eyes made me feel safe and good."

The pink one was unperturbed by this behaviour and continued to love the boy, nurturing him toward his divine potential. Despite the disturbing nature of these developments, the pink one never lost faith in the boy or himself.

Then I saw another vision, terrible and wonderful, and it shook me to my core. This vision came before all the others, yet it also came after them and its narrative runs through all of them. An ancient deity, powerful and wise, good and caring, created a world of beauty and light. He was pleased with his world yet sad, for its inhabitants denied him. In his loneliness, he reached out and had a child with one of the inhabitants, a young woman of great inner beauty. Yet his own iniquitous actions grieved him and in his distress, he destroyed his creation and every living thing within it.

When the deity saw what he had done, and that love was no longer within him or proceeding from him, he destroyed himself. The energy produced by this was so monumental it restarted the omniverses. In his final act, however, two eternal outcomes resulted. The first was that essential fragments of himself could not be destroyed. These fragments descended into a quiet world on the edge of the omniverse where they were embedded into the soil near a trickling, silver stream. They grew into a tree, grand and magnificent, which in time, and throughout time, came to have tremendous influence on the realms and dimensions of the omniverses. The second outcome was that despite his intentions and powers, he was not able to destroy the child that he had created with the woman. The child grew up to be known by many as "the boy who lived twice a million times".

I saw then that this was the same boy who had come under the tutelage of the pink one.

Finally, I saw a collection of boxes, some big, some small, spread out as far as the eye could see. Some of the boxes were simple, while others were ornately decorated. The pink one was very intentional about the order with which he opened the boxes and gave them to the boy. All of the boxes belonged to the boy, yet the pink one guarded them faithfully and kept them from being opened until the appointed time. There was one especially beautiful box, richly adorned with all kinds of precious stones and gold layerings. The pink one kept this behind him, out of site of the boy. Inside the boxes were the secrets of the omniverses. And inside the richly adorned box was the greatest secret of all.

While the boy was opening one of the boxes, a king, huge and powerful, appeared for a brief moment. He spoke in a foreign tongue, but for some reason it was completely understandable to me. He said, "Ah...second time around I see". As soon as he retreated another king appeared, this time small and weak, saying, "Somehow I knew you would be here".

The pink one moved to shield the boy from these kings and their statements, but the boy heard and became confused by what they were saying. In the movement, the boy saw the richly adorned box that had been hidden behind the pink one, and asked to see inside it. The pink one resisted but the boy's persistence overcame him, and he opened the richly adorned box and showed him its contents. This happened before the appointed time.

Inside the box was the boy's divine destiny. Having seen it ahead of the appointed time, the destiny was not what it would have been had it been opened at the right time. The boy's divine righteousness was laid bare, incomplete and compromised. Though the pink one had succeeded in purging virtually all evil from the boy, flecks of it remained, and these became as a virus working through a host. The boy, ascending to divinity, remained corrupted.

The pink one reached for the box before the boy could claim it for his own, and a mighty battle ensued. The enmity between them shook the heavens, and I saw galaxies and universes fall from the skies. Despite the boy's divine potential and burgeoning powers, he was defeated by the pink one, who overcame the boy's evil with the love that had arisen from protecting the boy.

In the final throes of the battle, I saw the pink one take the boy to his white room where the second Big Bang had occurred. There he committed the ultimate act of love to ensure his victory would be an everlasting one. He slaughtered the only other of his own kind - the boy - for the greater good of the omniverses, before bringing his white room and the omniverses together as one into perfect harmony.

Then I saw multitudes upon multitudes appearing from all over the omniverses, great and small, kingly and lowly, mighty and simple, and they bowed down before the pink one, and sang his praises for ever and ever.

The sphere of light before me then shrank to an infinitesimally small dot before disappearing altogether. I fell to the ground, overcome by these visions that were too wonderful for me to see, and too profound to fathom. Overcome and unable to speak for seven days, I duly wrote the visions down as they had been revealed to me. Though unworthy to witness such surpassing greatness, I declare that these visions are true and righteous. Blessed are those who hear and understand what has been revealed in them. Grace and peace across the tiers.